D0327445

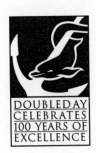

DOUBLEDAY
CELEBRATES
100 YEARS OF
EXCELLENCE

BY THE SAME AUTHOR

Bad Manners
Curtsey

D O U B L E D A Y

New York   London   Toronto   Sydney   Auckland

Marne Davis Kellogg

TRAMP

A LILLY BENNETT MYSTERY

PUBLISHED BY DOUBLEDAY
a division of Bantam Doubleday Dell Publishing Group, Inc.
1540 Broadway, New York, New York 10036

DOUBLEDAY and the portrayal of an anchor with a dolphin are
trademarks of Doubleday, a division of Bantam Doubleday Dell
Publishing Group, Inc.

Book design by Richard Oriolo

Library of Congress Cataloging-in-Publication Data
Kellogg, Marne Davis.
Tramp: a Lilly Bennett mystery / Marne Davis Kellogg. —1st ed.
p.   cm.
I. Title.
PS3561.E39253T7   1997
813'.54—dc21   96-29719
CIP

ISBN 0-385-48859-9

Printed in the United States of America

September 1997

First Edition

1 3 5 7 9 10 8 6 4 2

With all my love for Peter
who makes our life such a wild and excellent ride
and in special, loving memory of
Bill Ball
Founder
American Conservatory Theatre

ACKNOWLEDGMENTS

Part of the fun of writing fiction is doing the research. I am especially grateful to Tom Haney, chief of patrol, and Detective Tom Richey, Bomb Squad, Denver Police Department; Dave Gilmore, M.D., toxicologist, and Carol Rymer, M.D., radiologist, St. Joseph's Hospital; Arlene Hirschfeld and Rabbi Steven Foster; Karol Stoker, Cherry Creek Coin Company, Inc.; Peter Mark, general director, and David Grindle, stage manager, Virginia Opera, for all their expert guidance. My brothers, John and Andrew Davis, have been particularly helpful and are the only research associates I know who I can call at six o'clock in the morning and will work for shots of José Cuervo and burritos—and I really appreciate it.

Nick Ellison, my agent, has worked so hard and so enthusiastically on my behalf that it is nice to be able to thank him publicly for landing us at Doubleday and Bantam with Arlene Friedman, president and publisher of Doubleday; Judy Kern, senior editor, Doubleday; and Kate Miciak, associate publisher, Bantam. I cannot believe my good fortune in working with such an outstanding, supportive, and straight-talking group of individuals.

As always, none of this would be any fun if my family were not so engaged and engaging: Peter, my parents, Peter II, Hunter, Courtney, our grandson Duncan, and Gussie—I love you all so much it's ridiculous.

Marne Davis Kellogg
Denver, January 1997

TRAMP

1

M O N D A Y   M O R N I N G

Well, I thought as I hung up the phone, I've never shot anyone for making a pass, although I may have considered it on occasion. And I've certainly never shot anyone ninety years old, but if that old bastard tries to feel me up one more time, I will not hesitate to draw down on him and blast off whatever's closest.

"Who was that?" Richard asked.

It was early June and we were sitting in the warm morning sun on the flagstone patio off the living room having our breakfast.

Spring comes slowly to Wyoming, and when it does arrive, it only stays for a day and then it snows again and then it's summer. But today was the day when it was spring and out at the ranch, the Circle B, the air smelled of rich, moist earth and manure. Bone-numbingly icy water flowed from thawing underground springs and turned wide dry dips and ditches in the meadows into marshes and bogs, and randomly criss-crossed the roads with deep rivers of gooey black mud. Across the massive valley, beyond the swollen, rolling Wind River, the leaves on the aspen trees were still coiled in tight, tiny cones. In another week or so they would begin to open and turn the hillsides chartreuse.

Cyrus Vaile, what a lousy breakfast-time interruption, I thought as I looked across the grassy meadow that sloped gently down to the river and then curved up again just as gently on the other side, where Black Angus cows and quarterhorse mares grazed peacefully. Their calves and leggy colts slept quietly in the warm sun, oblivious to the thumming whine of the helicopter idling in their midst, waiting to take Richard and my younger brother, Christian, to town.

I looked over at him, Richard Jerome, the handsomest, most perfect man I'd ever known, and recalled the night I met the tall, good-looking, rugged cowboy in the well-cut tuxedo, and learned he was a former husband and Morgan Guarantee banker who'd had enough of his cheating wife and the high life in New York City and moved west to Roundup to run the Opera and learn to become a real team roper—not just an executive who practices with a paid partner one weekend afternoon a month. I never got tired of looking at his craggy, windblown, beaten-up face and wondered how much longer he was going to keep spending five nights a week out here at the ranch with me—this had been going on for months—and not pop the question. Sometimes I felt like whacking him over the head with a frying pan. Just like a mule. Just to get his damn attention.

"You men are really a problem," I said.

"Excuse me?"

"It was Cyrus Vaile."

"Ah. Hand-Man." He laughed and the sun flashed in his dark blue eyes. "Look, the guy's almost ninety. So what if he tries to tear off a little piece every now and then? You've got to give him credit."

"You are so sick."

"You know I'm kidding."

"He said he had a business proposition that might interest me."

Everything with Cyrus was always a proposition. Everything. I could picture the old rat perfectly—huge yellow teeth and a few dirty strands of white hair sealed to his sharp, rancid skull. A man entitled. A man who felt that every part of a woman's anatomy was fair game. A man who, even at ninety, at a cocktail party, would run one hand down the middle of your back to see if you were wearing a bra and at the same time pour his drink down your front and immediately, before you even knew what was happening, whip out his handkerchief and start to knead up the spill. The Hand-Man—a geezy letch. Just hearing his voice made my skin crawl.

"He wanted to know if I could come by this afternoon for tea, and then, if whatever his 'proposition' is turns me on, I'll no doubt want to stay for the cocktail party to meet the players." I smiled at Richard. "Turns me on? Can you believe it? But my day looks pretty quiet and, you know me, I love cocktails."

"So you said yes."

"It's spring. I can't help myself."

The winter had seemed particularly long, especially once I figured out that Richard's Christmas Eve gift from Cartier wasn't an engagement ring. Don't get me wrong, it was an absolutely exquisite Christmas brooch—a little platinum tree, decorated with every imaginable kind of precious and semiprecious stone—a real show-stopper. And besides, you'd think that I'd learn, after all these years of never getting the ring from the right guy, always from the wrong one, not to get carried away by all that romantic stuff. But I was really, really disappointed. And he knew it.

"Don't worry," he'd said, and kissed me. "Everything will be fine, you'll see. Be patient."

What the hell, I thought. I'd be fifty pretty soon. I'd waited this many years, what was a few more months? And then we made love, right there in the helicopter, on our way back to the ranch, and here it was almost summer and we were still crazy about each other.

I would be less than truthful if I didn't admit that I think nine months is enough time to make up your mind whether or not you love someone enough to marry her. Richard's excuse was that he'd been slam-dunked by his former wife and was gun-shy. Well, so what? That was twenty years ago. Time to get a grip, I say, and try it again. I'd been devastated a few times myself by marriage, but only by husbands who weren't mine, and now I was ready to quit dancing around and get on with the program.

Besides, who knew just how long this new face lift would hold out?

I haven't said any of this stuff to Richard directly, but I'm getting close.

A few minutes later, sunlight glinted off the windshield of my brother Christian's Land Rover as he left his house at the opposite side of the valley for the short drive to the chopper. Time to go. Richard kissed me good-bye and covered the distance down to the helipad in the meadow in long-legged strides, climbed aboard the big Sikorsky-76, which thundered into the sky, hovered momentarily, turned as though it were rotating on the point of a compass, and then shot off like a navy-blue bullet. They'd get to Roundup, our pretty little city that sits at the foot of the Wind River Range, about the same time I'd arrive in Bennett's Fort, a small windy tourist-trap town next to the ranch, from whence I run Bennett Security International.

My name is Lilly Bennett, and since the 1850s my family's successfully raised two black crops on the Circle B Ranch—Angus and oil—which have staked us all well. We could live lives of luxury in Monte Carlo if we wanted, but none of us did. We all worked, although when I was young, work was certainly not expected of me, except the work of a wife and mother. Not me. No way I was going to live my mother's life. I moved to California and became a cop, and for twenty years I worked hard and rose through the ranks and became chief of detectives of the Santa Bianca Police Department. But the wife of the Chief Justice of the California Supreme Court caught me and her beloved in bed together and I decided it would just be a lot better to head on back to the ranch than to have her sell the videos to Maury Povich.

Bennett's Fort also has a small Old West Jail and there's always been a marshal who has high-noon shootouts with bandits and bank robbers to amuse the busloads of gaping tourists who've spilled Grapette down the fronts of their white polyester STP shirts and glued their fingers together with peanut butter salt water taffy. And, when I was growing up, I thought the fellow who was the marshal for most of my life, Marshal Dan, was an actor. But when he died last year and I was asked to take his place, I discovered that the Fort is a legitimate federal district and the U.S. marshal position is the real thing. Primarily ceremonial, but I accepted the post nevertheless, delighted to receive the service's wide-ranging jurisdiction.

The district also comes with a young deputy: Dwight Alexander. I fantasize about him and Richard all the time, probably in the same groping, grasping way that Cyrus Vaile fantasizes about the entire female species. But he's ninety years old. It's gross. Well, I suppose, as they say, where there's life, there's hope, but I sure hope to God that if I have the bad luck to live until I'm ninety, I'll have the good taste and restraint to pretend I've got something on my mind besides sex.

2

M O N D A Y   A F T E R N O O N

High fashion has never been a distinguishing characteristic of the
Rocky Mountain West, the way it is in other parts of the country.
We don't have the slim sophistication of Manhattan women, or the
polished chic of San Francisco's society matrons, or the climate to wear
Palm Beach's beautiful chiffons and linens. Our fashion is influenced
more by the Southwest and Texas—neither known as a fashion mecca in
any sense of the word: lots of glitzed-up squaw dresses and rodeo-queen
jeweled bomber jackets.

Whatever mainstream haute couture is available can be found at the department store founded by Cyrus Vaile's ancestors in the late 1800s: the Roundup Dry Goods Company.

Cyrus was always a prominent, tolerated fixture in Roundup society. Prominent because the store had a very hard-working public relations girl who was always more than happy to loan out jewelry and gowns for special occasions, and tolerated because he had so much money and was so generous with it, which made it easier for people to overlook his behavior. In many ways he was the big, smelly, fat kid who owned the ball.

Cyrus's greatest claim to fame was the Roundup Repertory Company, which he'd brought to town from southern Connecticut twenty years ago because the people there wouldn't contribute enough money to support it.

Bidding for the company's presence was lively, and by using the same middle-of-the-night-we'll-build-you-whatever-kind-of-stadium-you-want tactics the really big power guys use to entice major league baseball, or hockey, or football teams, Cyrus bought the ensemble of actors, directors, set and costume designers, and stage managers right out from under those Connecticut Yankees. He installed George Wrightsman, the company's young founder and general director, and his troupe of classically trained, much-admired artists in Roundup's exquisitely restored beaux arts Vaile Theater, so named because Cyrus had personally paid for the restoration.

Frankly, I'd rather have a baseball team.

Still the company's greatest patron, Cyrus pretty much regarded the Roundup Rep, all the actors in its company, and all the students in its conservatory, as his personal possessions and himself as the Louis B. Mayer of Roundup.

Such were my thoughts and recollections that afternoon as I rode the elevator up to his penthouse apartment in the Roundup Grand Hotel. I got laughing about the last time I'd seen him, when he told me I was still young enough to be an ingenue, and I had all the makings of a great actress, and wouldn't I let him help me, and then he tried to French-kiss me and I slapped him. The truly funny part about the whole thing is that I was almost forty years old at the time and he thought I'd believe his ingenue bit. The unfunny part is that he was about eighty and, believe me, there is nothing funny about being French-kissed by an eighty-year-old man unless maybe you're a ninety-year-old woman.

Well, anyhow, today I had on a smart, hot pink linen suit, black patent high heels, and a little Glock 26 in my black patent purse, and, as I mentioned before, I'd already decided that if Cyrus tried anything I'd have to shoot him.

A young nurse opened the door. She had long, straight, glossy dark hair and wore a short, pressed white cotton uniform, white stockings, and white shoes—the way nurses used to dress in the old days—which made me think she probably wasn't a nurse at all but an actress over to play "doctor" with Cyrus for the afternoon—sort of a *Debbie Does Nursing* deal. Her skiff of makeup was so expertly applied it was almost invisible, just a blush on the cheeks of her clear young skin and light mascara on her long thick lashes.

"Miss Bennett?" She smiled and stood back so I could enter the foyer. I followed her into the living room. "Mr. Vaile will be right in," she told me. "Please make yourself comfortable."

The huge living room was straight from the sixties: black and white. The cushions on the sofas and armchairs were smooth surfaces of buttery soft fine white leather, and sculptured white area rugs covered the veined black marble floor. The tables were slabs of thick glass balanced on curved white pedestals, molded to look like elephant tusks. All the table and floor lamps were white twists of thick rope with white lacquered shades. I thought the place was all right. Not great.

But through the large picture windows the view was spectacular, especially on such a cloudless, bright-blue-sky day with the Wind River Range a glistening deep purple silhouette in the distance. It's hard to find a bad view in Roundup because you're looking either at the mountains or at the hill country and prairies, and in either case they're all vast, reaching landscapes that let you take a deep breath, refuel, calm down. It takes a real Westerner to appreciate our big empty sky on a permanent basis—we can just stare at it for hours.

Unfortunately, we're a rare breed—our towns are mostly full of newcomers who just want to fill up our prairies with prefab houses and trees and sprinkler systems, and to use all our water on their fancy landscaping. They may be here, but they aren't *of* here, and in my opinion they should go back where they belong.

I heard the unmistakable shuffling of an old man in leather-soled slippers on a hard floor, and turned from the window to see the nurse escorting Cyrus into the room.

He'd aged drastically since I'd seen him last ten years ago. He was tiny and thin and his back had hunched horribly, which made him leer up at me out of his bleary blue, white-lashed eyes, like the witch in *Sleeping Beauty*. His big yellow teeth seemed bigger than ever in his skull-thin face. White flakes of dandruff flecked his shoulders, and some kind of something had caked into a white crust in the corners of his mouth.

"Lilly, how are you?" he said. Even from across the room his breath flowed to me like the gutters of Calcutta. "You're more beautiful than ever. What a lovely lavender suit. St. Laurent, I believe, although I've not seen it in that color."

His eyesight obviously was wrecked. I didn't look that great and the suit was as pink as pink can be. I didn't say anything, though—it didn't make any difference.

"Thanks, Cyrus," I answered, feeling held in place on the far side of the room, not by acrimony, but rather by a deep sadness that the game, for him, was over. "I'm sorry to be late."

The girl helped him into a chair whose cushions were flattened with use, and his palsied clawlike hand patted her hip. I felt so sorry for him—not long ago he would have grabbed, or bitten, or at least blithely brushed her breasts and made sure I'd seen it. Now, I imagine, he was just glad to be breathing.

"Thank you, Kissy," he said wearily. "What would you like to drink, Lilly?"

"Jameson's on the rocks, please."

"That sounds so good." Cyrus grinned up at the sweet-faced Kissy. "Can't I have one? Please?"

"Sorry. Just tea. Doctor's orders." She turned to me. "He's got a little heart trouble, and unfortunately liquor and his medication don't mix," she said, and left the room.

"Lovely girl," Cyrus said.

"Yes," I said, thinking he had more than a little heart trouble. He looked terrible. Pale and clammy. He smelled of mildew and death.

Cyrus nodded. "Been with me for three years now, I think. This aging business is lousy. Now my eyes are shot. Everything's fuzzy, got yellow outlines. Makes me feel lousy all the time."

"I'm sorry," I said.

Kissy returned with our drinks, and while he fumbled around and she helped him to a small sip of his tea, I took a healthy belt of my whisky, which caressed deliciously all the way down, and then plunged right in to the matter at hand, which is one of the reasons I made a great cop and detective and would never have lasted a week in the corporate world: foreplay has never been my forte. Like many of my lovers, unfortunately.

"What can I do for you?" I said. "Why did you call me?"

Cyrus placed his bony elbows on the chair arms and leaned forward. "You know," he began, his voice thin and watery, "the Roundup Repertory Theater is the top in the country. I brought them here from Connecticut twenty years ago. George was just a young man then. And brilliant—absolutely brilliant. Best young director in the country," he said wistfully.

Past his shoulder, I saw a maid and Nurse Kissy arranging hors d'oeuvre around a massive white lilac centerpiece on the dining-room table.

"Over the years we've built it up into one of the largest theater companies in the country—our annual budget is ten million. Of course, once all the tickets have been sold and all the fund-raising is done, I still have to make up the shortfall of at least a million dollars a year while the board sits on their behinds congratulating themselves on what a great job they've done."

I took another sip and looked at him over the rim of my glass. "Cyrus," I said, "I don't mean to be rude, but I'm quite sure you haven't brought me here to give me a public relations pitch about the Roundup Rep. You said it was business and you're obviously expecting a number of guests. Let's work without pretense or else we'll run out of time."

He glared at me with hard, bad-tempered eyes. A look that, even in his greatly diminished state, still flashed the cutthroat steel that had made him always willing to pay the price of success at any cost. Son-of-a-bitch, killer eyes. I could tell it inflamed him that he could not control me. That he knew he had nothing I wanted, unless maybe it was an interesting case, and frankly, for me to work for him, it'd have to be a hell of a problem.

"You're a pretty tough cookie, Lilly."

"Yes," I said. "And I'm a pretty busy cookie, too."

"All right, then," he said, hurt.

I felt like a crumb. I didn't need to sit here and beat up this old guy. Pick on someone your own size, Bennett, I said to myself. Give him a break.

"I won't waste your time. I have two requests. First, I would like you to consider serving on the Board of Trustees of the theater."

"Me?" I almost laughed out loud. "I'm very flattered, but I can't imagine why you would want me on your board. I'm not what's known as a team player, Cyrus, and I know the Bennett Foundation already makes a large gift every year."

"This invitation has nothing to do with your money."

"Come on." I smiled. And I'm afraid my expression might have been patronizing, even a little cynical. "You know everything has to do with money."

He became very agitated. His quaking hands clenched into fists and his jaw tightened. "This is not a joke, Lilly, and it has nothing to do with your ability, or lack of ability, as a team player or a board member. It has to do with finding solutions, in a discreet and covert way, to what has become a twenty-million-dollar shell game."

"Tell me," I said.

"George and I have grown far apart the last couple of years, and now we're locked in a power struggle for control of the company. He's trying to convince the board to move me into the role as honorary chairman and freeze me out of all the decision making. I know I'm an old man, maybe not as sharp as I was, but this is my company and they can't just throw me out on the street. If they do, I'll stop the money." Cyrus had gotten very worked up. White foam appeared in the corners of his mouth. "George is crazy. He's a megalomaniac, a tyrant. He acts like Napoleon or somebody."

With every word, Cyrus spewed foam like he was spitting out his teeth. "He and Winston McMorris sit around and snort cocaine and smoke marijuana and make up outlandish rumors about me and spread them among the other board members—that I'm nothing but a senile, doddering old geezer—and he threatens to resign if they don't give him total financial and artistic control of the company."

Cyrus drew in a ragged breath and I bit my tongue against conflicting emotions, against snapping out the first smart-aleck thought that came to my mind: such as, if George Wrightsman and Winston McMorris—whoever he is—want to sit around and get stoned and tell a bunch of lies, I pretty much feel that's up to them. I'm more helpful when it comes to murder and larceny. And pity. Cyrus's eroding power base held no interest for me, but I felt terribly sorry for him. It's sad to watch the lions get old, even when they're old bastards like Cyrus.

"You mentioned a twenty-million-dollar shell game," I said. "Tell me about it."

The doorbell rang.

Cyrus leaned toward me. His tone became more urgent. "It's the new endowment fund I set up, and it's gone. Vanished. I'll tell you after the party," Cyrus said as Kissy helped him struggle to his feet. "Just watch George."

"I'm not sure George is coming," Kissy told him.

"It's my birthday party," Cyrus spat. "The bastard better show up."

He snatched his cane from her hands and started to shuffle.

3

A number of people arrived, bringing silver balloons with birthday messages and bottles of champagne with frilly ribbons. Actors and actresses. A couple of board members. Some staff members and conservatory students. No George Wrightsman.

Theater people are very strange. Like all the rest of us, they're really comfortable only in their own world, but their world is so different, full of fictional characters only they know intimately—generally more intimately than they know themselves. Their world is based on secret fantasy lives shared in public with a handful of other artists. Basically, they have no reality.

Socially, they are totally inept. And they like it that way. It's an elitism they call shyness. I call it out-and-out bad manners.

"People who claim to be shy are lazy and arrogant," Mother proclaimed when we were little. "They choose not to make an effort, and few of them will ever amount to anything." Need I say that shyness was not tolerated in the Bennett family, and my brothers and I all practically still have the bruises on our legs from well-aimed direct hits from Mother's pointy-toed pumps. Hits that no one saw or felt but us. And being a quick learner, and averse to pain, it is not surprising that my attitude about shyness turned out to be the same as Mother's.

Which is why my attitude about this inbred, almost incestuous gathering began to deteriorate even further. It was the quietest party I'd ever been to—full of shy violets. Whenever Nurse Kissy's back was turned, Cyrus, the only person I was acquainted with, shoveled Vienna sausages heaped with mustard into his yaw as though they were popcorn. He was engaged in an intense, angry conversation with Winston McMorris, who, I had learned, was the company's dope-smoking executive producer—the man in charge of the business side of the operation. It didn't look like a discussion I could, or should, interrupt, so after a few forays, feints, and volleys into the various family-like cliques and clusters, where I was greeted with bored disinterest, if not outright suspicion, I decided none of them was worth talking to anyway.

I got another drink and admired the view, and was thinking that if I left now I'd still have time to go for a long ride before dark, when a woman, identified to me by Nurse Kissy as George Wrightsman's secretary, Shelley Pirelli, walked to the center of the room and clinked her fork on her wineglass. She looked about thirty-five, small and thin with long wavy dark hair and bangs swept off to the side. Heavy makeup concealed large pores in her olive complexion, and a tightly fitted, low-cut, flowered print dress showed off her glamorous figure. She held a white index card in her hand, making the chips in the brown metallic polish on her too long nails stand out as though they'd been spattered with Wite-Out. I'd seen her type a million times before: Shelley Pirelli was an alley cat with capped fangs. A street-smart, on-the-lam-looking girl with a dusting of powdered sugar on her tongue and a grimy copy of *Etiquette* by Emily Post in her back pocket.

"Cyrus," she said in a sultry, measured voice. "George was so sorry he couldn't be here to wish you happy birthday, but he sent a message and asked me to have Gregory Donnelly read it."

"He could have been here if he wanted," Cyrus countered angrily, as one of the actors, a handsome, middle-aged, silver-haired man in a corset so tight that his chest and shoulders looked like they were about to fly off the top of his body like a champagne cork, stepped over to Shelley, took the card from her, and studied it for a moment.

"He really, really couldn't," she explained to Cyrus. "He's in rehearsal."

As soon as I heard the "he's in rehearsal" remark, I knew George was giving Cyrus the big kiss-off. And Cyrus and everyone else at the party knew it too. It was the same as an attorney's secretary saying, "He's in court." He might just as well have said, "Tell him that if he drops dead on the spot I could give a rip."

"Cyrus," Gregory Donnelly said, "I swear on a Bible that it's the truth. You know we're in rehearsal for the Scottish play, and the only reason I'm here is because they're not doing any of my scenes this afternoon. He's sent you a fine message, don't you want me to read it?"

"All right. So go ahead." Cyrus frowned.

Gregory gave his throat an important clearing and straightened his back as he waited for full silence and got himself in a proper frame of mind, and then his voice rumbled from that puffed-up chest like Moses on the Mount. " 'Because of your generosity and dedication' "—he smiled paternalistically at Cyrus over the tops of his reading glasses— " 'your leadership and vision, you have cast a radiant beam of light across all the arts in America. We are indescribably fortunate that that beam emanates from our midst—that we are the beneficiaries of your presence. Cyrus, you are the heart and soul of our company. We treasure and honor you with our love, our lives, and our art. George.' " The actor looked up with tears in his eyes.

Made me want to throw up.

Cyrus was clearly furious. "Same old bullshit," he seethed, glaring from face to face. "If he really loved me, he would have come himself."

Everyone ignored him, apparently accustomed to the feud. Instead, they clapped and then sang "Happy Birthday." Shelley went over and gave him a big kiss, making sure he got a good peep down the front of her dress into her slightly shopworn, stringy cleavage, which had seen a lot of action and better days.

"You know he loves you," I heard her whisper. "Please don't get so upset, Cyrus. We don't want anything to happen to you."

Cyrus stood there, feet spread wide for balance, his birdlike body hunched over like a running back with a ball, a look of impotent fury contorting his blotchy face. "You tell George it doesn't mean anything unless he wishes me happy birthday himself. In person. You tell him. Or else he'll never get another nickel."

"I'll tell him," she said. She looked nervously at Winston, who, for just a moment, had slid his hand possessively and unobtrusively over her rump, and then excused herself.

Immediately thereafter, the cliquish silence returned, and I was halfway to the door when Winston McMorris clapped his hands a few times and said, "Cyrus has something to say." Then he stepped aside and left the scowling relic front and center.

"Thank you, Winston." His voice was small, hard to hear, as though the angry explosion at George's absence had drained all the juice right out of him. His skin had turned gray. "I'd like to welcome our newest board member, Lilly Bennett, who will be joining us at the annual meeting tomorrow."

Well, everyone paused long enough to look me over and, after a few other brief remarks by Cyrus, gave me a couple of seconds' worth of halfhearted applause, and then returned to whatever they were doing. It made me mad, and childishly, the first thought that crossed my mind was, Fine. I'll just be sure at the next Bennett Foundation meeting to tell them the Rep doesn't need our hundred thousand a year and we'll give it to someone who's a little nicer.

Just as I began to point out to Cyrus that I'd not accepted his invitation and did not intend to, he clutched his chest and began to gasp and gurgle. "I'm numb," he wheezed. "I can't breathe." He grasped the edge of the table as he collapsed and pulled the cloth, the Vienna sausages, and all the lilacs down with him.

For a second everyone just watched, and then, since I was the closest, I was the first one there, but he was already staring wide-eyed at the ceiling. Dead.

The most interesting thing about Cyrus Vaile's death there in his dining room was that there was almost no reaction. No one offered to help. They all looked at Kissy, who in turn looked at me, an astounded expression in her eyes.

"Call 911," I told the cook, who peeked out of the kitchen door as I stood up and smoothed down my skirt. If Cyrus had been alive, he could have looked right up it. Better luck next time.

"No. No. No 911," Kissy said, finally seeming to regain herself and rushing to the body.

I made a mental note never to hire her as my nurse if I wanted any quick, decisive action, or anything more than a companion on a cruise.

"We all have very specific instructions not to resuscitate him." She bent down and pressed her fingers against his neck, feeling for a pulse. Then she did the same thing with his wrist. "No." She shook her head. "He's gone." She looked over at me, not sure she could trust me not to resuscitate him. "I'm going to call the doctor. Don't try to do anything to him."

"Don't worry," I told her, shuddering at the thought of giving mouth-to-mouth to those white, crapped-up lips.

Although there were a few predictable reactions to what should have been viewed as a major calamity in the life and fortune of many of the guests, dependent as they were on the liquidity and fiscal stability of the Roundup Rep, and its greatest patron lying flat-out dead on the floor, with his purplish tongue protruding disgustingly—still hoping for one last kiss—for the most part, the guests filed past Cyrus and gawked and squinted and squeezed out a few hard-wrought tears and then filtered out of the apartment like bubbles in dark glasses leaving an aquarium. Three of them even reclaimed their champagne birthday presents, tucking the expensive bottles back into their canvas tote bags among their thumbed-over scripts. But nobody bawled, and nobody flailed. Nobody keened or cried. Being actors, I thought they might have pretended a little.

I leaned against the dining-room table and watched them go, not quite able to believe my eyes.

Even Nurse Kissy, or whatever her name was, once she had made the call to the doctor, threw on her long, navy-blue nurse's cape with its Red Cross emblem on the breast. "You'll stay with him until the doctor arrives, won't you?" she said to me. "You know more about what to do than I do."

And then she disappeared, leaving Winston McMorris, the late Cyrus Vaile, and me alone in the dining room.

I had a feeling that, if I left, Winston would too, and while I don't know much about Judaism, I have had a handful of Jewish lovers, and I do know that a body cannot be left alone from the second the person dies. I came across this information first hand when one of the afore-mentioned lovers and I were caught literally with our pants down in his grandmother's powder room during his little brother's Bar Mitzvah party. She had opened the door, seen us, and collapsed and died right there on the spot, blocking the door so we couldn't close it. What a mess.

But I take people's religious beliefs very seriously, and evidently the duty to stay with Cyrus had been left to me. Which was all right, I didn't mind—I'd spent lots of time with corpses in much worse shape than his. But I must say, it really surprised me, because there had been several Jewish guests at this birthday bash, and I knew they knew better. I swear, I'm getting more and more like my mother every day. She bitches endlessly on practically every subject, but funerals and weddings really get her whopped up about people's lack of propriety and decorum, and brother, she's right. I mean, here I am, a rock-ribbed Episcopalian—well, okay, I know Episcopalians aren't rock-ribbed about much of anything except the cocktail hour—but here I am watching over this old dead Jewish fellow because I know enough to do so. Wouldn't you think that someone else in his household would have been prepared to assume that duty? I supposed someone was, but now Cyrus was dead and they figured he would never know the difference.

Winston and I stood there self-consciously in this incredible quiet for a moment or two, which gave me a chance to study him.

He was very handsome, sort of medium tall and, like Shakespeare's Cassius, had a lean, gaunt, troubled, hungry look. A slightly sad-eyed man who worked too hard for too little money. He lit an unfiltered cigarette and ran his hands through his longish hair.

"How long have you been with the theater?" I finally said, breaking the silence.

He looked at me as though he'd completely forgotten I was there. "Eight years."

"Where were you before?"

"San Diego."

"Funny," I said. "I would have picked you for a New Englander. You don't look like a Californian."

Winston blushed out a bashful smile. "You're right. I'm originally from Massachusetts. I was at the Old Globe for a few years before coming here."

"Ah." I nodded my head sagely. Obviously I'd missed some big story somewhere. I thought it was still in England. "How long has it been since they moved it?" I asked after a long pause during which air began to escape noisily from Cyrus's body.

"Moved what?" Winston looked perplexed. He was struggling to conceal his absolute horror at what was going on there on the floor.

"The Old Globe," I said casually, as a long blabbering burst shook the corpse. "Was it at the same time they moved the bridge?"

"What bridge?" he cried. He longed to escape.

"London Bridge."

Winston burst out laughing, a wonderful hilarious, hysterical yowl. "No. No. No. It's a repertory theater in San Diego. It's just *called* the Old Globe."

"Right," I said. I had no idea what he was talking about.

"I'd better call George," he blurted out as though he'd said too much, and then bolted through the swinging door into the kitchen, leaving me alone with Cyrus's fast-shrinking remains. He'd been so old and there was so little to him at the end, and now, as the air escaped like sputters from a balloon, he became an unrecognizable skeleton covered by a paper-thin, transparent membrane of skin.

"Don't be afraid, Cyrus," I said to him. "I'm here."

The doctor appeared surprisingly quickly, followed shortly by two very somber, dark-suited funeral home men wearing yarmulkes and wheeling a gurney. Without a sign of greeting or acknowledgment to me or the doctor, they quickly rearranged Cyrus so his feet were pointed toward the door, laying him out perfectly straight, and shrouded him in a white linen sheet. They whispered prayers the whole time. The doctor handed one of them the death certificate, which the man examined quickly, folded, and slid into his inside jacket pocket before turning to help his assistant gently bundle their charge into a large black zippered bag. The gurney's steel legs snapped into place, and then, without a pause in the incantations, it was all over. Cyrus was gone.

Winston and I rode down in the elevator together. His hands were thrust deep into the pockets of his tweed sport coat. He seemed lost in thought.

"What time is the meeting tomorrow?" I asked him.

He looked at me blankly. "Meeting?" he said. "You mean the annual meeting? The board meeting?"

"Yes." I laughed, a little flustered at his reaction. "I think I'm a new trustee." I felt like a jerk, and then I wondered why I hadn't kept my mouth shut, because if I had, I could have written off the whole afternoon's exercise as just that. Instead, I'd managed to get myself in deeper.

"You aren't planning to join the board anyway, are you?" Winston appeared incredulous, and not happily so. "With Cyrus dead?"

Well, if I hadn't been, I sure was now. I was frankly stunned that he wouldn't want me on the board. I mean, any nonprofit that said it didn't want a Bennett on its board was nuts. There just aren't that many of us, and even though we give a lot of money away through the foundation, we don't get directly involved very often. With Cyrus gone, they'd need the community's help more than ever, and believe me, I knew that Winston McMorris, for all his fumbling, absent-minded-professor charm, must have a brain somewhere inside that rumpled-looking head and that as executive producer he thought about business and money every second. So for him to try to put me off not only aggravated me, it also didn't make much sense.

Also, Cyrus had asked me to be on the board for a specific reason that didn't have to do with money. My money, at least. It had to do with a missing twenty-million-dollar endowment. A lot of money. Which more and more attached itself in my mind to Winston's negative reaction to my participation.

The afternoon was becoming a distinctly Shakespearean experience: first Cassius, and now the realization that something big was stinking in Denmark, or however that line goes. There was no way I would let it drop.

I asked Winston again when and where the meeting would be.

"At the general offices. At noon."

"Good," I told him. "I'll look forward to it."

"Righto." He pulled a pack of cigarettes from the breast pocket of his flannel shirt. "I'll tell George. I'm sure there won't be a problem."

The elevator doors opened and Winston quickly crossed the Grand's lobby, lighting his cigarette as he went, passed through the revolving doors into the magnificent spring evening, and disappeared down the busy, tree-lined street.

This George must be something, I thought. But then, so am I. Bennetts don't blink first.

CHAPTER

5

I trailed slowly after Winston across the Grand's elegant rotunda lobby that was surrounded by ten curving floors of ornate wrought-iron balcony railings leading all the way up to a dome with a stained-glass design of an orange-red Indian paintbrush, Wyoming's state flower.

The last time I'd been here was for the debutante ball before Christmas, when the lobby was cleared of furniture and rugs to make way for the orchestra and dance floor. Today, when I reached the center of the rotunda, I stopped and looked up, and then let my eyes descend slowly back to the ground. I could still picture Fancy French, in that exquisite ice-blue satin strapless gown, lying face down in the middle of the floor, thrown or jumped from several stories up, that huge diamond ring still sparkling on her finger.

Large Persian rugs now covered the floor but did little to baffle the rinky-tink cacophony coming from the harpsichord. The harpsichordist, one of the few in Wyoming, took her seat every afternoon at teatime and banged out deafening renditions of "Clementine" and "Oh, Susannah" and "I've Been Workin' on the Railroad," while the hotel guests sat in cozy little groups on red leather chairs and banquettes, having cocktails and grousing about how they thought it would be a lot warmer, and a lot less windy, here in Wyoming this time of year. Jeez, I wanted to say, it just stopped snowing last week, this is like Florida.

23

My Jeep was right where I'd left it at the front door, and so was Baby, my wire-haired fox terrier, balanced on the top of the rear seat, watching for me out the window. I gave the doorman another ten dollars.

"Thanks, Curtis," I said. "I hope she didn't bark too much."

"Been quiet as a mouse once you got inside, Miss Bennett." He held open the car door for me. "Seems like every time you go in the hotel a dead body gets carried out."

I laughed. "You're right. But I think it was Mr. Vaile's time. Don't you?"

Curtis nodded. "He'd really been going down fast the last couple weeks or so, and all these people rushing in and out for meetings—almost like they knew. We'll sure miss having all those pretty actresses visit him all the time, though." He slammed my door shut. The few remaining rays of sun gleamed on the gold braid of his brown uniform as he touched the visor of his cap. "Visit us again soon," he said.

"All what people?" I asked.

"Oh, you know. Mr. Wrightsman and Mr. McMorris and Mr. Bradford Lake and Cyrus's brother Samuel, Miss Gigi. All the regular people. No one special."

I'd planned to go home, and had even got as far as the interstate, but things seemed a little up in the air, unfinished. That's pretty much the way it is when people die. One or two people might be devastated by the loss, but the rest of us just pretty much walk off and keep doing what we're doing.

I'm not taking back all the awful stuff I said or felt about Cyrus Vaile, but the fact is, by today he was just a sick little old, old man who'd dropped dead among what he thought were friends, except none of them stayed to see that he was looked after. And if it hadn't been for his philanthropy, ninety percent of the people in that room wouldn't have jobs. The Roundup Repertory Company wouldn't exist, and neither would the Vaile Theater, and without the Roundup Dry Goods Company, neither would what we loosely call "fashion" around here. Of course, his younger brother, Samuel, had more to do with the department store than Cyrus, but even so, I found it terribly disturbing that literally everyone simply walked off when he expired. This was not right. Not only did it offend my sensibilities, it alarmed them.

The image of Cyrus's face as they pulled the sheet over it would not leave my mind. What was it? There was no abnormal deformity, just some little something about the way the skin had begun to tighten around his nostrils, widening them slightly, drawing the white-ringed rictus into a more ghastly grin. That, added to a couple of things he'd said, made bells go off in my head.

I took the next exit and headed over to Emanuel Cemetery, a small, green, sheltered graveyard where Roundup's oldest Jewish families are buried. Temple Emanuel, a small stone structure that was Roundup's first synagogue, stood sentinel at the wrought-iron gates.

Their cemetery was a lot nicer than ours, the Protestant one, the Wind River, which stands on a lonely, blustery mesa outside of town, equidistant between the Roundup Country Club and St. Mary's Psychiatric Hospital—the joke being that most of the people buried there died either in the bar at the country club or at St. Mary's drying out. It's probably not true, but some things are just too serious to contemplate seriously, especially now that I've started on the downhill side of the slope.

It's possible to think about death too much—to think about it to the exclusion of thinking about life. Especially as we get older, it starts showing up everywhere, all the time, closer and closer to home. I now make a special effort to look for life, otherwise—especially as a homicide investigator—my heart and soul could die from overexposure to sadness and grief and loss, and I would never know they were gone until it was too late.

I turned left before entering the cemetery grounds and circled around to the business end of the operation, a one-story, windowless, blond brick structure. A black canopy extended out from above the simple glass front doors across the drive, protecting visitors from the elements, and although it wasn't visible from the front, I knew that around back was the large, double garage door that had swallowed the station wagon with the blacked-out windows that carried Cyrus's remains.

I had an autopsy in mind.

Many Christians don't care what happens to their bodies after they're gone. They say, Sure, go ahead, take it. You need some eyes? Here they are. A liver? Couple of kidneys? No problem. Need to do an autopsy? Go ahead. Embalming? Absolutely.

Jews? Forget it. Absolutely not. Nothing is touched. Nothing. If you are a Jew and you die and there is blood on your skin, your blood, it stays with your body because it is part of your body. There is no embalming. Plus, there are family members and friends who look after you the whole time. They wash you, cleanse you, purify you, wrap you in clean linen, and lay you in a plain pine box. They never leave your side until it's over, and never stop praying for you, not for one second, until you are buried. I think it's wonderful.

I learned all this from David Loeb's grandmother's funeral preparation. David's mother had told him he'd murdered his grandmother, which fatally affected our torrid affair in the most specific and embarrassing way, and if he ever was able to make love again, I am confident it was not to another Gentile.

David Loeb's grandmother did not have an autopsy, because dying of shocked sensibilities is not technically homicide, or even manslaughter—unless you listened to David's mother's opinion on the subject. But I learned at that time that for a Jew to have an autopsy is a very, very big deal, and as I drove along, I hoped that Cyrus had not been Orthodox, because then it would be completely out of the question unless I could prove, beyond the shadow of a doubt, that he had been murdered. But, on the other hand, he'd been eating all those little sausages, so I don't think there was a chance he was Orthodox. Conservative, maybe. Whatever he was, I had to move fast, because by Jewish law he had to be in the ground within twenty-four hours.

It was almost dark when I parked in the empty lot and entered the surprisingly spartan, silent lobby. Wide hallways led off to either side, and small glowing candles provided the only illumination. One of the dark-suited men who had been at Cyrus's apartment appeared from an invisible, silently opening door. His eyes looked especially black in the dim light.

"May I help you?" His voice was soft.

"Yes." I took out my badge. "I'm Marshal Bennett. I was at Mr. Vaile's when he died."

"Yes, Miss Bennett, I recognize you. My name is Robert Goldman." He extended his hand. "How may I help you?"

"Nice to meet you," I said. His grip was cool and firm. "I'm here because something about Mr. Vaile's death seemed irregular, and I have some very strong suspicions about it."

Mr. Goldman's eyes grew large. "But Dr. Allen issued the death certificate with no question, and I saw nothing abnormal about the body."

"I know. I'm sorry. But I'd like you to request an autopsy."

At that moment the front door opened and Cyrus's brother Samuel strode inside. Fifteen years younger than Cyrus, Samuel had always looked as though he came from an entirely different family. There was some resemblance, but the same elements that had made Cyrus craven and ghoulish had rendered his brother handsome. He was a little taller, more filled out, and his white hair looked distinguished against his tanned skin. He had always been the gentleman, his brother the rogue.

"Mr. Vaile," said Mr. Goldman. "I'm sorry to be the one who had to bring you the tragic news about your brother's passing."

Samuel shook the man's hand. "I understand. What happened?"

"He went very peacefully at home during his birthday party. Dr. Allen said it was a heart attack."

Samuel just shook his head and nodded. "Poor Cyrus," he said. "God bless him." And then he noticed me, waiting, in the dim light. "Lilly? What are you doing here?"

"I was present when Cyrus died, Samuel. And I'm sorry to be presumptuous, but it didn't look like a heart attack to me."

"What do you mean?"

"There's a lot of severe pain associated with a heart attack. You don't simply collapse. Pass out. Just run out of steam."

"So? I don't understand what difference it makes." Samuel frowned. "He was an old man and he died."

"Cyrus said he was numb and couldn't breathe, and then he fell. He was dead almost instantly," I explained. "I'd like your permission to have an autopsy."

Samuel was floored. "Autopsy? It's out of the question."

"Why?" I asked, sensing an unexpected uphill battle.

"Although Cyrus's behavior may have been occasionally excessive, even *un*orthodox, we are Orthodox Jews. Cyrus will not be touched. Cannot be touched. It is against Jewish law."

"Samuel, this is one area in which I know what I'm talking about."

I chose my words carefully, speaking as respectfully as I could, aware that no matter how close, or estranged, these men had been, this was an emotional time, and for me to get adamant would be totally unprofessional, not to mention uncalled for. "Autopsy is not against Jewish law if there is some suspicion of murder or poisoning, which my instincts are telling me there is."

"It will take more than your instincts to convince me," Samuel said. He struggled to contain his indignation, but red patches on his cheeks gave him away.

"I have my master's degree in toxicology, Samuel, and have been involved with dozens of cases in which, against all indications, I have suspected poison was the cause of death and been right. Please understand I am not making this request lightly."

Silence. I forged ahead.

"There are typically three ways in which autopsies are called for." I counted off on my fingers. "If someone is murdered. If someone is killed in an accident, such as a car accident or a fall. Or if the family requests it."

I stopped and looked from one man to another. Both had extremely tense expressions on their faces. They had lost control of the situation and they knew it.

"Now, in the first instance, murder, the autopsy is court-ordered, which is a public action, which makes the fact that it is taking place available to the press, and the results may or may not be made public. In the case of an accident, the autopsy is routine and the results are generally released privately to the family. In the third instance, when the family requests the autopsy, no one needs to know it was done and the results are private, unless there has been foul play."

They listened quietly.

"Samuel," I said, "I have huge respect and affection for your family, and I would never want to draw attention to you unnecessarily. Please request the autopsy. Don't make me do it through the court. And then, if I'm wrong, no one will ever need to know."

Samuel was very quiet. His blue eyes focused on me with total concentration and then shifted to Mr. Goldman, who nodded slowly.

"She's right," he said.

6

MONDAY NIGHT

I never get tired of driving from town out to the ranch—no matter what time of day, it is always beautiful. Tonight, the four-lane out of the city across the hill country was quiet, and when I turned into Crazy Squaw Canyon, mine was the only car. I pushed the accelerator up to eighty and opened all the windows. Baby balanced with her rear feet on the back seat and her front ones on the console and leaned into the well-known curves like a pro at a rally.

The fact that the federal government let go of its fifty-five- and sixty-five-mile-an-hour speed limits on interstates and back roads a few years ago passed without much notice in Wyoming, since we had always regarded it as just one more lame suggestion from all the lamebrains back there in Washington. Of course, it also explains why we have one of the highest highway death rates in the country.

Don't get me wrong—I'm not one of those anti-fed militia wackos. I'm a government girl through and through, and like most people, I find blowing up government buildings and government workers the sickest, most terrifying kind of terrorism imaginable because it's homegrown. You can be talking to one of these people and not even know it until you see his picture in the paper, and it turns out to be your fifth-grade teacher's nephew or something.

When the Oklahoma City Federal Building was blown up, Congress held hearings to talk to various militia leaders and members from around the country. These people came in with unbelievably outlandish claims, such as the reason there had been more killer hurricanes in the last ten years had nothing to do with nature—it was because the federal government was manipulating the weather system.

Or that the government had a conspiracy against the people and was controlling them with subliminal messages through the airwaves.

I had a guy say to me once that the reason George Bush stopped running mid-campaign, just quit—which he did—was because the government was actually run by a small, powerful, international cabal, and they told Bush they didn't want him to win, and he had to do as they ordered.

"Let me get this straight," I said. "Are you saying that one day George Bush is sitting at his desk in the Oval Office and the phone rings and he picks it up and someone says to him, 'George, Oscar here. We want you to quit now. You're through.' And so Bush said, 'Oh. Okay. Sure. No problem.'?"

And the man who was telling me this theory said, "Yes. That's exactly what happened." Well, if it is, which I'm sure it isn't, I'd sure think George Bush would be a lot richer, and might not be living in such a modest house in a Houston suburb. Personally, I think he quit because his mother died and he finally could say, "Now I'm doing what I want."

In any event, the claims and wild-eyed proclamations these folks made to Congress were so nuts, they were laughable. But the problem is: they aren't funny. They're absolutely terrifying because these people are serious, and, as they have shown, they are so caught up in their paramilitary fascist world that they've lost the ability to differentiate between fact and fantasy and they'll stop at nothing.

No. When I start bitching about those poor people whose brains are getting baked in all that hellishly Stygian heat and humidity on the swampy banks of the Potomac, I'm talking about the fact that the federal government is always coming up with these harebrained schemes to rip off the ranchers because these workers sit back there in these little tiny airless cubicles in Washington, and they don't have a window within a hundred yards, and they think about all the land we have out here. They just sit there and envision all our land, all our space, and they don't like it, and they think we have more than enough. Well, the fact is, we don't. This land isn't cultivated—it's straight prairie, pastureland—mostly dried out and windblown, and it takes fifty acres to raise a single steer and get it to market and break even, forget making any money. Try explaining that to one of these bleary-eyed bureaucrats. Forget getting across the concept of open range. The only way to make even a tiny bit of headway is to get them to understand that we need all this land so McDonald's doesn't run out of hamburgers.

So the speed-limit laws don't carry much water around here, and tonight I put on my "Best of the Beatles" tape and powered through the canyon, pushing the edge of the envelope the whole way. I blasted past Bennett's Fort, which was all closed up and dark, and hit the rise on the leading edge of the cattle guard at the entrance to the Circle B doing ninety-five. I shot through the air, sailing right over it, to the accompaniment of the final crescendo of "Twist and Shout." It was excellent.

I cruised on, through the cold manure- and pine-scented air, past the cattle pens and barns and the big main ranch house where my older brother, Elias Caulfield Bennett IV, who runs the ranch, lives. But other than the big farm light that illuminates the whole area down near the equipment sheds and cow barn, and a couple of lights back in his staff quarters, the farmyard and his house were dark.

Far off to my left, across the river valley, up on a distant hillside, Christian's house blazed like a Mississippi river boat. He runs the family newspaper and banks, and he and his wife, Mimi, are very social. If they aren't giving a party, they're going to one. They are involved in virtually everything that goes on in Roundup, which is why Christian just keeps getting richer and richer. Opportunities never stop walking through his door. I think I remember hearing that tonight's party was for some high-toned British publisher whose publishing house Mimi thought she might buy. Poetry and literary treatises, stuff like that. The kind of stuff that I admire people who read it, but I'm not one of 'em. And frankly, half the time I don't get it, not because I'm stupid, but because I don't much care about David Lloyd George's formative years at Eton, or whatever.

I like simpler things. For instance, I never tire of coming around the bend and seeing my house sitting there on the riverbank. Built by my great-grandfather for his mother, the house is constructed of typical ranch materials—chinked logs and stone chimneys and a tin roof—but its design is what makes it unusual: for some reason, it's more Australian than American West, except that my great-grandfather came from England. The ground floor, which contains the living room, dining room, kitchen, library, guest room, and bath, has three sets of French doors on each side of the house that open onto a wide, surrounding veranda. Upstairs, where my bed and bath and dressing rooms are, French doors with little balconies are cut into the sloping roof in each direction. There is a fireplace in every room.

It is just about as perfect as a house can get, and when you add Richard into the picture, it is complete. But the truth is, the house was built for one woman, and that's all that's ever lived in it, and if he were to stay permanently, which isn't looking too promising at the moment, we'd have to build something bigger—I'm way beyond thinking that sharing a bathroom with someone is a pleasurable or romantic experience, and it's not fair to make him go downstairs all the time.

Richard's old Mercedes convertible was parked in front, and as I drew closer, I could hear music pouring out the windows—*Rigoletto*. Verdi's tearjerker would open the Opera's outdoor summer season in three weeks.

I turned off my car and sat there for a moment, watching him through the open doors—my big old beaten-up cowboy with the craggy face and sun-scorched skin, faded Levis and mud-caked boots—sitting at the grand piano belting out *"La donna è mobile."*

Before I could stop her, Baby jumped out of the open car window, raced into the house, onto Richard's lap, and then onto the keyboard. The concert was over. He stuck her under his arm and met me at the door.

"How's Cyrus?" he asked. "You're so late, I was starting to get jealous."

"Don't bother," I said as we kissed hello. "He's dead. Let's have a drink."

"Coming right up."

I went upstairs and put my hair and makeup back together and sprayed on a little gardenia perfume, and by the time I got back down, he had the fire going in the living room and two dark-looking cocktails in crystal tumblers and a platter of chips with a bowl of Celestina's green chili salsa sitting on the coffee table.

"What's up?"

I told him about the party and Cyrus's death, the invitation to join the board, and about the endowment.

"Cyrus Vaile gave the theater company a twenty-million-dollar endowment?" Richard whistled. "That's incredible. What was it for?"

"I don't know," I said. "I didn't ask. Why? Does it make a difference?"

"Well, sure it does." Richard looked at me as though I were stupid, and frankly, when it comes to managing the arts, I sort of am. It's not exactly like anything else. For instance, if the books don't balance, you just ask for more.

"It could be for funding new playwrights," he said. "Or a special program in the conservatory to bring in directors and actors and teachers to teach master classes, or for design, or for production of specific classics. It could be for a dozen different things."

"Well," I said, trying not to be defensive, "it's missing."

"What do you mean, missing?"

"I'm not too sure. Cyrus said it was gone and that's why he wanted me to go on the board to try to find it."

Richard shook his head and stared into his drink as though the money might magically appear there. "Doesn't make any sense," he finally said. "An endowment fund can't simply vanish."

I shrugged. "I don't know what to tell you except that the annual meeting is tomorrow at noon and I'm going. Do you know George Wrightsman?"

"Sure. I know him well. He's crazy. Totally paranoid."

"What do you mean?"

"He runs the Rep like he's the dictator of a secret organization. Almost like a cult." As he spoke, Richard took my glass from my hand and went to the bar and added more ice and whisky to our drinks. "The management turnover is like a revolving door, except for Winston McMorris, who's his hatchet man, keeps all the nuts and bolts in place from the production side, and keeps his hand on the financial tiller. He's one of the top executive producers in the country.

"But all those elements that involve people from outside the company: board members, donors, volunteers, subscribers and the general audience, media—basically, anyone who isn't an actor, director, designer, or stage hand—George regards as the enemy because they all have to do with money, which, as you know, keeps us all going. He's an interesting guy. Very, very talented as a director. Very personable. I like him."

Richard handed me my drink and then settled back in the corner of the couch and stretched his legs across the coffee table. "Do you want to hear my favorite story about George Wrightsman?"

"Of course." I sat forward in my chair and reached for a chip. They were corn and sesame—about a million calories each. "I don't know anything about him at all."

"A few years ago," Richard said, "he decided to try to run the company in a full classical repertory style." He paused and looked at me. "Do you know what I mean?"

I could lie and say I did, but then I'd probably miss the whole point of the story. "I haven't got the slightest idea," I admitted.

"That's okay. Most people don't," Richard said, pleased to be enlightening me for a change. "Repertory theater is when there are two or three shows running and the performances are alternated. For instance, maybe the matinee is *Hamlet,* and the evening performance is *Romeo and Juliet* and the next night is *Othello,* and they just revolve around in continuing repertory."

"Always Shakespeare?" I asked, thinking the whole affair sounded pretty dreary.

"No, those were just examples. The shows and the performing art itself can be anything. If we had a bigger budget at the Opera, we'd do it. Anyway, back to George. He decided he wanted to run three shows—not just up and performing on a revolving, matinee, evening, day-to-day performance basis as they do now—but literally at the same time. So he rented two other little theaters in the neighborhood and launched three productions at once—one enormous opening night—and they ran for two weeks that way. Some of the actors were in two of the plays, and they were running up and down Cheyenne Street changing their costumes as they ran. It was wonderful. Almost killed everyone, but the national publicity—they got four pages in *Time*—and the thrill, were unforgettable. The actors want him to do it again, but I doubt if the board will let him. It cost—and lost—a fortune. The market here's not big enough to carry such an effort. Neither is the attention span," he added as an after-thought.

"Cyrus said George and Winston McMorris sit around and smoke dope all day."

Richard laughed. "Sure," he said, not even slightly surprised. "I'd believe that. Not all day, maybe. But I imagine a lot of that goes on over there."

I think of two-bit jerks and losers and high school kids as dope smokers. Not grownups, people who are admired, seen as leaders. It ticks me off. "Is that what you do at the Opera?"

Richard shook his head. "Nah," he said. "Whole different crowd. We just eat and drink a lot and have hysterics on a regular basis."

Celestina came in from the kitchen. "Ready?" she asked.

"*Sí,*" we both answered, and sat down as she placed a steaming casserole of hominy, beef, cheese, and green chilis, and a big green salad, down before us.

"*Bon appétit.*"

I was starving and ate my dinner the way I ate two whole Sara Lee strawberry cheesecakes once when I was twenty and smoked marijuana the first time. I only smoked it twice—the second time I lost fifty dollars' worth of those little whiffle golf balls at a miniature golf course and thought it was the funniest thing I'd ever done in my life. Evidently my date didn't, because he never asked me out again, which helped me figure out that smoking grass was not only illegal, it was also fattening and expensive, in terms of money and men, so I never did it again. But, boy, that cheesecake was fabulous.

CHAPTER

7

TUESDAY MORNING

When we set out for the barn at five-thirty for our morning ride, the sun had broken the horizon and turned the high, thin overcast in our big glorious sky into a purple, pink, fiery-red, and golden wonder. I don't know how God does it every day. I know this goes on all over the world, but the truth is, there is nothing like dawn out West. That is, if you like your view uncluttered, uninterrupted by trees or houses or skyscrapers. Or people.

When I was chief in Santa Bianca, I had an offer to move to Manhattan, not as chief, but way up there, certainly as the top-ranking female detective inspector in the history of New York law enforcement. It would have been a big deal, and a great and challenging position, and I seriously considered it for a while. But I found myself waking up in the middle of the night thinking about living in a place with no dawn and no sunset, no ability to get a sense of where the sun was coming from when your day began, and where it was going to when it ended. There would be only the growth and diminishment of light. No way to push away the horizon. I couldn't do it. I turned them down.

A lot of women, some of whom I knew, some I didn't, who were closely involved in a number of women's issues organizations, went nuts over my decision, said I'd let the sisterhood down. What a load. What is all this *sister* deal anyhow? Other than a propagandized attempt at imposing a guilt trip? At least fifty percent of the world's population is female, and believe me, ladies, they may be your sisters, but they aren't mine, and I don't consider their plight my own just because we are of the same gender. Sorry. Seeing a sunrise is more important to me than being the crime prevention poster girl for the sisterhood.

But then, I'm a Westerner and we pretty much think and do what we want, whether it's socially acceptable or not. Every time someone uses the initials "P.C." to mean "Politically Correct," I still think they're talking about personal computers.

By the time Richard and I got down to the barn, Art, our ranch manager, had our horses, Hotspur and Ariel, saddled up and ready to go. A homemade cigarette sat glued to his bottom lip and he rolled it over to the corner of his mouth with his tongue and took a gulp of coffee.

"Have a good one," he said, swatting Ariel on her hind end, and we set off across the meadow, following the river toward the canyon country—the creaking of our saddles and the soft footfalls of our mounts the only sounds in the silent morning. We were the only two people in the world, except for the birds who began to sail and sing as we passed, lining our route like Londoners greeting the Queen.

"What are you thinking about?" Richard turned toward me from the back of his gigantic palomino stallion. The wrinkles around his eyes deepened into crevasses and his eyes smiled at me through the deep morning shadows. "You're never this quiet."

"Cyrus," I answered, ready to put my sleepless night into words. "I've been thinking about what he said, about how things were yellow, had a halo effect. He thought my pink suit was purple. I thought about it all night, and finally the bell went off. A few years ago in Santa

Bianca, when I began to specialize in poisons and was working on my master's in toxicology, one of the scenarios had to do with digoxin poisoning. Digoxin is synthesized from digitalis, and it's commonly used to slow and regulate the heart. If you put Cyrus's vision together with his heart problems, and if he was taking digoxin, he could have been poisoned with it, if someone increased his dosage a little. That's what it does."

"What?" Richard remarked, as we broke into a slow, comfortable canter along the flat road. Our horses' hoofbeats echoed off the tree-lined corridor and sounded fake, like wood blocks on an old radio show. "Turns everything yellow and then you die?"

"Yup. That's pretty much the way it works." I grinned over at him. "Unless you get help first, of course. It's pretty simple to correct."

"How do you know this stuff?" Richard asked. His voice gave away his bewilderment.

He loves what I do. He loves the danger, the hours, the guns, the power as much as I do. My bravado, which he mistook for courage, attracted him like honey. But the attraction was incredibly equal. I didn't care much for his hours—nights and weekends—and there was little physical danger in opera, and the guns were, hopefully, props. But his self-assurance, his masculinity, his ability to talk anybody into any-thing, his ability to rope a running calf cleanly without raising his butt off his saddle, the way he could set me on fire with the smallest caress, left me breathless in the same stupid overheated schoolgirl way that Troy Donahue did in *A Summer Place*. Another thing: I felt so incredibly safe around Richard, although I'd never been aware of feeling unsafe before.

My knowledge of poisons turned him on, and I could tell he wanted to tackle me off my horse and drag me into the trees.

"It's what I do." I blew him a kiss and then leaned forward and squeezed my knees into Ariel's withers, giving her the green light.

My little bay quarter horse mare took off like a rocket, leaving the palomino in the dust. Sooner or later, I knew, they'd catch up, because even if we could go faster, they could go farther. Richard and I were a real tortoise-and-hare combination. I think that's why we got along so well—one of us was always standing there holding the net for the other.

I dressed in what I thought was a very smart red tweed suit with red and navy kid pumps. A perfect theater-board-of-directors-meeting en-semble. Even if I couldn't play the part very convincingly, I could look it, and sometimes that's half the battle. I headed to the office, swinging my Jeep into the dirt lot behind the saloon, next to Linda's little four-wheel-drive truck, which had a pine-tree-shaped air freshener hanging from the rearview mirror, and clipped up the steep, rickety, wooden stairs that were attached precariously to the outside of the old clapboard building.

No matter what time I get to the office in the morning, Linda Long, my secretary, is always there first. She's about fifty and left her husband when she caught him and the neighbor's sixteen-year-old daughter in the hayloft.

"Don't think I'm telling you this to get sympathy," she told me when I was interviewing her. "I was glad to get out of there. That ranching life is too tough when you get to be my age. Too tough and too lonely. He needs a young wife. She can have him and the ranch and the cows."

It turned out that during all those long, lonely years on their ranch outside of Riverton, Linda had read every book and journal, paper and periodical ever written, and while she might not have been ready for a big city like Denver, she quickly found her legs in our little city of Roundup and took like a duck to water in my small, thriving operation with its Bennett's Fort international headquarters. She knew hardware, software, and telecommunications cold, watched the bottom line like a banshee, and studied foreign languages in her spare time. She was speaking French into the phone when Baby and I walked in.

"Très bien, madame," she said, her voice enthusiastic and friendly. *"Oui, oui, oui. Je la dirai, toute à l'heure. Au revoir."* She hung up. "Hey, hi." She smiled at me like a twelve-year-old who'd just gotten an A.

"Bon jour," I answered. Bright springtime sun streamed into my office through the tall windows that opened onto the main, and only, street of Bennett's Fort. I looked down toward the jail and saw my deputy crossing the street in my direction. "What's Dwight doing around so early?"

U. S. Deputy Marshal Dwight Alexander's main job is to work the make-believe shootouts and talk to the tourists. He's as handsome and sweet and dumb as marzipan and the crowds just love him.

Dwight's the failed son of a Grosse Pointe tycoon. A bastard, a miserable drunken son of a bitch, according to Dwight, who accused his only son of being a slacker, of malfeasance and drunkenness, of hedonism, sexual addictions, and just general goofiness, for his whole life. And for Mr. Alexander, Sr., it had become a self-fulfilling prophecy.

His young heir is a nice kid who basically will never be more than a heart-stoppingly handsome guy with little gray matter between his ears and an enormous, highly talented snake in his pants. This is according to not only the scores of bosomy young girls who hang around the cheesy shops in Bennett's Fort in midriff-length, sheer white cotton, skin-tight T-shirts and short shorts that are cut way high on their backsides, showing off their perfectly toned little honeydew bottoms, buying gifts of after-shave for Dwight; but also, it is based on Linda's and my visual assessment of maybe not scores, but certainly dozens, of Roundup's unhappily married society ladies who normally wouldn't be caught dead in Bennett's Fort but think of reasons to jump into their Jaguar sedans and Mercedes wagons with their tinted windows and rush out here between the hours of ten and four and slip into the jail cleverly disguised in their Valentino suits and Giorgio Armani sunglasses. At least Dwight has the judgment to draw the blinds and lock the door during their visits and put out the sign: THE MARSHAL IS OUT WITH A POSSE— PLEASE CALL AGAIN.

He wandered in and took up his customary perch on the edge of my desk, where he likes to swing his booted foot slowly back and forth, using it like a cat's tail to hypnotize his prey. I had to struggle not to look. Police work, to Dwight, is incidental, a scam, a camouflage. He makes no attempt to conceal the fact that sex is his single raison d'être, and I'm pretty sure he is very, very good.

"I thought when I became a deputy I'd get to do some real law enforcement stuff," he said, twisting a paper match between his fingers. His biceps bulged beneath the short sleeves of his khaki uniform shirt.

"I tried to tell you, Dwight, that my duties as a U.S. marshal are more window dressing than anything. I told you you'd be bored."

"Well, but we've got this nice little jail and all, and . . ." He tossed the match into the wastebasket and drummed his fingers on his belt buckle. "I am getting kind of lonely, Marshal Lilly. We haven't had a single prisoner since that Witness Protection Program fellow last Christmas. You don't even come to visit."

Of course I didn't go visit him in his jail with its CALL AGAIN sign and snap-roll shades and Jean Naté Splash he keeps alongside the lavender soap and fluffy hand towels at the sink in one of the little cells where the bunk is always freshly made—because all I could do was picture me sitting on the edge of Wyatt Earp's desk with my whipcord skirt and lacy petticoat around my thighs. And my high-necked blouse ripped right open—the little buttons dotting the floor like pearls—and my pink, hard nipples in Dwight Alexander's talented hands, him standing between my legs, rocking back and forth in long, deep, slow strokes, telling me how good it was.

"Maybe one of these days I'll come up with another prisoner," I said, forcing my eyes away from his buckle. "You know, our jail is only for high-profile prisoners the feds want to keep out of sight, and I guess there just aren't any of those around right now. Look at the bright side—you're an actual, fully trained, sworn-in U.S. deputy marshal—charged with 'enforcing the laws of the United States.' That's a pretty tall order."

"Yeah." He grinned. "What I like best is working around you. One of these days, you'll give in."

"Have a nice day, Dwight," I said. My mouth was so dry I could scarcely make the words come out.

Linda followed him out with her eyes before heading back into my office; her no-nonsense stacked heels clomped sturdily on the wooden floor. "That boy." She shook her head and blew out her breath. "Takes my pulse about an hour to slow down when he leaves. Buck just pulled up with a whole load of new rocks. I can't believe how much he sells that junk for, and that people actually buy it."

"I know," I agreed, following her gaze down the street away from Dwight, who was kicking dirt clods and tugging down on his trouser pockets with his thumbs, rearranging himself. I cleared my throat and recrossed my legs and decided to buy a lacy petticoat and a pearl-buttoned blouse, just in case.

Of course, looking at my cousin, Buck Bennett, had the same effect as a dose of cold water. Buck owns Bennett's Fort—lock, stock, and barrel—and rakes in millions every year from tourists with too much money and too little taste or brains or both. He was supervising two wranglers in the off-loading of several large cardboard barrels from the bed of his old Ford pickup.

"It's scary, isn't it?" I added.

Even though he wasn't actually doing any of the lifting, Buck was already sweating heavily in the early morning sun. His checkered shirt was soaked with perspiration and had come unsnapped around his enormous belly. He took off his hat and wiped his bearded face and shiny bean with a bandanna and cracked jokes with the workmen as they hefted the barrels of petrified dinosaur manure, geodes, flint chips. "These rare and priceless flint relics are left over from the arrowheads of Ancient Native Peoples," he assures the gawkers from Arkansas. Fool's gold, mica, asbestos, and huge rough chunks of rose quartz go past him on the men's straining backs into the Rock Shop.

Buck buys the goods for almost nothing from a supplier in Denver and sells them to the tourists for an arm and a leg, claiming he's found it all out there in the prairies and hills right outside of Bennett's Fort. "Had to kill dozens of rattlesnakes for each one. See these fang marks on my arms?" He asks, showing them the scars left over from where he scratched himself when he had chicken pox when he was eight. They don't care. They buy it faster than he can bring it in.

He is the son of my father's late, and only, cousin and, as a Bennett, has full access and opportunity to all of the family benefits. But like so many of these men—Vietnam vets, now in their fifties—Buck just never did get it all back together after he got home.

"Don't try any of that delayed stress bullshit on me, Uncle Eli," he'd said to my father. "There's nothin' wrong with me I can't handle, I just choose not to get into that corporate bullshit situation—askin' permission to take a crap. Just give me Bennett's Fort and mind your own goddamn business."

Putting a request and an insult in the same sentence is a common Bennett family trait. Like, "Give me the gun, asshole." Or sometimes we reverse it. "I can't imagine who on earth could have told you that color was right for you. Why don't you just give the sweater to me?"

But at least my father had one solid successor to the Bennett empire—my brother Christian—and that's all that's necessary. More than one, things start to get messy. Elias, who was older and born the heir apparent, made it clear when he got home from Vietnam that he wanted to run the ranch. Period.

Buck saw me in the window. "Hey," he yelled, the sun glinting off his mirrored highway patrol glasses. "Come on down and have a cup of coffee."

"Maybe later," I called back.

Buck keeps his office in the large rear booth of the Golden Nugget Saloon, directly below my office, and I try to meet him and Elias at least once a day for a couple of shots and some uplifting conversation, just to stay in touch with the alternate lifestyle element of the family. I love both these guys so much.

"Suit yourself," he said and disappeared into the saloon for his first cup of the day of Irish coffee. Buck drinks more than anyone I've ever known in my life. He's a big old bull elephant—nothing seems to faze him. He just keeps bulling along. One time, I watched him lie on his back and single-handedly jack up a dump truck to change a tire, and it wasn't one of those fancy hydraulic jacks, either. The other hand held a can of beer straight up on his laundry bag belly. Never spilled a drop. He's divorced and his daughter will be starting her senior year at Vassar this fall.

"This is a good one, I think." Linda held the notes from the French conversation in her hand. "Three leading vintners have died in the last two years, each unexpectedly and under mysterious circumstances, but apparently not mysteriously enough that the prefecture of Sûreté in Beaune—that's the capital of Burgundy," she primly informed me, "sees anything amiss. So the widow of the latest to die, let me see"— Linda glanced at the slip and articulated the name first silently to herself—"the Countess Louisa de Rochefoucauld, wants to know if you'll look into it for her."

"Hmm," I said, sorting through the mail and messages stacked on my desk. "How did she get my name?"

"The marchese. She's his first cousin."

"What a wonderful little world," I said.

"Tell me about it."

A few days earlier, Richard and I had gotten home from Tuscany, where we'd spent two weeks softening up and tricking Vincenzo Cortini—the evil, larcenous, broke first cousin of my client, the Marchese Enrico Cortini—into selling us the Titian he'd stolen right out of the music room in the marchese's ancient seaside villa and hung in the library of his own falling-down palazzo in Saturnia. The family was scandalized.

"There!" The tall, handsome, graying marchese had glowered imperially when we arrived in Porto Ercole. His pale blue eyes glared down a long, thin, arched beak, and he pointed an accusing finger at a small square of music-room wall that was several shades of ocher darker than the rest of the high-ceilinged, slightly mildewed drawing room. "Since the 1600s it has been there. Right from under my nose. He is no good." He flipped his fingers in the air as though he were tossing a newspaper out the window of a moving car.

"I'll get it back for you, Enrico," I said.

We sealed the deal with a lot of great wine and then, the next day, Richard and I drove off to a snug little mountainside hotel in Montefollonico, where the view had not changed for five hundred years. Over the next two weeks we posed as a newly rich, newly wed, delightfully naive American couple wanting to buy a Titian—any Titian would do—for an insane amount of money as our wedding gift to each other. Finally, through a set-up introduction by a major auction house, the marchese's cousin sold us his. As we passed through the gates of his villa and down the cypress-lined drive, Richard saw him in the rearview mirror, literally jumping for joy over his good fortune. Unfortunately, our check wasn't any good.

The night before we left Italy to come home to Wyoming, the marchese gave, in our honor, in the music room under the candlelit gaze of the rescued Madonna, the most opulent, excessive dinner party I've ever been to in my life, with Chianti from his private vineyards and olive oil from his orchards, *orecchietti y vongole*—little ear-shaped pasta and tiny fresh clams gathered that dawn on his beaches—spring lamb and fresh rosemary, succulent figs with fresh pecorino and prosciutto. It was literally a fountainhead bacchanal that had taken centuries of practice to create.

And later, as the springtime moon came through the window of our bedroom and tiny lights twinkled on the boats in the harbor, I was pretty sure Richard was going to propose, but he didn't. But I'm pretty sure he's about to.

Linda handed me the notes she'd taken from her conversation with the French countess and went to pour me a cup of coffee. "Do you want a blueberry muffin?"

"No, thanks. I've hit the bottom. I'm never going to eat again as long as I live."

"Okay," she said, and closed the door. God, she didn't even try to change my mind. I must be even fatter than I thought. I checked my watch. Eight o'clock. I dialed the morgue at Christ and St. Luke's Hospital, our regional medical center in Roundup.

"Dr. Leavy, please," I said when a technician answered.

"I'm sorry, she isn't in yet. I expect her any minute. Can I have her call you?"

"This is Lilly Bennett and I'm calling to get a status report on the Vaile autopsy."

"Just a minute," he said, and put me on hold. He came back a minute later. "Are you a member of the immediate family?"

"No."

"Well, I'm sorry. The autopsy is being conducted at the request of the family. I can only discuss it with them."

"Don't make me come down there and show you my badge," I said, irritated. "Just tell me if it's been done, and if it hasn't, when it will be."

"I don't think I'd better. I could get in trouble."

People like this used to make me crazy; now I'm relieved to find a half-wit every now and then who does *not* have decision-making responsibility. "Have Dr. Leavy call me," I said, and gave him my number. I didn't want to start out my day like this. I wanted to go back to Italy.

At about ten o'clock Linda stuck her head in the door. "A woman named Shelley Pirelli is on the phone. Wants to know if you can meet with George Wrightsman at eleven before the board meeting."

"Sure," I said. "I'd love to. Tell her I'll be there."

I'd never been to the Roundup Repertory Company's offices before. They were directly across Cheyenne Street from the Vaile Theater. There was no identification on the glass front door and, once inside, I peered down a narrow dark hallway and saw the bright blue metal door of a small cage elevator and an adjacent steep narrow staircase. Beyond it, the hallway seemed to compress and darken even more into the sort of dangerous site women are taught to avoid. The chipped black and white linoleum floor was filthy with layers of grime and littered with paper. A small hand-printed sign thumbtacked to the elevator door frame—RECEPTION–FIFTH FLOOR—emerged from the gloom.

I pushed the button. Nothing happened. I pushed it again, but the only sound was that of my breathing in the oppressive, dank atmosphere. I pushed it again. Nothing. I could feel the skin on my back start to prickle and my pulse quicken. I must be in the wrong building.

Suddenly, loud voices began to echo and ricochet deafeningly down the stairwell into big cannonballs of sound that rolled across the floor, and almost simultaneously the front door opened and a knot of young men and women, shrouded more than dressed in several versions of black leggings, turtlenecks, and scarves, and carrying heavy book bags and notebooks, squeezed into the tiny entryway and banged impatiently on the elevator call button. One or two of them eyed me suspiciously and returned to their jabber, leaving me uncomfortably, and self-consciously, aware of being an outsider, and an old, plump one at that, caught in the undertow of their swirling, exclusive mob.

"This thing's never going to come," a long-haired, bearded young man said, slapping his hand against the side of the silent elevator shaft. "I'm late for Voice." He started up the stairs, squeezing past the flow that thundered down. A number of other students followed him.

I wasn't really too sure what to do. And then the front door opened and a small, pudgy, slightly jowly man in clip-on dark glasses entered. Trimmed, dark brown hair circled his balding head. He wore white sweatpants, a hooded white sweatshirt, and tennis shoes. A long, bright yellow jersey muffler, perfectly arranged as though it had been ironed in place, was draped two or three times around his neck. A bursting navy canvas tote bag with the Roundup Rep ascending angel logo painted on the side was slung over his shoulder, and he clasped the straps in a plump, pink hand. An awed silence came over the rabble.

"It's not working?" he asked.

"No." Almost all the students answered at once.

He twirled and departed, leaving only a lingering scent of lemons and a fluttering yellow fringe in his wake.

"Oh, God. He is so brilliant." A young man broke the quivering hush.

"I saw some of *Macbeth* yesterday," said another reverentially. "You won't even believe what he's getting out of Ray. He is the most righteous, indignant MacDuff since Dustin."

Hoffman, I assumed. I also assumed I'd just experienced my first sighting of George Wrightsman, and frankly, he didn't look all that brilliant to me. And besides, we had a meeting in a few minutes. Which evidently had just been canceled due to elevator failure.

Nevertheless, I joined the crushing migration up the stairs, pulled along like a refugee swept up in the crowded maelstrom of a foreign country, wondering in the back of my mind if the fire inspector had visited this place recently. At every landing, a few students cut away from the herd while others wedged themselves in, and even when I'd reached the fifth floor, the horde kept surging, up and down, in and out of doors, bumping and buffeting me, until I somehow spun out of the whirl and found myself eye to eye with a black receptionist whose desk was heaped with books and scripts, a cheap vase of dead flowers, and a large, old-fashioned PBX board. A headset crossed her closely cropped head.

"Good morning, Roundup Rep," she said into the mouthpiece as she looked at me with flat, black eyes. The skin around them crinkled. "One moment, please." She pushed a button and yelled over her shoulder into an open office door, "Winston, Glenn Close's coming through."

"Righto," he called back. "Thanks, Celia."

"May I help you?" Her wary expression let me know she was experienced, guarded, and savvy, prepared for friend or foe, with an alarm bell next to her knee and a .45 in her drawer.

"I'm Lilly Bennett," I said. "I have an appointment with George Wrightsman."

"Oh, sure, fine," Celia said with a little more warmth, but not much. "Just have a seat and I'll let Shelley know you're here."

From a broken-down, red vinyl couch across from her desk, I watched Celia in action. Every person in that unrelenting, unabated stream of students, actors, managers, and whatever who passed her bulkhead was greeted by name, and she handed out message slips as though they were numbers at a drawing, sometimes adding little personal observations to the recipients, little compliments on what they were wearing, or how wonderful they'd been at last night's performance, or how she was going to stop in at their rehearsal on her lunch break. She never stopped moving, she never stopped talking—deftly integrating the phone into the surrounding live action—she never got rattled. Everything about her was smooth and even, like a perfectly engineered perpetual motion machine.

"Miss Bennett," she said to me, neatly working me into her process without a bump, "Shelley will be right out. Would you like a cup of coffee or something to drink?"

"No, thanks," I said, glancing up at twenty years of posters listing the company's seasons. "I'm all set."

The posters all had the same design, only the colors had been changed from year to year. Didn't look very fun. Except for the plays, which were all classics. Nothing weird or avant garde, which was fine with me.

A woman in a dove-gray suit and chunky silver jewelry, from the public relations or development department, I imagined—she had long red fingernails and a burning cigarette—came in. "Where's that goddamned photographer?" she said to Celia, who shrugged. "Kindly find that son of a bitch and tell him if he isn't at this shoot in five minutes, I'll can his ass." Then she noticed me and smiled sweetly. "Good morning. Happy to see you," she said, and stomped out.

From the corner of my eye, I saw Winston McMorris's lanky frame disappear down a hallway, followed by a West Highland white terrier.

It was, honest to God, like being in Oz.

CHAPTER

9

I waited for about five more minutes, straightening and restraightening my white cotton gloves across my nubbly red tweed knee, and reminding myself I'd had about ten chances not to put myself in this dirty, junked-up waiting room with all these long-haired Hamlets and Cordelias, so my wasted time was no one's fault but my own, when finally Shelley Pirelli's narrow, olive face appeared.

"I apologize, Lilly," she said, walking toward me with her hand extended. "Just as you arrived, George got a call from Vienna about the tour the company is doing there in July. But, unless he's gotten on the phone again, I think we're all set."

She guided me along, shoulder to shoulder, indicating the direction with an extended hand, through a claustrophobic passageway with offices on either side. "I love your suit," she said with a phoniness that made me want to laugh out loud. But when I looked at her eyes, they sparkled with humor and intelligence. There was also cunning there. And envy. "I'd never have the nerve to wear that color."

"Why not?" I asked, wanting to add, "What possible harm could it do?"

There was something of Eliza Doolittle about Shelley that made you want to take her in hand and lead her off to Elizabeth Arden for a complete makeover, the potential seemed so great. Yesterday's voluptuousness was hidden beneath a poorly fitted, cheap, teal-blue suit. The twill sleeves reached her knuckles, and the skirt fell just below her knees, giving her an air of vulnerability. She had on the same open-toed sandals and dark brown stockings as the day before, except that I hadn't gotten close enough at Cyrus's to notice that her big toe extended way past the others. It looked awful, like an old woman at a bus stop. I didn't tell her that with a little concentrated guidance and very little money she could be stunning. Mother would have; she regards such helpful tips as Duty.

"There's nothing to it," I said to her instead. "As long as you get the right red. The wrong one can make you look lousy."

"Oh, I don't know." She wrinkled her nose and shook her head; her kinky hair rippled down her back. "I had my colors done and I'm strictly autumn. Red's never for me. I usually wear jeans to work, but I wore this today because of the funeral. Is that what you're wearing to Cyrus's thing this afternoon?"

I'd been so wrapped up in Cyrus's autopsy, I'd completely forgotten he was going to be buried at four o'clock. "A red suit at a funeral? Heavens, no." I sounded exactly like my mother, whose tone of voice always left the implication of "you fool," hanging at the end of such statements. "I'll go home and change after the meeting."

I followed her up a short staircase into a large open room, one side of which was floor-to-ceiling windows that hadn't been washed since the building was built, maybe fifty or sixty years ago, and around another corner into her office, where a window alongside her desk opened into what I assumed to be George Wrightsman's office. "Here we are," she said.

The man in the white sweat suit sat in a swivel armchair, leaning way forward, giving angry orders to Winston McMorris, and when he saw us through the window, he waved and smiled and jumped to his feet.

"Oh!" he exclaimed when Shelley opened the door. He clapped his hands together with what appeared to be genuine unbridled joy, and his face absolutely beamed. I'd never seen a more beautiful smile. "Oh!" he said again. "I am so delighted to meet you."

It was remarkable. I felt caught in an incredible energy field that was so strong, so seductive, it almost made me dizzy. I was instantly and intensely drawn to him, not in a sexual way, but rather in a way of the cosmos, the eternal universe. The discovery of a shared soul, a teacher. I felt amazed and exhilarated, like laughing out loud.

"Please come over here and sit down." He took my arm and led me to a brown canvas director's chair. "You know Winston?"

"Yes." I smiled and we shook hands. His bony grip was clammy and uncertain. The little Westie slept beneath his chair. "We met yesterday at Cyrus Vaile's. Nice to see you again."

"Yes," Winston answered tentatively. He was wearing dark glasses.

George had unwrapped the yellow mantle by a turn or two and held the ends in his hands, like a flight officer using paddles to direct traffic on the deck of an aircraft carrier. I guessed it might have been a stage director's device to provide emphasis. Without the scarf: Walk this way. With it: Walk THIS way.

"Please, please sit down," the right paddle indicated. "What would you like to drink? How about some nice herbal tea? It always calms me down before a board meeting. Yes? Shelley, bring Lilly a cup of tea. Winston? Nothing? All right, that's it then."

George's desk was actually a large Queen Anne dining-room table shoved into a corner, so that he sat facing out from it into a semicircle of a half-dozen directors' chairs and little wooden box tables. The desk's surface was extremely well ordered, with a neat stack of files and typed correspondence on small-sized letterhead, his name emblazoned in navy blue at the top, and two magnificent black and white photographs in sterling silver frames—one signed by Sir Laurence Olivier and one by a woman I didn't recognize—and a tall cut crystal vase of purple lilacs. A large, dusty, three-dimensional gold sculpture of the ascending angel hung above the desk, and around the room the same indistinguishable framed posters from each of the company's seasons hung on the pale yellow walls. Plush, new green carpeting covered the floor.

Shelley crept back in with my colorless, odorless, lifeless tea in a gold-rimmed cup and disappeared again without a word. She had a grungy old Band-Aid on her heel and the edge of it had caused a run in her stocking.

"Winston tells me you've joined the board?" George picked up a large glass of water and took a big gulp. As he spoke, I noticed that his mouth looked and sounded as if it were full of cotton balls, almost glued shut with dryness, the way some people get when they're extremely nervous. He set the glass down deliberately and blotted his lips meticulously with the scarf. His eyes were large and black behind wire-framed glasses.

George Wrightsman was probably gay, but his mannerisms were not those of an effeminate man so much as they were high-performance, precision-machined actions—specific, well-thought-out, unequivocal movements. No wonder this theater was not an improv operation; that would be anathema to him, a surprising characteristic in an individual whose profession it was to encourage gut reactions from his artists. But then, actors are only spontaneous within the boundaries of their characters, and I wondered which role Mr. Wrightsman, whose bookshelf displayed a number of golden Tonys for his own Broadway performances over the years, was playing for me.

"Yes," I said. "Cyrus invited me onto the board yesterday—just before he died," I tacked on almost as an afterthought.

"Hum. Yes." George breathed in deeply and let out a long sigh. "Poor, poor Cyrus. He did so much for us." He slumped back, his hands falling limply between his legs, and then he seemed to sink into some sort of deep gloom.

Winston and I waited quietly, respectfully, but not for long, because without any warning at all, not even so much as a precipitous grin, George—followed a split second later by Winston—burst into outrageously disrespectful laughter, which made the sleeping Westie jump to its feet and lap the room, barking.

"He's dead. He's dead," George cried. "Thank You, God. Thank You, God."

I realized they were both completely stoned. Totally blasted.

What to do? What I wanted to do was place my teacup on the edge of his desk—I hate herbal tea anyway, it's, like, Why Bother?—and say, "Thanks, have a nice life, and good luck on your future."

But there were just too many questions floating around. What I was witnessing with this stupid behavior could be important, or it could simply be two grown men wasting my time. But what if Cyrus *had* been poisoned? What if twenty million dollars *had* been stolen? I wished Dr. Leavy would hurry up and beep me on my pager about the autopsy. Let me know if I should stay in this nut house or go back to the ranch and take my phone off the hook.

Through the window, Shelley, waiflike in her too large jacket, sat focused on her computer screen. From behind, her shoulder pads were so high and so wide, she could have had electric frying pans stuffed in there. She was either oblivious to, accustomed to, or ignoring what was going on in George Wrightsman's office. She folded a stick of gum into her mouth with one hand while the other flew along her keyboard. A Dicta-phone headset cut across her puff of hair, which swayed slightly to what-ever was on either end. I don't think it was dictation. I think it was Yanni.

"You boys haven't been smoking marijuana, have you?" I asked once they'd calmed down a little. "You do know it's against the law." Which made them laugh all the harder.

Finally George removed his glasses and blotted his eyes and cheeks with the soft sleeve of his snowy white sweatshirt. "Please don't arrest me, Lilly," he said. "You can't imagine how happy I am that Cyrus Vaile is dead. He was strangling me and this company to death."

"How?"

"How? How? Oh, God," George said. "A million ways. Every day he thought up a new torture to jam his business head onto my artists. He insisted that the company run the same way a profit-making corpo-ration operates, and it's just not the nature of the beast. This is a *theater,* a nonprofit organization, we're not meant to make money—we need patrons, we need contributed financial support to survive." George leaned back in the canvas chair and rolled his eyes at the ceiling, and I saw that the laughter was gone. He looked quarrelsome. "But the big-gest betrayal, the last straw, came two months ago when he launched a campaign to get the board to agree to sell the air rights over the theater for thirty million dollars. A big Japanese hotel company apparently had made such an offer."

George's smooth face was flushed, and his plump, clean, soft hands had balled into fists around the ends of the armrests. "It's *my* theater, it exists only because *my* company brings it life, *my* vision, and I'll die before someone puts a big hotel or office building on top of it. This is a classical repertory company we're running, one of the best in the English-speaking world—not a shoe sale in some third-rate frontier general store."

He leaped to his feet, took a giant stride toward me, and jammed his fists into his thick waist, addressing me. Like Yul Brynner. "And I'll be goddamned if some *businessman* is going to turn it into a real estate operation. And I'll tell you another thing," George hollered down at Winston and me. His face was red and furious. "The only reason Cyrus wanted to pull this off was because he needed to control me, needed to control the company. He didn't give a damn about the money or the hotel. He cared about the control. He wanted to break my back because I didn't love him.

"He was nothing but a second-rate, overweening, tyrannical, immoral old fogey shyster who decided that if I wouldn't be his lover he would destroy me and my work and my life. I am so happy he's dead, I am even considering closing the offices this afternoon during his funeral and throwing the biggest party this company's ever seen."

I could see why he'd won all those Tonys. He was beyond fury. He was a controlled frenzy of thunderbolts. Consumed with rage. He was Marlon Brando in *On the Waterfront*. He was fabulous.

"We have suffered, Miss Bennett." He paused and drew in a deep breath. His shoulders sagged and I thought I'd never in my life seen anyone so downtrodden. "Suffered as you cannot imagine. We have been artistically and financially suffocated and strangled, and now we are free because Cyrus Vaile is dead. Thank God." He whispered out the last words and collapsed into his chair, his eyes heavenward, his arms stretched up toward the sky, as tears poured down his cheeks.

I am quite sure my mouth was hanging open. I know my eyes were wide. I'd been pushed back into my chair by G forces, and I felt like applauding. Winston looked down at his hands, but I couldn't look away from George's eyes. They burned like dark diamonds—bright and brilliant. They burned with the fire of a cornered mother bear. Electricity singed the air and I found myself so drawn to him, so aroused, so smothered in the field of his personality, I could scarcely move.

"I need your help," he said to me softly.

"What do you need?" I whispered, drawn back to reality only by a light knock on the door followed by Shelley's unobtrusive entry. She closed the door and quietly leaned against it, fidgeting with her fingernails like an usherette waiting for the show to be over. If she'd been Southern, I would have called the way she was eyeing Winston just downright "slatternly."

"I need allies on the board. Cyrus has turned them all against me," George said, slowly regaining his composure. He took a drink of water and rearranged the scarf, smoothing it across his round chest and stomach. "Even Bradford Lake, my leading director, has turned his back. Bradford and I have been together for years, since the start. Since Yale. And now I think someone is trying to kill me."

"Why?" I asked.

"Someone tried to run him off the road the other night," Shelley said, picking up the glasses and cups and placing them on a silver-plated tray. "It's time to go up to the meeting, George," she added as if it were a footnote, before continuing. "He had to swerve into a wall to avoid being killed."

"How do you know it was on purpose?"

"Mine was the only car on the road until this other one showed up and started squeezing me off the edge—it was up in the mountains—and my brakes had been cut."

"I haven't heard of anyone cutting brakes for years," I said. "You must have a really old car."

"Well, you know," George said, "I'm not mechanical at all. Tampered with, I guess I mean."

"Did you call the police?"

"Of course. My car was totaled."

"What did they do?" I asked.

"Arrested me."

"Arrested you?"

"I might have had a little too much to drink."

"What did they say about the brakes?"

"I didn't tell them."

"Why not?"

"You have to understand, Lilly," Shelley joined in. "George was very frightened and it was only after, not until the next morning, that he remembered how terrifying the drive had been and how he couldn't get the car stopped."

"Did you have them checked?"

"What," George asked. "The brakes?"

I nodded.

He looked up at Shelley, and she nodded. "They'd been readjusted by then."

Oh, boy, I thought. This is a bunch of coconuts.

"Who do you think it was?" I asked, going along. "Who wants to kill you?"

"I think it was Bradford," George said, his eyes blazing.

"Bradford and Gigi," Shelley said at the same time.

"Bradford," Winston muttered. "Or *Macbeth*."

"It's not *Macbeth*," George said emphatically. "I think Bradford and Gigi and Cyrus decided the only way they could get rid of me was to kill me. Cyrus wanted Bradford to run the company after he sold the air rights to the Japanese and got me out of the way."

"Gigi?" I said.

"You know," George snapped impatiently. "Our grand, grand, grand, grand, grand leading lady: Gigi Dorrance-Downs." He tossed a scarf-end in the air for dramatic emphasis.

"Plus," Shelley said, almost as though she were egging George on, trying to feed his paranoia, "there's that stuff with Patrick."

George gave her a get-a-life look and rolled his eyes in my direction. "Honestly, Bradford is so dramatic sometimes. He's apparently sworn out some sort of a blood oath against me and is bent on revenge because he thinks it's my fault that Patrick—one of his protégés—is dead. He died of AIDS a few months ago."

"And he thinks you gave it to him?"

George nodded.

"Do you have AIDS?" I asked.

He gave me a very stern frown. "Certainly not," he said. "Besides, Patrick was never my type."

"The point is," said Winston, "Bradford blames George for everything that goes wrong, and now if you were to ask him, he would simply blame everything on *Macbeth*."

"Ah," I said sagely, pretending I knew what he was talking about, and thinking that unless you were on drugs you could never make any of this stuff up.

"As I'm sure you know, *Macbeth* is a very bad-luck piece of work." Winston kept going. Slight patches of color were returning to his gaunt, gray cheeks. "Ever since it was written, every time it's produced, terrible calamities occur. People break legs, theaters burn down, a couple of people have died mysteriously."

"Right," I said, and just because this seemed as good a time as any to float my potential trial balloon, I added, "Then that might explain— if it in fact turns out to be true—why Cyrus was murdered."

"Murdered?" George drew out the word.

"Yes," I answered, unable to control my smile. "How would that strike you?"

I thought George was going to erupt into another display, but after a moment he spat out Bradford Lake's name.

"*Macbeth*." Winston insisted.

Shelley just looked at them and shook her head.

T U E S D A Y   N O O N

All I could think about after I left George's office and followed Winston up another single-file staircase, next to another coffin-sized elevator, was how I couldn't wait to tell Richard all about this bizarre experience. Of course, he'd just tell me it was business as usual.

I already knew I'd be virtually no help as a board member, but the opportunity just to be around this crowd was enchanting—like being around a group of children, or people from an underdeveloped country who were dazzled with the smallest trinkets—Indians with mirrors. They lived in the world of make-believe where fantasy became reality and reality just got folded into the batter, so totally unlike my world of homicide and grand larceny, where the word "fantasy" always referred to sex—usually the dangerous, sick, and lethal kind—and "reality" was the cold hard fact of a gunshot victim on a slab at the morgue. My reality was the brutality of the living and barely living and dead—the victims, survivors, the criminals—and there was never anything fun or fey or whimsical about it at all.

"The second, third, fourth, and sixth floors are all rehearsal rooms and classrooms," Winston explained as we climbed the steep stairs. "As you can see, they're all named after classical characters." We paused on the landing outside a large bright room with the name OBERON over its door. "I'm so glad George liked you." He grinned. "As I'm sure you've discerned, being a nominee of Cyrus's is not a desirable condition."

"And?" I said.

"He's very nervous around rich people. Especially board members. Better around rich women than men, but still, very uncomfortable, very paranoid, as if they're going to steal his company, his soul, everything about him."

"His air rights?"

Winston laughed nervously. "Exactly."

"Well, I liked him very much."

"Yes." Winston stuck a cigarette between his lips with slightly shaking fingers and clicked a disposable lighter. "I think he can see that."

He turned to two strikingly handsome young men—one dark, one fair—who were talking quietly at the other end of the long landing. They wore long, dark-colored, loosely knit scarves draped around their necks, à la George, and the way they huddled with their faces close together reminded me of the cloaked young guards in *King Lear,* plotting murder.

"You two'd better get going," Winston told them. "George is waiting for you."

They bolted down the stairs immediately like gamboling, rambunctious young bulls racing for the heifers.

"Those are George's interns." Winston's face tilted into its tired, apologetic smile, and he took a long drag on the cigarette. He seemed reluctant to leave, but I didn't know if it was the spot on the landing that held him, or I. I sensed there was something he wanted to tell me but couldn't make up his mind.

"I wouldn't take too seriously what George and Shelley were saying about Bradford," he finally said. "Brad's been swearing blood oaths against George since Yale. He's always been jealous as hell of him. Bradford and Aldo Franciscus were George's interns when they were undergraduates and George was already the big rising star at Yale Drama. So right from the start, Bradford and Aldo needed him, and no matter what they've done in the years since, they've never been able to get that step ahead. Besides, Ozzie and Harriet—that's what we call Brad and Aldo, they've lived together for so long—thirty years—they're like old hens that just bitch and peck and bitch and peck and bitch and peck. They and George are totally codependent—they're his requisite Greek chorus."

"Can't they go somewhere else?" I said.

"Not a chance." Winston shook his head. "This company's the top. And don't get me wrong, they're good, but they just don't have the touch. Nobody can match George's power—the sheer charismatic force of his personality—but it makes him vulnerable, too, and that's why he's always so sure they're plotting behind his back, which in fact they always have been. As they say, even paranoiacs have enemies. And George isn't the easiest man in the world to deal with."

Boy, marijuana turns people into blabbermouths. Even the loyalest of lieutenants.

"Well," he finally concluded, "why don't you go on in and grab some lunch? I'll be right back."

A number of acting company and board members had already gathered in the sunny corner rehearsal hall, and they snaked slowly down a long buffet table, picking up chicken baguettes and vegetable croissant sandwiches and fruit, herbal tea, Perrier, and white wine. No caffeine-laden products. No sugar, except for the fruit and wine. Clearly, George wanted a docile, clearheaded group. Nothing too aggressive to jar the bliss of his marijuana coffee break.

A double circle of folding metal chairs had been arranged, interrupted only by an easel draped with elaborately gilded brocade. And again, my sense was what it had been at Cyrus's: one big unhappy family. Outsiders not welcome.

11

I had met Bradford Lake, George's leading director, at Cyrus's deadly birthday party the day before, and recalled him as tightly wrapped, with tense, bloodless lips and nostrils that twitched and trembled in what seemed to be a state of perpetual sensory insult. With his buttoned-down, Black Sheep Club way, I would have cast him as a commuter on the Yale–New Haven–New York line, an insurance or advertising executive who wore khaki shorts and pristine Top-siders and sailed a seventy-foot yawl—the *Whisky Sour*—on the weekends, before seeing him as a person who had a single artistic bone in his body.

He was sitting across from the door in the first row of the large circle of chairs, pretending to study some papers while peeking surreptitiously above his tortoiseshell reading glasses at the board, company, and staff members as they entered. They came in almost timidly. Here and there one or two people spoke to each other, but for the most part they passed singly through the buffet line and took chairs where they pretended to be just as preoccupied with other business as Bradford.

I circled around and sat directly opposite him, silently thanking all the hours I'd spent refining my lip-reading skills, mostly at long, boring dinner parties pretending to listen to whatever my dinner partner was blathering about while I was actually paying attention to what the handsome man across the table, who should have been my dinner partner in the first place, was saying to the dog next to him.

I recognized Bradford's partner, Aldo Franciscus, from a number of movies and television shows as one of my favorite character actors—a lovable, avuncular, human golden retriever.

He crossed the room toward Bradford in a shambling sort of lope, like a tall sail luffing gaily in the wind, large and loose and rumpled in baggy corduroy trousers and flannel shirt and a stretched-out, homemade, loose-knit cardigan sweater badly misshapen by the size, weight, and volume of items he carried in its pockets. Glasses, car keys, ballpoint pens, chalk, rolled-up scripts. His gray hair was slightly long and waved elegantly back from his deeply lined face. His hazel eyes lay beneath heavy lids and bushy eyebrows, and peered kindly above half-glasses.

"Well," he interrupted Bradford's covert ogling and sat down beside him. He shook out his napkin with a flourish and settled his plate on his knees. "What do you think?"

"About what?" Bradford answered curtly.

"About that Cyrus might have been murdered."

Wow, I thought. News sure does travel fast in this place. I wondered if George's office was bugged, and I realized that, in an organization that appeared to be as inbred and paranoid as this one, information, whether rumor or fact, was a specific and legitimate currency. Access to George was power, and now that Cyrus was dead, the ensuing struggle over control of the company and its assets, including the unsold air rights, might very possibly be to the death.

I could tell Bradford's heart had skipped for a second at Aldo's gossip, but no sign crossed his face. He and Aldo, both in their midfifties, had seen, and done, and been, everything one could in the world of the theater, and probably would not have known an honest emotion if it came up and cracked them over the head with a snow shovel. I studied Bradford's face for signs of murderous revenge, but saw only his bland, wrapped-up, WASP-y good looks.

"Where did you hear that?" he asked. Beneath his dark pencil mustache, his thin lips clamped over the edges of his chicken sandwich and his small, sharp teeth took such an antiseptic nibble, the hard crusty bread didn't shed even a single crumb.

Aldo, on the other hand, swirled and mixed and chopped and pared his food, loading bites of it onto roughly torn hunks of baguette, which he chewed and swallowed with incredible relish. All the while he smiled and waved to practically everyone who entered.

"George and Winston and Shelley were in there meeting with Lilly Bennett." He indicated obliquely across the room with his sandwich to where I sat, legs casually crossed, pretending to eat my lunch, regarding them from behind large dark glasses.

"What exactly did she say?" Bradford blotted the corners of his mouth and then folded his napkin back the way it had come and placed it carefully on top of his neat plate.

"That it was possible. Possible."

"We were there, Aldo," Bradford said tiredly. "Cyrus was old and he was sick and he just fell down and died. He wasn't murdered."

"I didn't say he was," Aldo said. "I simply said she brought up the possibility. There's Maude Ballentine." He laid his plate on the seat of his chair. "I'd better go say hello."

Bradford watched him kiss Maude Ballentine on both cheeks and say something to make her almost smile. That was as good as it got with Maude—a smile was as close as she ever got to outright hilarity. An extra-wealthy, extra-conservative, severe old biddy—except that she wasn't that old, only a couple of years older than I—she resented anyone who looked better or had more fun than she did, which was about ninety-nine percent of the people in the world. Her life consisted of going around from one board meeting to another, throwing cold water on good ideas. And the only reason she was invited onto all these boards was because the possibility always seemed imminent for a major gift, which so far had not materialized, but no one wanted to give up the fight. Her hair was dead-mouse brown and cut in a straight line above her shoulders. She didn't pluck her eyebrows, always looked like she needed a shave, and got her clothes at the Junior League Second Hand Rose thrift shop.

I knew a lot about Maude Ballentine because she'd been in my older brother Elias's class through elementary and junior high. They'd gone to dancing school together at the Roundup Country Club, and my mother, who'd never felt it was too early to begin to line up potential life partners for her children, had started pushing Maude early on. But Maude had gone off to Bennington and dragged home some Dartmouth yukko who liked to spend our long windy winters wrapped up in coyote furs trudging around the country club golf course on snowshoes pretending he was Grizzly Adams or something. He always kept a silver flask of brandy lashed to his wrist with a thin leather thong, and had vanished immediately into Roundup's social wilderness the moment he arrived, leaving Maude out there to trudge around alone in her late mother's moth-eaten mink, which still provided warmth, so why replace it, and black rubber galoshes. I couldn't even imagine what a dreadful, deadly, lifeless life they had.

Bradford dismissed her as easily as I did. He returned to his papers, and while he might have been an expert at concealing his feelings, I was an expert at looking beneath the surface, figuring out what people really meant or felt, getting beyond the lies. Studying him, I could almost see the wheels turning as he considered the possibility that Cyrus had been murdered. He looked up when Shelley and Winston came in and sat together. They were muttering, laughing, touching, and I watched his gaze dismiss them a little too quickly. He didn't trust them.

Finally, George burst through the door with the two boys in tow like young centurions, their scarves waving behind them like battle standards. The air grew electric with possibilities and the seated circle stopped slouching and posing. We all slid forward a little toward the edges of our chairs. A cool breeze of pure white energy rode around him, replacing our earth-bound fog and smoke and torpor. George had suddenly blown the breath of life back into us—just like God blowing in Adam's face in the Sistine Chapel.

"I am so, so happy you all are here." His voice brimmed with enthusiasm and he stopped in front of his chair next to the brocade-draped easel and clasped his hands together as though in prayer. Sunlight glinted off his glasses and made his eyes invisible.

"This is the beginning of our twentieth year. Can you believe it? Oh, my." He clapped his hands on his cheeks. "I never thought we'd make it this far. I never thought we'd survive that first season."

Gentle, friendly laughter warmed the air and George planed over its smooth surface like a baby on its belly gliding on shallow water, arms and legs extended, a big smile on its face.

"As you know"—he smoothed the yellow pennant across his chest—"today's the day we introduce the new season and define what it will mean to us as actors and directors and trainers and designers. But first I want to talk for a moment about Cyrus."

A murmur chugged around the room like fans doing the Wave at a football game, and as he spoke, I studied all the faces.

Most of the board members had their eyes glued to George, their faces illuminated and enraptured as though they were in the presence of a divine being, or at least Elmer Gantry—except for Maude, whose mind had tumbled into some black hole located on the floor ten feet before her. Through an elaborate series of hand movements, reminiscent of a policeman directing traffic in Mexico City, Aldo silently instructed one of the students in the back row to close the door. Bradford kept his eyes carefully on George, but I could tell he wasn't listening, he'd heard all this crap a hundred times before. He was a million miles away. Shelley Pirelli sat ruler straight, a rehearsed expression of transcendent joy and adoration on her face, and next to her Winston slouched way back in his chair biting his nails and watching their leader with a guarded look of nervous affection. It looked like tinted contacts had replaced his dark glasses; no one's real eyes were that blue.

"Without Cyrus Vaile," George continued, "there would have been no seasons at all. He provided us with all the tools we needed, all the money we required to realize the mission of our company. We are on a strong course to the future because he gave us a strong past—and therefore, without tears, but with joy and celebration and gratitude for all he did to make our company possible, I want to dedicate next season, our twentieth, our most radiant season ever, to our greatest patron, the late Cyrus Vaile."

George began to clap his hands together the way a seal does, in big loose flipper-like flaps, and the noise it made was terrific and pretty soon everyone was standing and applauding and cheering and yelling "To Cyrus!" and George removed the golden brocade with a flourish and revealed the list of plays that would open the season in October.

The room was filled with good cheer and happy faces, except for Bradford, Shelley, and Winston, who clapped and smiled, but their eyes stayed dead, hard, cold, and suspicious, still registering, processing the news of Cyrus's possible homicide.

George kept up the performance, controlling his audience with the expertise of a get-down, Bible-thumping, Jimmy-Crack-Corn, Assemblies of God preacher, as he announced the plays—Turgenev's *A Month in the Country,* Noel Coward's *Hay Fever, The Little Foxes* by Lillian

Hellman, *Buried Child* by Sam Shepard, Chekhov's *Three Sisters, Hotel Paradiso* by Georges Feydeau and Maurice Desvallières, and Shakespeare's *Cymbeline,* to be directed by Bradford "the most brilliant director in the history of our company" Lake, which would open the season and which, in fact, had already had read-throughs.

"You've got to let it go, Brad," Aldo Franciscus whispered to his friend. "Put a smile on your face. They're clapping for you. Patrick is dead. He would be dead anyway. We can't do anything to bring him back."

"It's not just that, Aldo," he muttered, showing all his teeth in what looked like a genuine smile, and doing theatrical half bows in three directions. "You know how many things I have on my mind right now. And I'm so upset about Cyrus—it throws so many things up in the air. How does George expect to support this company with Cyrus gone?" Bradford retook his seat after the ovation, carefully straightening the creases in his light flannel trousers and arranging his navy blazer, shooting his cuffs. He was George's main contact with the outside world—so buttoned up, so normal-looking with his close-cropped hair and Brooks Brothers shirts and ties and cordovan loafers. So easy for board members and major donors to relate to. So mad. So jealous. "The bastard's going to make it my problem."

"The strength of this company," George was saying, "aside from the oceans of classical choices available to us thanks to the greatest playwrights in history, lies in the creative abilities of our actors, our directors, our designers, staff members, and, yes, to a great extent the creative abilities of our board members to continue to raise the money."

"You've got that right, George," called out Andy Beckett, a board member I'd known well since we were children. He looked just the same except that he'd grown a beard, which he kept well barbered—not one of those big wild, dirty things you can smell from a hundred miles away and don't even want to begin to think about what's in it.

We'd gone out a few times when we were in our teens, even messed around a little on the red leather back seat of his white Impala convertible, until I figured out he was a promiscuous, philandering, fortune-hunting braggart, something I've become a true expert at spotting over the years. But to his credit, he was a good-looking, nice guy, fun to be with, and he finally married a Barbie doll with enough money to launch his cable television business, which had become stratospherically successful. He played around on her. It's easy to tell when people do. I had a feeling she didn't mind.

I was sitting next to him and could also tell he'd had enough sitting

around listening to all this glad-handing, self-congratulatory, artistic pa-
laver. He'd spent the whole time, so far, looking up Shelley's skirt,
trying, no doubt, to concentrate her legs into spreading a little farther.
He frowned pointedly at his watch. "We've got to make money to raise
money," Andy announced. "And I've only got ten more minutes. Do
you mind if we just move right to the budget?"

"Oh, you're so right." George rolled his eyes. "Let's keep going on
our agenda." He picked up a sheet of paper from his chair. "I think
Maude Ballentine is next with the report on special events."

Andy shook his head in disgust and glanced across the circle at
Shelley, who caught his eye before looking quickly away. She rolled her
head around on her shoulders, as if to loosen some tension there, and
then began to undo the teal-blue, poker-chip-sized plastic buttons on
her suit jacket. She unbuttoned each one slowly so as not to call attention to herself while Maude dragged along about the Designers' Show
House Boutique, which would bring in a remarkable thousand dollars.
But when Shelley wiggled toward the front of her chair, straightening
her back and thrusting out her chest, I realized she was undertaking a
little burlesque for Andy, the sole male corporate executive in the audience, who would just as soon write a check for the measly thousand
bucks if Maude would shut up.

Shelley picked a far corner in the ceiling as the anchor for her big
brown bedroom eyes, as the jacket fell open. She drew in her breath,
making her large, low-slung breasts strain against her shiny burgundy
satin blouse, and thrust forward huge, excited nipples. I couldn't take
my eyes off them. They looked like she'd shoved twenty-millimeter
cannon rounds into her bra—if she'd been wearing one, which she
clearly wasn't, judging by how the long double strands of gray pearls
danced and skidded and binged along over the slick polyester surface.

Andy Beckett sniffled and cleared his throat, crossed his legs and
laced his fingers over the end of his knee.

She pulled her jacket off, very sedately, one sleeve at a time, and
revolved very slowly to hang it over the back of her chair, then turned
face forward, placing her body at right angles, knees clamped together,
hands folded in her lap, like a little girl at dancing school. Her eyes now
drilled straight into Andy's and she ran the pointed tip of her tongue
over her lips. He had crossed and recrossed his legs several times, and
now I could hear him breathing. His mouth had fallen open slightly and
his eyes were glued to those astonishing howitzers aimed directly at him.
Very, very tentatively, almost imperceptibly at first, she flexed her fin-

gers, rubbing each tip with her thumb and then her hands crept from her lap to her waist, where they paused and she spread her long-nailed fingers and pressed them across her stomach. A small smile curved her lips and she tilted her head slightly as her hands moved casually up her body and flicked like fireflies over her inflamed burgundy satin breasts, as though she were brushing off lint.

Andy was breathing openly now, fully engaged in her from far across the room. He slid his hand into his pocket and the contact was like an electric jolt. He trembled and sighed and ran his hand over his mouth, wiping away a film of perspiration that had formed on his upper lip.

Shelley's hands continued up—her fingers blotting her sharp collarbones and slender neck as though she were drenched and dying of heat in a tropical rainstorm, and traced along her cheeks, until they paused at her temples, where they moved into her long hair, lifting it up into a large, dark fan. And as her hands and hair rose, so did her breasts, until they had taken on the perfect dimension of soccer balls.

It was then that I realized Shelley didn't shave under her arms. I almost screamed and fell out of my chair.

So did Andy, but not for the same reason.

Seconds later, she let go of her locks and shook her head and settled back into her chair and it seemed as though nothing had ever happened—she had simply removed her jacket and lifted her heavy length of hair free of her neck to cool it. I looked around the room and everyone seemed to be interested in Maude's description of the series of dinner parties that would raise gobs of money in the fall and would we please all sign up on the sheet she was passing around.

"Lilly," she said, "I know people would especially enjoy coming out to your ranch for a picnic."

All I could do was smile at her as though she were speaking to me in Urdu. "I'm sure they would," I finally blurted out like an idiot, still trying to figure out if Andy and I had been the only ones to witness this hot exhibition. It was hard to believe, but it seemed we were.

Andy cleared his throat again and straightened his tie, showing off the tone-on-tone monograms on his cuffs and eighteen-carat gold cuff-links in the shape of little satellite dishes. He took his cellular phone out of his briefcase and made a call. I thought about Richard and all the things I planned to do to him when I got home.

Watching Shelley had reminded me that this morning, when we were leading our horses into the barn, I'd noticed a small tear in the back of his jeans, just a small corner-shaped flap, about two inches long on each side. It was about three inches below his rear and just a little off center, in toward his crotch. There was nothing much to the rip, except that it was almost large enough to see into, but not quite. All I could see was a hint of light as he walked and then inky shadow. It had only been for a few steps, but I couldn't take my eyes off that tear. I wanted to reach in and touch Richard's cool, smooth, golden skin and trace my fingertips up his leg, the way Shelley had moved hers languidly up her front. And then he'd turned and smiled from under his hat and said, "What in the hell are you looking at, Bennett? Get a move on."

My pager vibrated against my waist.

CHAPTER

12

The silent summons was like a breath of fresh air, a rescue sent by the
gods. Not only from the meeting, which held virtually no interest
for me (I'm not all that nuts about theater, and frankly, it's tough
for me to get all whooped up about *Cymbeline* and Chekhov. I truly
love opera, but way down deep, I'm really more interested in rodeo),
but also from the fact that between Richard, Dwight, and Shelley, I'd
been thinking about sex practically nonstop since dawn. I needed to
catch my breath and deal with a little reality. Even I know there's more
to life than just one big roll in the hay. So when my pager went off
beneath my jacket, I breathed a huge sigh of relief.

Whenever I get buzzed, I always hope it's Richard, and sometimes it is, but today, when I checked the number, I saw it was Dr. Leavy's direct line at the morgue.

Shelley Pirelli followed me into the hall. Her jacket was back on and she was rebuttoning it as fast as she could.

"Is there somewhere private I can make a call?" I asked her.

"Oh, sure." She led me down the steep staircase back to her office. "Right in here."

We stopped in front of a door that was visible only once you were all the way in the room, and I looked around and realized there were six separate doors in her office. I wondered if there were stained cots behind each one.

"This is George's inner sanctum." She pulled the door open to reveal what probably at one time had been a large walk-in closet or storeroom, but now was like a small English garden. The walls and furniture were covered with flowered chintzes, and the chairs were shiny white wicker. A large basket of fresh flowers sat on a wicker coffee table with a stack of *Architectural Digest, Harper's Bazaar,* and *Elle* magazines, and a telephone with five lines sat on a small stand in the corner. At that point, the garden mystique ended abruptly. The air reeked with the acrid, distinctive smell of stale marijuana smoke. I mean, it was so strong, you could get stoned just being in there.

"Perfect," I said and closed the door and dialed the morgue.

"Dr. Leavy speaking," the trim, fit blonde answered on the first ring. She was one of Wyoming's top tri-athletes, and who could blame her with the business she was in. Also, Kim Leavy had come to the table with a lot of baggage.

Her brief career as an actual physician—a general practitioner who worked with actual, real live patients—had been a disaster. Her patients kept dying because she consistently misdiagnosed them, and when a ten-year-old died of kidney failure after waiting on the liver transplant list for two years, and it turned out there was never anything wrong with his liver, the state—Illinois—and the insurance companies pulled her ticket. This had occurred several years ago, and since then she'd gone back to school with a forensic specialty, got all her anatomy, organs, chemicals, and toxins straight, and even been relicensed to practice medicine. But she swore to herself she'd never touch another living human being as long as she lived. She moved to the wilds of Wyoming, where nobody knew or cared anything about her, and established herself as a highly competent, respected, and dedicated forensic pathologist. She was so dedicated and enthusiastic, it was a little scary.

Many of us wondered if she'd ever stop doing penance for the souls she'd taken and now the ones she ministered and whispered to. Chatted with as though they were sitting there having a cup of coffee. Kim worked out four hours every day and spent almost all the rest of the time in the morgue. She was addicted to endorphins and damaged beyond repair.

"Kim," I said. "It's Lilly."

"I've got news that I'm sure you'll be semi-happy with, being the sick individual that you are." Her voice was bright and energetic.

"What did you find?" My pulse, which had just slowed down, began to pick back up.

"His digoxin level is elevated way beyond where it should be. His system is completely saturated, and unless he was inadvertently doubling or tripling his daily medication over a period of time—and you know digoxin is a once-a-day drug—there's no way this could have been accidental."

"What if his nurse was accidentally repeating his medications?" I asked, not sure if Nurse Kissy had even been able to read.

"Well, if she were, and if I were his family, I'd sure have one heck of a strong malpractice suit. That kind of repetition would be considered criminal. It's outright negligence, but proving criminal intent, well, that's something else." I could almost hear her wiping her brow and saying, "Whew, and thank God for that."

"Thanks," I said, my adrenaline almost deafening me. "I'll come by in a couple of hours, see if you've turned up anything more."

I tracked down my brother Elias, who filled in occasionally as a deputy. He was at my office, where he was no doubt discussing dinner and a movie with my secretary, Linda. Their flirtation had grown into something a little more serious but no one was too sure just what. My mother had spent an inordinate amount of time trying to dig up Linda's background, except she didn't exactly have one as far as Mother's book was concerned. But Linda was so nice that we were all happy for both of them, Mother included.

"Do me a favor, Elias," I said. "Meet me at Cyrus Vaile's funeral at Temple Emanuel at four o'clock. I have to go home and change, so if I'm late, keep a sharp eye on the theater people."

"How will I know which ones they are?" he asked.

"Believe me, you'll know. And also watch Samuel Vaile, Cyrus's brother. I just got the autopsy report, and it's possible Cyrus was poisoned."

"Cool," Elias said.

"Keep it to yourself, and stay in the background as much as you can," I told him. "I'll see you there."

Just after we hung up, I noticed the first whiff of smoke. Not marijuana smoke, real smoke. And then the fire alarm went off.

The noise was crippling, unrelenting, and because of its deafening, disorienting, excruciating effect, it took me a second to realize that the door to this little piece of England was locked. From the outside. The door was locked, and thick, chemical, toxic smoke flowed in a wide, flat sheet from beneath it into the small, windowless room where it choked me and burned my eyes.

"Hey," I yelled, pounding on the door. "Hey. Let me out."

"I can't get the door open," Shelley yelled back. "It's stuck."

"Well, go get some help, for Crissakes," I told her over the din.

This is ridiculous, I thought as I ripped my jacket off and stuffed it into the crack along the floor to block the flow of smoke. I picked up the phone and it was dead, and then I started to get worried. I pounded again on the door, and screamed at the top of my lungs, but the fire alarm was so loud, nothing could overcome it. I watched the smoke begin to wind around the door frame and the wall grew hot.

Then Shelley was back, struggling with the doorknob, pounding on her side. "It's locked. I can't find the key. It's gone from my desk." I could hear her coughing. "I can't see anything." Her coughing grew worse as she continued to rattle ineffectually on the door.

"Please get some help," I called out. "Tell someone I'm in here. Go for help."

Stay calm, stay calm, I ordered myself. You can handle this. Just stay cool. I drew back as far as I could, but it was really only four or five feet, and hunkered down into the corner and drew my blouse over my mouth and tried to breathe as slowly as possible.

"Panic is not an option," I said out loud. "Stay cool." But after a while the smoke became so thick and so sickeningly pungent, it was difficult to breathe without choking. It was everywhere. It had permeated everything. I couldn't even see the door anymore, and I had no choice but to breathe it. I began to cough. I knew better, but I couldn't help it. And the more I coughed, the more smoke I drew into my lungs.

"Help! Help!" I screamed, but I don't know if any sound came out. Oh, God, I thought, this is stupid. Stop this from happening. Give me some air. Oh, please. Save me. The alarm had stopped but my throat and lungs were too paralyzed to make any noise. I literally could not make a sound to save my life. I couldn't breathe anymore. Oh, no. No. Richard, save me. Richard, save me, please. Okay, you win. If you ask me to marry you, I will. And that is the thought that carried me down for the count into the bitter, acrid, lethal darkness where the air was always fresh and sweet.

W E D N E S D A Y   M O R N I N G

I was smiling up at Richard and the rip in his jeans and the snappy, laughing look in his golden-blue eyes as he said, "What in the hell are you looking at, Bennett? Time to get a move on." But then a mumble of voices interrupted and I became aware that there were tubes shoved up my nose. What the hell is going on here? I thought. My smile evaporated into the blue of my dream.

For some reason, I was way, way out of the loop, and I decided just to keep lying there quietly and try to gather my wits a little before I opened my eyes.

Someone or something had ahold of my hand. It was a light, soft touch, gentle as a paw.

"Well, she's frowning," a man's voice said. "I'd take that as a good sign."

"Don't frown, Lilly," my mother's voice ordered. "It'll ruin your lovely forehead."

I opened my eyes. Good God, I thought, am I dying? It seemed everyone in my life, including Roundup's chief of detectives, Jack Lewis, was gathered around my bed, staring down at me. I smiled. They smiled. Richard's paw squeezed mine.

"Well. Thank heaven, that's over." Mother let fly with a gasping sob into my father's shoulder. Here's the deal with my mother. I've thought quite a lot about this and decided that her being a Gemini explains her behavior perfectly: she's an armadillo who is regularly and predictably moved to tears by cheap melodrama, but is uncrackable by real-life tragedy, thanks to that primordial armor. I knew instinctively that throughout whatever I'd just been experiencing, whatever and however long it was, she had not wavered for one second and had not tolerated weakness on the part of anyone around her. Plus, now that it was over, there would be no time for more than that quick sob because it would be time for all of us to get back to work, and anyone who had time for more than that was a slacker.

I saw right through her. I smiled at her and my father, and the look in their eyes told me all I needed to know.

Elias stood at the foot of the bed, and my dog, Baby, peeked out from beneath his canvas jacket. He set her on the bed and she ripped up it and kissed my face and wiggled all over and then curled into a tiny ball right next to me.

I looked at Richard and shook my head. "How long have I been here?" I asked. I felt absolutely awful. My mouth and every breath I took stank of bitter smoke and my lungs burned and struggled for air against an invisible thousand-pound weight on my chest.

"About eighteen hours."

My eyes wandered around the room and I realized I was in a Critical Care Unit, hooked up to beat the band. I had oxygen, two IVs, a blood pressure cuff on my arm, EKG tags taped to my chest and a catheter, which, the moment I realized it was in there, started to hurt like hell.

A uniformed police officer stood outside the door.

I turned my gaze to Jack Lewis, who had been leaning against the window sill, a Styrofoam cup in his hand. Our relationship was unofficial, but he and I both knew all those awards and citations he'd been receiving lately from the mayor and the police commissioner were thanks to my behind-the-scenes detective work. Jack, who was always so meticulous, so squared away in his dress and demeanor, actually looked a little rough around the edges. Like maybe he'd been a little worried about me. He actually needed a shave.

"What's happened?" I said. "What am I doing here? Why are you all here?"

"The fire," Richard said. "At the theater's offices. During the board meeting. You went downstairs to make a call. Any bells?"

I listened to him, studying his tired face hard, trying to put his words into my brain, to comprehend, and then it started to come back, first as vapor, and then the whole picture flowed in like a wide, smooth river and I started to laugh, but it must have come out sounding like a painful moan.

"What?" Richard whispered, leaning close, his voice deep with concern.

"Shelley Pirelli doesn't shave under her arms," I practically yelled, and laughed harder until a coughing fit grabbed me and made me think I was probably going to die.

"Oh, for heaven's sake." My mother frowned. "What in the world is she talking about? It must be the drugs."

"The fire was set on purpose," Jack said, gruffly ignoring my delirium. "Whoever did it tried to make it look like a spontaneous flareup in a wastebasket, but the closest basket was usually under a desk six or seven feet away. This one had spilled right along the base of the door. No question you were the target."

It was all coming back to me: the call to Dr. Leavy, Cyrus Vaile's elevated digoxin level, the locked door, the smoke, the promise to marry Richard if he asked me. I looked at him, saw nothing especially new there except bone-breaking fatigue and worry, which made me feel special.

"Was anyone else hurt?" I asked.

"Wrightsman's secretary, Shelley Pirelli, was treated for smoke and released last night," Jack said. "She's the only one."

I wiggled up onto my elbows, which sent all the monitors into orbit, and started to unpop the little suction cups that were placed strategically here and there. A stabbing pain from the catheter made me wince. "Let's unhook all this stuff," I said impatiently. "I'm fine."

A few minutes later, once the nurse had disconnected, withdrawn, and removed everything and the doctor had checked me out and declared me out of danger as long as I stayed in bed and took it easy for a couple of days, everyone crowded back into my room, and Richard asked if I wanted anything to eat or drink.

"I'd love a glass of water and a cup of black coffee." My voice sounded thin and shaky, not like itself at all. But aside from that, and the burning in my eyes and lungs, my mind and all the rest of my body seemed to be in pretty good order. I didn't even want to think about what my hair and face looked like. Jack Lewis's saying I had been the target had moved me quickly into the fast lane mending-wise. "Have you talked to Kim Leavy?" I asked him.

"Yes. Several times. She wants me to call her as soon as you feel you'd like to see her. She has more information."

"Go ahead and get her on the phone," I told him. Mother frowned at me. "Please," I added, and swung my legs out of the bed. "I'm going to take a shower."

"The doctor said," Mother warned, being of the old school where doctor's words were gospel.

"The doctor took his best shot and I'm taking mine. I'm much better than he thought I'd be," I snarled, trying to look and sound as authoritative as one can in a hospital gown. Richard held me up as I tiptoed across the cold floor into the bathroom.

"I think she's hungry." I heard Mother say before I closed the door. "Do you think her hair will be okay? She looks like she put her finger in a socket."

The shower came from heaven. I stood still in its strong hot mist and then began to scrub the stink of smoke and medicine off my body and out of my hair, which felt like a Brillo pad. If one takes processed hair, such as mine, and cooks it at a high temperature in toxic fumes for a while, things really get rough. And it's true: I do get a little coppery-bronze touch-up from time to time. Quite regularly, in fact, because I have no interest in seeing how much, if any, gray hair I have. Maybe when I'm seventy I'll quit. But, I thought, after this fire, I'll be lucky to have any hair left at all. I touched my eyebrows. Same extra crispy texture. Fried chicken feathers.

By the time I turned off the water, someone had hung a clean, pale pink cotton nightgown and robe from home on the back of the bathroom door and placed my frayed old overnight kit with its overkill of bottles and tubes of skin care products on the edge of the sink. And, by the time I got back into my room—where the only persons remaining were Richard, Elias, Jack Lewis, and Kim Leavy—aside from a deep, hacking cough, I felt and looked—not great, but all right.

"What's up?" I asked Kim as vigorously as I could once I'd climbed back onto the bed. It was a huge effort. I hated to admit it, but the shower had sapped my strength; I wanted to fall into the pillows and close my eyes and just rest. I wanted to go home and crawl under my own soft, sweet, cedar-scented covers.

"I kept running tests on the blood," Kim bubbled enthusiastically. "Because it kept looking like something else was there, just tucked right alongside the digoxin. Know what it was?" Her eyes twinkled and she smiled her mad scientist smile. "Full-strength digitalis."

"Digitalis? You mean, like digitalis from foxglove?" I said.

Kim nodded. "Brilliant. Whoever did this is brilliant."

"How was it delivered?"

"Food or drink." She bounced on the toes of her white cross-trainers, which sported some brownish-red spots that suspiciously resembled dried blood. "He didn't have any puncture wounds. And there was nothing unusual in his digestive system. So, as to the actual delivery method? No idea. That's your department." Kim looked at her watch. "Got to get back downstairs. For some reason we've practically got them lined up in the halls taking numbers today."

Jack and I looked at each other once she'd gone, and he shook his head. "I'm so glad she's not in my department," he said. "I've been over to talk to a few of these theater people, and they're all completely crazy, except the nurse, Kissy, who's a local party girl—I can't remember her real name. She's been questioned thoroughly and wasn't able to shed any light. I'd appreciate your help with the rest."

He said it with a straight face. And it didn't look like it hurt.

Last winter when the baroness was murdered, he'd asked for my help and I knew that the nose of this camel had just poked itself under his big tent, which was filled with unlimited support and access. Now I had my whole head in there.

Hot damn. Except that by now the trail was as cold as a dead fish, and I was as limp as a dead puppy.

"I'll get started right away," I said and fell into a deep sleep.

It was afternoon when I wakened because the western sun seemed to have focused itself directly on my bed and had heated me up to about fifty million degrees. That, added to the disgusting residual roasted plastic taste in my mouth, and the fact that every breath I drew was like smoking old tires, made me wake up feeling extremely grumpy. So when I opened my eyes and saw Andy Beckett standing at the foot of my bed, I was in no mood to be polite.

"What do you want?" I snapped. He had on so much cologne, it gave me an instant, blinding headache.

"I just thought I'd drop in and see how you are," he answered, a little surprised I wasn't happier to see him.

"I thought there was a NO VISITORS sign on my door," I snarled, trying to kick my legs free from the sheets and blankets that had wrapped themselves around me like hundreds of strait jackets. I was so tangled and so hot, I was afraid I was going to panic. I felt like Houdini, wrapped in ropes and trapped underwater with the oxygen clock running out. Finally, I broke free and hurled the covers off the bed onto the floor in one huge, liberating gesture. "Jesus Christ," I growled down at them and then turned my angry eyes back on Andy. "And an officer out there to make sure people read it."

He was completely taken aback, as he should have been, and began to grasp for a graceful exit. "Uh, well, I'm on the hospital board with your mother, and she said it would be fine for me just to stick my head in. It obviously isn't. I'm sorry."

My body temperature dropped, and as it fell, my attitude improved. I drew in a deep breath and ran my fingers through my crunchy hair in much the same gesture Shelley had used the day before. But there any similarity ended, and I could tell Andy saw no connection, no parallel in the movement. I was just an old, middle-aged friend he was visiting in the hospital, which was fine with me.

"Does Shelley Pirelli always act like that at board meetings?" I asked.

"Like what?" His expression was maddeningly innocent as he poured me a glass of water, and it reminded me of another reason we had not progressed beyond the back seat of his car a hundred years ago. There had never been any possibility of a connection between us because he was always so sly, always working the angles, so determined to dominate, to keep his agenda on the front burner and negate that of those around him: *I* am what is important. How *I* see it is what counts. I am right. You are wrong. Listen to *me*.

He left no opening and no opportunity for review or rebuttal. It was lucky for him he'd gotten so rich.

"Are you serious?" The glass of water had cooled me more and I straightened my wrinkled nightgown around my legs. "She was practically doing a strip tease."

"She was? I'm sorry I missed it."

This was the message he had come to deliver: not to divulge to his wife, or my mother, or whoever else might have some proprietary interest, what I'd seen. That Shelley Pirelli and her rocket launcher tits had practically given him an orgasm in the middle of a meeting. And I imagined that was only a tiny glimpse of what went on between them outside the boardroom.

Why couldn't he just come out and say it? His philandering was no secret. What a loser.

"Who do you think set the fire?" I asked. "Did you see anyone leave the room after Shelley and me?"

"Winston checked his pager and I think he left. I wasn't really paying attention."

"How much money do you give to the Rep every year?"

"My annual gift's ten thousand. Plus some odds and ends—subscriptions, special events—adds up to about twelve."

"I read in the paper the other day that you made eighteen million dollars last year."

Andy's neck pinkened. "Well, that's really all on paper. It wasn't really anything like that at all. You know how that stuff works. Besides, most of our business is out of state. International. We don't make much money here in Roundup per se."

"I think you should up your annual gift to a hundred," I said.

Andy and I looked each other in the eye and understood one another perfectly.

"All right," he said, fingering his sterling silver TV-and-rabbit-ears cufflinks.

Maybe I would turn out to be a pretty good board member after all.

14

FRIDAY MORNING

Richard had driven me home on Thursday morning and tucked me into my big, sweet bed where I'd lain quietly for the last twenty-fours, trying not to be too demanding.

I know this doesn't sound very coplike of me, but the truth is that I don't think that when people are really sick or messed up, the way I was from the smoke, they should try to be heroes and stagger on. Unless their lives depend on it. I think they should go to bed for twenty-four hours, never more than forty-eight, lie there and sleep and get well. Otherwise, you just drag around, and it can take days, even weeks, to get back to one hundred percent. I realize that my method takes you completely out of the action for a while, but when you come back, you're like gangbusters.

Which is the way I was by Friday morning. Except for the cough, which was almost gone, and in any event wasn't nearly as bad as the cough I'd had when I used to smoke.

I started smoking for real when I was thirteen, and was still at it twenty-seven years later when I turned forty and I felt like hell and was pretty sure I was getting emphysema. Dolly Parton and I happen to be the same age, and I was reading an interview with her about how she'd lost lots of weight, or something like that, and the interviewer asked her why she'd done it. And she said, "Well, I just turned forty and I realized that there are just some things you can't get away with forever." Or words to that effect. Anyhow, the "can't get away with forever" got me right between the eyes and I realized I couldn't get away with smoking anymore or it was going to kill me. I mean, two packs a day (of course, like all smokers, I said it was a pack and a half) for twenty-seven years is pretty strong moojoo.

So, thanks to Dolly Parton and the American Cancer Society literature, which I then started seeing everywhere I went—on park benches, the sides of buses, airport billboards, vending machines, television—and the fact that I realized I'd worked my butt off to be a good cop and was killing myself to be the best chief of detectives Santa Bianca had ever had, and I didn't want to die from smoking, I quit.

It gave me the creeps that smoke almost killed me anyway.

It was that sort of second-grade, second-rate, numskulled reflecting I did while I lay among my white, puffy covers letting Richard treat me like a queen.

He'd put a little silver bell on my bed table, in case I needed him, next to a bouquet of pale pink sweetheart roses from my mother. George Wrightsman had sent a vase of the biggest Casablanca lilies I'd ever seen in my life, and they hovered at the end of my bed on the coffee table in front of the fireplace like a flight of white doves. Their distinctive sweet-tart fragrance filled the sunny room and occasionally, when the wind blew across them in a certain way, they made me sneeze.

I kept them around because the fact that they were from George kept my mind on the subject at hand: ergo, someone had murdered Cyrus Vaile in a most sophisticated, meticulous, beyond-premeditated way. The long-range strategy, careful planning, patience, and just outright deceit required to pull off a well-organized and imperceptible poisoning, whether its goal is death or merely discomfort and distraction, have historically been the handiwork of individuals who are consummate masters of deception, which didn't help me much at all, since Cyrus's poisoning happened possibly in conjunction with a theater company, where the whole point is deception.

And, conversely, someone tried to murder me in the opposite fashion—a ham-handed, clumsy, obvious attempt that, thank God, failed. But only just.

I knew so little about any of the people involved, except Andy, who had no obvious need to kill Cyrus because they were both businessmen who lived for the deal and a little on the side. Murder—the ultimate coup de grâce—was not, and would never be, their style.

All the rest of the possibles were as unknown and exotic to me as Martians.

By Thursday evening I'd been well enough for a Jameson's on the rocks, a couple of them, actually, and when George rang up at noon on Friday to ask if he could come out and see me, Richard, who had kept the phone in my room turned off, urged me to say yes.

"He's been calling here practically every hour on the hour," he told me. "What do you want me to tell him? I personally think you're fine."

I think Richard's largesse had peaked, and I didn't blame him. I'd tried to keep the bell-ringing to a minimum, but I think the four trips to town he'd made in the last day and a half to get me things I urgently needed—polish remover; hand lotion; pink grapefruit; *People* magazine, which had a story on George Wrightsman and the classical perfection of his staging of *Macbeth,* scheduled to open in less than a week; a couple of books I'd been meaning to read; the new *Vogue;* and a bag of lemon-chip-white-chocolate candy—had demonstrated his devotion to the max. Especially during this time of the year just before rodeo season kicked off, when he and my brother Christian needed to sharpen their team-roping skills and timing and shave off every second they could.

They were the champs and would start defending their gold buckles next week at the first big rodeo of the summer, the Cody Gateway. From then on, every weekend until Labor Day, they'd be the sport's major targets, dragging themselves and their ponies from one end of the

Rocky Mountain West to the other to keep those big gold bas-relief dinner plates holding up their knife-starched Wranglers.

"Absolutely," I agreed. "I feel perfect."

"Good." He breathed a deep sigh of relief. "I'm going to the barn. Give George my regards."

FRIDAY AFTERNOON

George Wrightsman didn't exactly fall out of his car when he opened the door of his silver Jaguar sedan. More like lurched, as marijuana smoke billowed into the air. Like when Sean Penn opened the van door in *Fast Times at Ridgemont High*. The two interns appeared to be asleep in the back seat. George slung his canvas tote over his shoulder and made his way dreamily up the walk.

"I'm surprised you found your way out here," I said.

"I've been at it for *hours*." He laughed, flipping up the shaded covers on his wire-rimmed glasses. "A lucky fluke. I'm not a particularly good navigator." He spread his arms wide, turned slowly, and drew in a deep breath. "It is so beautiful here. How do you stand it?" And with that, he fell backward, straight as a stick. Wham onto the porch. Lights out. The fringed ends of the yellow scarf floated down beside him like dancing canaries.

I had enough experience with drunks and dopers to know that trying to revive him was a complete waste of time, so I left him where he lay and went inside to tell Celestina to hold up for a while on the cocktail quesadillas and to call me when Mr. Wrightsman was back on his feet. Then I went into my study, where the doors were open to the outside, and the afternoon air that flowed in from over the wide, spring-swollen river was crisp and fresh and clean.

I'd only been out of the office for two and a half days, but my desk at home was stacked with faxes, most of them from one of my investigators who was down in Puerto Vallarta spying on a fellow and his secretary. The lowest possible level of work—real bread-and-butter stuff—the sort of incriminating video sleaze Wink Harrison's wife used to cost me my job in Santa Bianca.

It still made me cringe—the sight of myself, big and plump and deathly white as a shark's belly, sitting on my haunches on top of the Chief Justice of the California Supreme Court, whose eyes were squeezed shut in his straining red face as he guided my dimpled hips to heaven. Oh, God. Why couldn't the guy at least have waited to film us when I was on the bottom and gravity was working in my favor? The existence of that tape in the justice's wife's safe pressed permanently against my neck and made me waken in the night needing to stretch. I prayed she would stick to her promise to destroy the tape in five years almost as hard as I prayed their house would burn down. I swore never to make love completely nude again.

But I must admit, the faxes from Mexico were probably as funny for me to read as that video had been for the judge's wife to watch.

My client was the hurt, angry wife. Here was her husband, fifty-five years old, married to her for thirty years, has a heart transplant, leaves his wife, and takes off with his twenty-two-year-old secretary, who is absolutely screwing his brains out down there at the Princess until he gets Montezuma's Revenge from eating the lettuce and unpeeled tomatoes at Carlos O'Brien's. So two days later he's still sick as a dog and she's yelling at him through the bathroom door that she's met a really nice girl named Monica on the beach and she'll be sitting in the sun with her.

What she doesn't tell him is that Monica is there with two Navy helicopter pilots who are on leave and partying like there's no tomorrow. Old Frank finally struggles out of the john long enough to crawl down to the beach, spots the situation before they see him, for which I'm sure he will be grateful the rest of his life, and calls his wife and asks her to come down and get him. Poor Frank. A gigantic scar from a heart transplant on a fifty-five-year-old body has a limited lifetime of sex appeal when it runs into a body that has less than thirty years on it. No matter how much money it has.

Monica and the two studs were actors on my payroll. I faxed the investigator to give them their bonuses and come on home.

George appeared at the windowpaned interior double doors of my study, which, to keep her mind occupied during World War II, my grandmother had painted with scenes of various momentous family occasions. His face had an intensely remorseful expression, and I was suddenly filled with compassion for this man who, according to what I'd read, had been literally abandoned by his mother, left as an infant on the doorstep of a convent in Bordentown, New Jersey. There he'd been raised by the nuns who occupied a mansion built for Napoleon's older brother, Joseph, during his seventeen-year refuge in the United States in the first half of the nineteenth century.

The convent, given to the order fully furnished, was a limestone building of exquisite proportions, located on a high cliff above the Delaware River, and I could imagine what it must have been like for a little boy to be raised in that opulent, ornate, icy palace of silence and regimented affection. It was also easy to understand why he'd become an actor, required, as he evidently had been, to create his only friends from his own imagination, and why he now drew such artistic comfort and security from the classics, since he had been raised in a house where the clocks had stopped in 1841.

"May I have a glass of water, please?" he said.

I filled a glass from the full pitcher on the bar and gave it to him as he circled the room deliberately, picking up pictures and little porcelains and studying the art.

"Thank you so much." He drank the water quickly, as he casually examined a Bierstadt landscape of the Circle B in the autumn, aware he could run his company for a year on the value of the frame alone. "Hmmm," he said, pretending not to be impressed. He handed the glass back. "I'm so dehydrated."

"Really?" I said, trying to keep a straight face. "Can I get you anything else? Herbal tea? White wine?"

"White wine would be wonderful." George settled himself into a deep, comfortable chair. "My, my, isn't this lovely." He trailed the end of the scarf along the side table, letting it flow over a small stack of antique volumes, and looked around. I could hear the cash register going in his head. "Oh, hello," he said to Celestina, who had come in quietly and set a platter of grilled, sliced jalapeño quesadillas on the coffee table.

"Buenas tardes, señor." She smiled. George had finished two quesadillas before she even had the doors closed.

I handed him a glass of wine.

"I don't even know how to begin to apologize for what happened on Tuesday." He shook his head miserably as he rummaged around deep in his tote bag. "I haven't slept for three nights worrying about you. And, as you know, the police are looking into it, but if there's anything I can do, just say the word and I'll do it. Ah, here it is."

A square wooden box bound with a flat strip of seaweed and sealed with black wax appeared from the canvas sack. "This is oolong tea I have brought in especially from China. It works wonders for every part of your physiology, particularly to calm and heal. I thought it might help you get well more quickly." He offered me the elegant, simple package.

"Thank you," I said. "I'll have some later this afternoon."

I was very touched by his sincerity and friendship and had to remind myself that this was one of the English-speaking world's finest actors. It was his profession to manipulate, to make himself loathsome or irresistible. But, on the other hand, I thought, even if he was stoned out of his gourd most of the time, it was sort of like having a Buddha visit your house. Not only his rotund fleeciness, but the promise of a greater wisdom, some sort of adoring salvation and peace, emanated from him as well.

Of course, he could have had the fire set by one of his devoted minions, and he certainly could have poisoned Cyrus. God knows there was motive enough.

"Who do you think started the fire?" I said.

George looked me straight in the eye. "I haven't got any idea, because Bradford was still in the meeting when it happened, otherwise I would have said for sure it was him."

"Are you serious about Bradford Lake?" I said. "Because if you are, you really need to get specific. You and Winston and Shelley mentioned him several times on Tuesday as the one who murdered Cyrus, and if you have good reason to believe he is the killer, you have to tell me what it is."

"Oh, poor Bradford." George said his name the way a parent does over a chronically wayward child. "I'd better lay off him. We're like brothers—Cain and Abel sometimes maybe—but we're linked for eternity and we'd never seriously hurt each other." He gathered up a string of my great-grandmother's amber beads from the table and ran them sensuously through his fingers into the palm of his hand, where they clicked like dominoes. "It's just healthy sibling rivalry."

I noted what he'd said and tried to remember if Cain had murdered Abel or vice versa.

"Did anyone else leave the meeting?"

"Just Shelley, as you know. And she almost died trying to save you." If he felt any anxiety over his executive secretary almost losing her life trying to rescue me, he hid it well. He finished off his wine as quickly as he'd drunk the water, and popped another cheese snack into his mouth. "She is a real trooper."

"Yes. She certainly is," I said. "How is she?"

"She'll be fine," he said, twirling the empty glass by its stem. Again I was struck by how clean everything about him was, especially his hands and fingernails, which were small and cut straight across, leaving a little length, but there was nothing effeminate about them. They were precise, specific, Prussian in their motion. He placed the glass carefully on a side table, with a quick, longing glance at the full bottle on the bar. "The doctor just told her to stay in bed for a day or two. She was back at work on Thursday. Shelley has a great deal of backbone and she is the most brilliant person I've ever known. She runs everything for me." His voice was apologetic, defensive, as though he needed to explain her role and actions. "I suppose you noticed what went on during the meeting."

"Yes, I believe I did."

"I overlook a great deal because she has a mind you wouldn't believe and she says that this job is the first time in her life that anyone's gotten past her chest to see the rest of her."

"I can believe that." I got up and poured him more Pinot Grigio, changing the subject from Shelley's mind, which I was pretty sure was one-track: the prevailing theme being penetration. "You know," I said, "Cyrus was murdered. Poisoned."

"Yes." He looked up at me, eyes shining. "Isn't it tantalizing?"

"Tantalizing?"

"Oh, I love intrigue. I know it's terrible of me to say, but you know how I felt about Cyrus—I'm glad he's dead—and I think it's thrilling that it was by such a creative means. It's certainly the most exciting thing that's happened to me in real life. Poisoning is such a classically dramatic, powerful statement. Just look what it did for Romeo and Juliet, and King Lear. I could go on and on."

"But this is real life," I reminded him. "Real death."

"Oh my, yes." He suddenly frowned. "I know. That's one of the reasons I came out to see you today, in addition to seeing how you are recuperating—the fact is, I'm absolutely scared to death." The second glass went down the hatch. "And I was wondering if you would be my bodyguard, because I'm certain I'm next."

I couldn't help laughing. I got up and took the bottle of wine over to him. "I'm just going to leave this here next to you," I said. "I've got more. Why do you think you're the next target?"

"Look at how determined Salieri was to get rid of Mozart," he said. "He didn't give up until he succeeded. The fire was a diversion. Someone, and maybe it was Brad, or even Winston—I love them both but I don't completely trust them—poisoned Cyrus once he had figured out how to structure this air rights business. Now I'm the only thing standing in the way. Cyrus worked hard on loading the board with cronies, and the control is about fifty percent him and fifty percent me. If something were to happen to me, my supporters would completely fall apart—leaderless, purposeless legions." His hand fluttered in a series of motions, phalanxes falling before slings and arrows. "And that would be the end of the Roundup Rep. It would become a real estate company.

"You know"—George stood up, wandered over to a bookshelf, and ran his finger along the titles—"a lot of people think I should retire. That I'm a has-been—so lost in the classics I can't see the real world. They think I've lost my artistic vision. They don't understand that we need grace and the lessons of the past. Besides"—he pulled out a volume of Voltaire and began to read through it—"the company is my home, and I'll die before I give it up. I love Dr. Pangloss, don't you?"

"Absolutely," I said, happy to try and keep up. "What I like best is everybody's irrational optimism, no matter how bad it gets. And as you know, for them, it gets very, very bad. But they just know it's going to get better. And finally, it does."

I didn't add that it was just this sort of blind, mindless, positive faith that kept me hoping a proposal from Richard might be right around the corner. That we'd been through enough travails, we were each other's pots of gold, and that bright light of eureka would shine on him any day now.

"George," I said, returning to the subject, "Cyrus asked me to come on the board to investigate what he claimed was a missing twenty-million-dollar endowment fund. What was he talking about?"

"That miserable old bastard," he grumbled. "That was one of his tactics. Start throwing dust and sand and smoke into the air, get everyone confused. The endowment fund is sitting right in the bank where he put it. End of story."

"Which bank?"

"Roundup National."

That was a helpful answer since my family owned the Roundup National Bank and I could confirm the fund's existence with a call to my father.

"I've got a copy of the guest list from Cyrus's birthday party and I think we should go over it to double check a few people." I handed him a fax.

He covered the perimeter of the library as he studied the list with what I was now coming to recognize as routine meticulousness, and after probably a full minute of complete silence, he came to a halt and stood almost at attention as he said every name out loud once with painstaking articulation. Then he went through again and put them in groups.

"Some of these can be eliminated quickly—the acting students for instance: Vanderbilt, Cary Scott, Jane, Annette. They're all kids from out of town and didn't even know Cyrus. Now, let me see, in the company: Deborah. No, I don't think so. She was never his type." George looked up at me over the tops of his glasses. "You do know what Cyrus was like, don't you? With women, I mean?"

"I know what he was like with me," I said.

"All hands and promises?"

"Yes."

"They're strong inducements for young actors. Gigi Dorrance-Downs, for instance. She was one of Cyrus's longtime protégées. He's been cramming her down my throat for the same amount of time he's been cramming himself down hers." George smiled at me, delighted at his own humor. "About ten years."

I pictured her right off. She looked exactly like Maureen O'Hara—a beautiful redhead with picture-perfect makeup and a movie queen demeanor—ideal for the sorts of period pieces the Roundup Rep did. And I also recalled that the few times I'd seen her onstage, even though she looked like Maureen O'Hara, she wasn't as good an actress.

"So that's one bunch of baggage I can unload before next season. She has become her publicity," he added dismissively.

"Would she have any reason to murder Cyrus?" I asked.

"Plenty," George said. "But I don't think she would have waited this long. I think she would have done it years ago. But, then again"— he paused and looked out the window and tapped a finger on his lips— "she saw him regularly. She's always been an ambitious girl. Maybe I've been thinking in the wrong direction.

"Now," he continued. "Let me look at the board members. Maude Ballentine. Poor dear Maude. She's such a lost soul. I think she will go whichever way the wind takes her.

"And Andy?" George laughed. "Let me tell you about men like Andy Beckett. He wants to be associated with the theater because, to him, it's like voyeurism, like peeking behind the curtain. He lives in a world of numbers and blue suits and stock issues and venture capitalists. The theater is a little bit naughty—a demimonde where homosexual men can be so masculine and where the plainest women are trans- formed into goddesses. Nothing is what it seems, and for someone like Andy it's like eating popcorn. He can't get enough of it because he can't believe the way it works, because it doesn't make any sense. He'll stick with me—he can get air rights anywhere he wants. He doesn't need mine."

"Do you think either of them murdered Cyrus?" I asked, grabbing a quesadilla before George finished them all.

"I cannot imagine why one of them would. They have nothing to gain." He glanced again through the list. "And the rest of these people? Winston. Shelley. The nurse, Kissy. The other board members. I can't see any way that any one of them would benefit from Cyrus's death." George poured himself the last of the wine. "How long do you need to think about the bodyguard question?"

"I'll tell you what," I said. "I won't do it personally, but I'll pro- vide someone through Bennett Security. Do you want him to start today?"

"No, the boys can keep an eye on me tonight. Have him come to the theater tomorrow at ten and ask for me."

"It's very important that no one knows he's a bodyguard, George. And that means no one, including the boys or your secretary or Winston. I don't want one of my crew unnecessarily endangered or compromised, and if people know why he's there, it'll be a complete waste of his time and your money."

George considered my words and I could tell the money part had got his attention. "No one?" he said.

"Absolutely no one."

"All right." He thought for another moment. "Have him tell Celia he's the Shakespeare scholar I've been expecting. You probably couldn't provide anyone with an English accent, could you?"

"Not one that you'd believe," I said.

George nodded. "That's all right. There are a few Americans who fill the bill. Well, I'd better get back to town. I wish I could stay at your house," he said wistfully. "It's so compact and comfortable. Really feels like a home."

"You're welcome to stay as long as you like."

"No. I'm sure the boys have set the car on fire by now; they're so wild on their day off." He stood up, lifted his tote off the floor, and slung it over his shoulder.

"Who are these boys exactly?" I asked.

"Brilliant young actors in our conservatory. They work as interns for me as part of a work-study program for their tuition."

"It seems to me all they do is sit around and smoke dope."

"Oh, my." George's smile was both sad and mischievous, and I was struck by how empty his life must be. "They keep me going."

He looked into my eyes, and the loneliness and pain in his gaze cut straight into my heart.

"I am a fifty-year-old gay man, Lilly. I have no family. No mother, father. No wife, no husband, no children, brothers, or sisters. My friends are dying in droves. I hear of, or go to, at least one funeral a week. Boys like these keep my mind off the reality and on the hope—it's all I have—like Dr. Pangloss."

My eyes filled with tears. "I can't imagine how awful it must be to have so many friends die."

"It's not anything I ever thought I'd experience, that's for sure. But Cary Scott and Vanderbilt are so full of life, neither one of them ever had anything and everything's an adventure to them. It helps you forget."

"Cary Scott and Vanderbilt?"

"Yes. Cary Scott Douglas and Vanderbilt Belmont."

"What are their real names?" I said.

"What difference does it make?" He kissed me on the cheek. "This is the theater, you know. Good-bye, my dear. Oh, who will you be sending?"

"Bertram Chiswick," I said.

"Now you're getting the picture. Bye-bye."

Through the foggy car windows I could make him out taking a long drag off a small cigarette and laughing hysterically as he lurched through a tight U-turn and wove away down the dirt road. The boys roughhoused in the back seat like oversexed, physical, pubescent, on-camera teens in a Calvin Klein ad. Sort of like dogs, if you get my drift.

B ertram Chiswick?" Elias leaned way out of his saddle and spat a long brown rope of tobacco juice onto the ground. He pushed his hat back on his head and regarded me. Complete contempt, scorn, and disdain creased his tanned, windblown, bearded face. I think he's the only cowboy who wears a tie. "Methinks you've picked the wrong writer."

"Well," I said defensively, "I didn't think of Falstaff Plantaganet soon enough."

"Do I need to tell you it'll be a stretch for me to pose as a Shakespearean scholar?"

"Oh, you can do it, Elias. Surely during all those years hanging out at The Hill and Harvard you read some Shakespeare. Weren't you a Rhodes scholar or something?"

"Well, yes, in fact, I was, although all it's ever done is make me even more of a disappointment to my family."

I looked him in the eye. "Elias," I said, "you're fifty-two. Get over it."

"Don't worry," he said. "I have. Sometimes I just forget I have. Know what I mean?" He smiled sheepishly. He was such a kid sometimes. "And I quite enjoyed reading Shakespeare, even though I regard it as high-toned crap. What play are they putting on?"

"Macbeth," I said, wondering if that were good or bad.

Elias nodded sagely. "Fair enough." He wiped his sleeve across his mouth. "Bertram Chiswick?" he said again. "Why not Chiswick Fezziwig?"

"Too obvious."

I'd found him in one of the upper meadows visiting with the hands. It was starting to get dark, and the peaceful meadow was wall to wall with beautiful Black Angus cows and calves. His Australian shepherds, Gal and Pal, slowly cruised their herd, hoping for instructions.

Elias laughed and shook his head. "What do you want me to do?"

17

SATURDAY MORNING

Richard had stayed in town Friday night and I'd slept deeply for twelve hours, as my ravaged lungs took in the healing hill country air, so by the time I got to the office on Saturday morning for the first time in four days, I needed all the coffee I could get. Linda seemed to sense that, because she had a steaming cup poured and on my desk when I walked through the door.

"Gigi Dorrance-Downs lives close by." She handed me typed directions. "It'll just take you about ten minutes to get there. Flat Gulch Road for twelve miles, right onto Chugwater for another two-point-one and the Auberge de Joie will be on your right."

In ten minutes in Wyoming you can cover some major ground. "Auberge de Joie?" I asked.

Linda smiled. She'd started wearing a little bit of makeup and had pulled her full red-gray hair up into a topknot. I cannot tell you how much better it looked. Someone must have said something to her. Wasn't me. Must have been Elias—lovers can get away with just about anything.

"*Oui.* That's what it says in the Social Register."

We have a Social Register in Roundup. Can you believe it? Of course it only has about three hundred names, basically everyone who has expressed an interest in being listed and doesn't mind paying the five hundred dollars for the privilege. Naturally, my mother shakes her head over it, but they're in there every year, so evidently she always sends her renewal fee on time.

So do I for that matter. It's a great little phone book—not as good as the one in Newport, Rhode Island, which is one typed page titled "Everyone You Know in Newport"—and it's also a good gauge of whether or not you've accomplished anything new in the last year, since it lists all about your business and education and clubs and boards and church, and winter, summer, spring, and fall addresses.

For years and years, I didn't add anything new. Same old stuff:

Episcopal Church. Roundup School for Girls.
University of Wyoming, BA, History of Art.
University of California at Santa Bianca,
MA, Law Enforcement. MA, Toxicology. MA,
Criminalistics. Chief of Detectives, Santa Bianca Police
Department, Santa Bianca, California.

This year, it changed:

Director, Bennett Security International. Circle B
Ranch. Bennett's Fort, Wyoming.

I was getting used to my new life. To like it even. A lot. I think Richard might have a great deal to do with that.

Linda handed me the book, opened to Gigi Dorrance-Downs. Sure enough, there it was: Auberge de Joie. I read further.

Eleanor "Gigi" Dorrance-Downs, Auberge de Joie,
Bennett's Fort, Wyoming.

The Bennett's Fort post office covers basically everything from
Roundup east to the Nebraska border.

Actress. Catholic Church. St. Mary's School for Girls, St.
Louis, Missouri. L'Ecole Arcadie, Bar Harbor, Maine.
Madame Emilia's, Paris. La Châtelaine, Genève.
Académie Française, Paris. American Conservatory
Theatre, MFA.

Gracious, as my mother would say.

For the first time, a cloud of suspicion passed over the credibility of
our Social Register listings, and I wondered if anyone ever bothered to
check their veracity. This listing was too, too much, and I knew I was
looking at Lie Number One from Gigi Dorrance-Downs, because if
there were a thirty-five-year-old woman anywhere within a five-hun-
dred-mile radius of Roundup with this sort of background, my mother
would have been all over her like a gold mesh gill net, and if she failed
to rope her into matrimony with Elias, she would have found some
other major role for her to play in what passed for high society in
Wyoming.

Gigi's listing went on to say that she was a member of SAG,
AFTRA, and Equity—all acting unions—the Roundup Country Club
and L'Alliance Française. She had a summer place in St. Tropez and
winter places in Paris and Palm Beach—each with the appropriate listing of clubs. Apparently there had never been a Mr. Downs, except for
her father. I wondered what he did back there in St. Louis, if that was
where he'd ever been at all. He was obviously good at it, because she'd
been well provided for her whole life, unless I'd missed something. I
knew that if she'd had to support herself on her acting wages, she
couldn't have afforded to pay for her hair dye, much less the dues at one
of those tony spots.

"She's really into this French stuff, isn't she?" I commented to
Linda as I finished my coffee, took my quintuple magnification mirror
out of my desk and checked my makeup, added a little lipstick and
blusher, and put on my dark glasses. "Check her out."

"Oui." Linda handed me the file. "Don't forget, she pronounces

her name 'Zjhi-zjhi.' Like the movie. Not 'Gee-gee.' Are you sure you don't want me to drive you? You look a little pale."

"No. I'm fine. Just a little ragged around the edges. Have you had any luck tracking down Nurse Kissy?"

"Not so far."

We both turned at the sound of heavy, familiar footsteps thunking up the outside wooden stairs and then the door swung open to reveal a wonderful vision.

"Bertram," I said, "I would know you anywhere."

Elias beamed, his white teeth sparkling through his sandy gray beard and mustache. He leaned on a walking cane and was dressed in banana-colored, wide-wale corduroy trousers, brogans, a brown tweedy hunting jacket with leather patches on the elbows, a tan cardigan buttoned up over a pressed white dress shirt and a scarlet bow tie. He'd smoothed his pale hair straight back, showing off his receding hairline to best advantage, and put a lot of slicker gel or something in it because a couple of thick clumps fell down to the side, giving the impression not so much of slicker gel as of hair that hadn't been washed because its owner was too busy squinting into the dusty tomes in the basement of Anne Hathaway's cottage.

"Where did you get those excellent clothes?" I said.

"They were Grandfather's. They've been in the cedar closet for years. What do you think?" He smelled more of mothballs than cedar.

"Perfect. Your cheeks are so healthy and pink, I'd believe you'd been out stalking the moors. You look wonderful."

"Rooojh," he said daintily. "I got it out of that hundred-year-old box of theatrical makeup we used to play with. Too much, do you think?"

"No," I laughed. "Not at all."

Linda was giggling and blushing and circling him like a dressmaker fussing over a bride. And all I could think was why some wonderful woman hadn't scooped him up and dragged him off into the sunset. He was good-looking, a little hefty maybe, but smart as a whip, charming, funny, and fun, and rich. Of course, I was all those same things and I hadn't exactly been dragged into the cave myself. But Elias really wanted to be in love, to be married. Of course, so did I. I mean, who didn't? But he was truly a fine catch. I was getting to be a bargain. And the way I looked and felt today? I would be considered a complete excuse-my-French mercy fuck.

"Let me show you what all I've got."

He pulled a Cliffs Notes *Macbeth* out of his side pocket and laid it on the desk and then opened his jacket to reveal a Glock 19 in a shoulder holster. Then he moved his right arm in a swift, whipping motion and a slim black knife appeared in his hand.

"CIA letter opener," Elias said proudly. "What do you think?" He held it up for inspection. "No metal. It's fiberglass-filled nylon. Hard as steel." He banged the handle on the desktop. "And completely unde-tectable."

A pepper spray canister and a set of handcuffs were clipped onto his belt. From one of his jacket pockets he took three Japanese throwing stars, and when he lifted his pants leg, a little pearl-handled gambler's pistol came into view. He pulled a cellular phone from another pocket.

"And," he glowed, "the pièce de résistance." With that he picked up the walking stick and unfurled a sword. "I'm ready."

"You certainly are," I said. "I can't think of anything to say, except I hope you don't need to use all that stuff. But if I needed a bodyguard, I'd want him armed the same way." What I wanted to say was that it concerned me a little that Elias had so much available weaponry.

"Damn right," he said, and began to restash his armaments.

Linda just stood there watching him, batting her eyes like a maiden in a melodrama.

"*Allez. Allez.*" I ordered Baby, who jumped into my arms, and we struck out for the Auberge.

"*Bonne chance,*" Linda called after me.

CHAPTER

18

When I left the office, the sky was so heavy with rain, the dark gray, slate-colored clouds hanging a few hundred feet above the ground looked like they were about to descend and smother the earth. I could still see as far as usual into our endless nothing, but the clouds put a top on it, as though I were looking from beneath the dark branches of a tree, or from under the covers of my bed. The air was cool and still, thick with iodine and ozone, as I sped out to drop in on Gigi Dorrance-Downs.

This "dropping-in" aspect of police work upsets my mother so much, we don't even discuss it anymore. Obviously, it's a key investigative tool for smoking out, or uncovering, criminal activity, or suspected criminal activity. But, as Mother contends, it's also unspeakably rude. Well, yes, that's true. You catch people literally with their pants down. Which is, of course, the whole point. It can also be extremely dangerous, but based on experience, I didn't think that visiting Gigi's farm, or whatever it turned out to be, would rate too high in the danger department.

However, before leaving the office, I double-checked the little 9mm Glock 26 I always keep loaded in my purse. Who knew? Gigi could be housing the Aryan Nation out there at the old Auberge. Or, more likely, a greenhouse full of foxglove.

If I hadn't seen the Auberge de Joie with my own eyes, I'd never believe a place like it existed in Wyoming—a formal, gray stone, French country house. A charming little three-story château with a slate and copper mansard roof, shiny black wrought-iron balconies, and copper fittings. The window boxes, as well as giant urns on the front porch, exploded with flowers, and as my car crunched to a stop in the deep gravel of her circular driveway, gleaming black, double front doors flew open and there was Gigi herself, in an honest-to-God hostess outfit. The kind with a flaring full-length cape skirt, skin-tight Capri pants, wasp-sized waist, three-quarter-length sleeves, plunging neckline, and large, upturned collar that would make even Elvis jealous. The whole affair was a shimmery chartreuse taffeta with colors that shone and flashed around the full spectrum of greens and yellows. High-heeled, strappy mules completed the picture.

She was much smaller than I'd expected. Petite. Her flaming hair was waved back off her face, and she had the most beautiful creamy, clear, perfectly made-up complexion I'd ever seen in my life.

Five small white French poodles rushed past her out the doors and barked at me with all their might, whipping her skirt into a maelstrom of poufs and billows. Each had on a different-colored collar with matching bows above its ears: pink, blue, green, yellow, and magenta.

"Why, hello," Gigi exclaimed. "What a wonderful surprise. I wasn't expecting company."

I took this to be Gigi Dorrance-Downs Lie Number Two. One does not dress in straight-up martini garb to do one's chores.

"I'm sorry to drop in this way. I couldn't find your number," I said, telling Lilly Bennett Lie Number One. "You aren't listed."

"You're Lilly Bennett, aren't you?"

"Yes," I called out over the fluffy white barking jumble.

"That's all, *mes chéries,*" Gigi ordered the dogs, who stopped instantly. "I can't imagine what you're doing out here, but I hope you'll come in and have a cup of coffee before you leave. Or, actually, I don't think it's too early for a little apéritif."

"I'd love to, thanks." It was ten o'clock.

I followed her past a family of cement geese, each with a bow around its neck, who waddled across the porch, into a tall, breezy entrance hall that opened into a surprisingly cozy living room packed with a disagreeable, tooth-jarring assemblage of what appeared to be authentic Louis Quatorze and Quinze furnishings, and cheap little geegaws and curios. Fragonard paintings and plastic flowers. Lillian Vernon Meets Marie Antoinette.

Gigi was steeped in Arpège.

"Let's sit in the sunroom." She swished along ahead of me, the hostess gown making a wonderful brisk noise that reminded me of watching my mother go downstairs to meet my father for the cocktail hour. The Arpège floated on the air and the mules slapped against her bare heels. "It's become my favorite room since the panels were installed."

The sunroom was up to its name. Even on such a dreary day it was warm and bright, scented with the delicate fragrance of freesia from a small adjoining greenhouse.

Antique ivory panels, painted with elaborate country scenes, covered the walls. Lords and ladies leaping and picnicking. Giving chase. Skirts flying, bodices ripped, trousers unbuttoned. Lying in the verdure doing it. As I looked closer, I realized the paintings were pornographic.

"Where did you get these?" I said.

"Aren't they *irrésistable? Jolie. Jolie. Jolie.*" Gigi smiled and caressed a couple of them as she passed by. "They were out of a small country house where Marie Antoinette met Count What's-his-name. She had them especially commissioned for their trysts. If you look closely, you'll see that she is one of the ladies."

It was true. I could recognize Marie Antoinette from a million miles away, because for years, I don't know how many, but a big part of my life anyhow, I studied her with the contention that she was not the empty-headed idiot history had painted her to be, but was truly the victim of her time and circumstance. I had intended to reform the tragic French queen's image.

I think I wanted to do this because it has always been hard for me to accept that sometimes people who come from backgrounds overflowing with privilege and opportunity just throw the whole thing out the window. Sort of like when I first discovered that handsome rich men and beautiful rich women could also be actual criminals. What an eyeopener that was, and a reality my mother still steadfastly refuses to accept.

I wanted to believe, and prove, that Marie Antoinette had no control. That she was bought for Louis only so the French government could get its hands on some of that Hapsburg family money (absolutely true). And, if the real, real truth were known, if she could have, she probably wanted to be a doctor, probably working to save poor people in Africa. Sort of like Albert Schweitzer's great-great-great-grandmother.

So I read and studied and visited, hoping to discover one or two redeeming features, but bottom line, the facts remained: even though she was born a Hapsburg princess, daughter of Empress Maria Theresa and sister of Emperor Joseph II, into an aristocratic family of brilliant world leaders and rulers, and had access to inestimable wealth, *she never learned to read or write.*

She spent money compulsively, self-indulgently, like a child movie star. There was no one to tell her *Non!* except her husband, the king, whose advisers kept saying, "Look, Louis, you've got to get her under control." But he was so paralyzed by shame over the fact that he could not perform even the most basic marital function in bed and, after years of marriage, his wife was still clearly childless, and perhaps even a virgin for all he knew, that he would not and could not stop her, for fear that she would tell everyone and humiliate him in public. So he kept eating and she kept spending.

Instead of venturing out and seeing actual people every now and then—beyond the occasional midnight masked ball in Paris—she built a complete village on the palace grounds and had peasants come and live in it and pretend to farm and be happy, and she would ride through this village—La Ferme—in her cabriolet and wave to them, and every now and then she'd get down to visit.

One day she saw a little boy standing next to his mother, holding onto her skirt, and Marie Antoinette thought he was so beautiful and precious—*she took him.* And *kept* him. And treated him as a son-pet. But then, when she had a son of her own three or four years later (whose patrimony will be eternally in question), she pushed the little kidnap victim aside and made him a child of the court. All he wanted to do was go home. Well, he got even a few years later—wrote his name in the history books—when the mobs were looking for her and the king, and he told them which direction they'd gone in their escape attempt. That they were on the road to Varennes. Seeee 'ya.

The point is that after years of study and research I discovered the historians were right: Marie Antoinette was a complete and utter boob. But the panels in Gigi Dorrance-Downs's sunroom were testimony to the fact that she definitely knew how to get down and have a good time.

Instead of sofas, two delicately curved, painted iron sleigh beds flanked a large coffee table in front of a small white marble mantel, and a wide, comfortable chaise ran along a wall of windows that opened onto a small private garden where, among the rose trees, boxwood, and ivy, a number of marble statues of Hindu gods with multiple horse-sized penises and spreadeagled goddesses whose chests were moguled with a dozen breasts, were engaged in illicit activities, primarily involving their mouths and oversized tongues, which arched into pointed hooks.

The furniture was upholstered with pink silk satin and the cushions were such fine down that, as the various dogs took up their various spots, they practically disappeared. Sterling silver picture frames with photos of various luminaries—the governor, Senator Walker, a couple of astronauts and movie stars—and of Gigi in various stage and screen roles in movies and plays I'd never seen, sat on the tables and sideboards. Some of the frames looked like the kind that swivel, and I wondered what was on their other side, but I didn't have the nerve to look. More orgies, I supposed.

A maid in a short black taffeta dress and tiny white apron brought us Lillet in lovely little glasses.

Gigi arranged herself in a bergère, the full skirt making a wide lily pad around her. She crossed her shantung legs and sipped the apéritif. "Why are you here?" She smiled, not at all discomfited by entertaining a female stranger in this erotic lair. I felt as if I were being interviewed by the Belle Watling of Roundup to join her high-class stable of working girls.

I couldn't wait to hear what Linda's background check turned up.

"I'm investigating the murder of Cyrus Vaile," I said, once I'd settled into the facing chair. "How well did you know him?"

"Pretty well," she said casually. "I've known him for years. He and my father were business associates. Daddy owned a string of manufacturing plants, and I met Cyrus when he came to St. Louis on business. I'd gotten my MFA and had been auditioning in Los Angeles and San

Francisco for several months, but I hadn't gotten any roles that were going to get me anywhere, and he said he could help me in Roundup. So, here I am."

"When was that?" I asked.

"About ten years ago."

"Were you lovers?"

Gigi looked down at her dainty feet in their high-heeled slippers. Her fingers and toes gleamed with hot cerise polish. "Did you know him?"

I nodded.

"Then you know what he was like, how he played the game, and you'll know what I mean when I say that was not one of the finest periods in my life. I was fairly young, twenty-three, and desperate to become a great actress. He was already old. And so disgusting." She shuddered and grimaced. "I'll never forget that first evening, going to dinner with him at La Nuit de Paris—do you remember that place?"

"No, I think it opened and closed while I was living in California."

"It was like a New Orleans whorehouse. All red velvet and gold. All older men and younger women. We sat in a circular booth—the booths there had very high sides and narrow entrances, so you could only see in from directly in front—and he wanted me to sit right next to him. One hand was instantly high up on my leg, and with the other he laid the menu out in front of us and said, 'What do you want?' And pointed his finger—it was an awful gnarly old thing with a chipped nail—and ran down the side with the prices, not the food."

Gigi rolled her eyes and laughed brightly. "I'll never forget it. I thought, My God, what have I gotten myself into? And later, when we got back to his apartment, those godawful cold, black and white, heartless rooms at the hotel, and he came toward me, both hands outstretched—one targeted on each breast—his tongue quivering through his thick lips, I asked myself, Just how much do you want to be an actress? This much? And you know what the answer was? Yes. And I've been giving Academy Award performances ever since."

We've all been faced with such choices in our lives, and I wondered if I'd ever come across anything I wanted to do so much that I'd become the mistress of someone I found repugnant, just to make my dreams come true. I don't think so. I mean, I wouldn't even dance with Dickie Chamberlain because he sweated so much, and he had loads of money. I could never fake sex on a regular basis.

"How often did you see him?" I said.

"Oh, I went by three or four times a week. We were no longer lovers, he'd finally come to terms with that, but I owed him a great deal. So I'd go by and have a drink on my way to the theater. It was the least I could do."

"Who do you think murdered him?" I asked.

"I suppose I should say I was surprised to hear he'd been poisoned." Gigi looked me directly in the eye. "And probably a number of people are saying I did it. Which I did not. But I've thought about it a lot. He was very controversial. Besides, if you knew him, then you know he was a mean, grasping, grabbing old bastard. He was involved in a number of projects other than the theater, but from the theater's point of view, which is the only one I'm familiar with, I'd have to say George did it."

She had been balancing the small glass of Lillet on the palm of her left hand, holding it straight between the thumb and index finger of her right hand, and she now paused to take a small sip and then set the delicately etched glass soundlessly on the table next to her. "Their relationship had completely disintegrated. It was total acrimony, and George had become so paranoid about the air rights deal every time Cyrus opened his mouth, George saw it as a stab."

"What about Bradford Lake?" I asked, wondering about, and trying to listen for, all the things she wasn't telling me, recalling that George had said she was one of the first items he would cut. She'd been the Rep's leading lady for a number of years and I was certain the history between her and George was volatile.

She'd known all these people well for a long time and was being grand and gracious, playing to perfection the role of helping the authorities. I admired her poise and elegance. I decided to buy an iridescent hostess outfit with Capri pants and an Elvis Presley collar and learn to make canapés and sip a tiny glass of Lillet in the morning, instead of wearing old Levis and belting shots of whisky. I could just see cousin Buck's eyes if I asked for a *petit apéritif* in the Golden Nugget Saloon. He'd take away my cowgirl papers.

She raised her eyebrows and her shoulders a little. "I can't think of any reason why Bradford would do it, or Winston. The minute I heard Cyrus had been poisoned, my only thought was that it was George. I really haven't thought about anyone else at all."

"What about Cyrus's nurse, Kissy?" I said. "How long was she with him?"

"I have no idea. Probably not long. Those girls were all interchangeable, and as you can imagine, looking after what Cyrus wanted tended to . . . well, one could swallow just so much. I mean, my dear, you don't really believe that girl was a nurse, do you? She was from another sort of agency—the kind where girls dress up and pretend to be different sorts of things. I know you know what I mean. He didn't really need a nurse," Gigi said. "Did he leave her anything?"

"I don't know. Did he leave you anything?"

"He gave me a case of gonorrhea once, but nothing since then."

Gigi looked up as the maid came in and handed her a note. She glanced at it and then folded it up and slid it into her deep pocket, making the taffeta rustle like tissue paper. "I'm sorry to cut our visit short, but I have guests arriving soon and I need to put myself together."

The second she stood up, all the dogs were instantly alert, on their feet in the deep cushions, barking. She lifted an engraved calling card off a small silver tray and handed it to me. "Here's my phone number so you can call to make sure I'm home next time and not have to make a useless trip all the way out here."

"Do you mind if I take a second to look in your greenhouse?" I said. "I grow roses and violets myself, and would be interested to see what you've been most successful with."

"No," she said graciously, not wanting to appear to rush me. "Not at all."

As she prattled along about this flower and that aphid, I looked at every single plant—under, over, and around the leaves and benches. There was no foxglove in sight.

"Please be sure to call if I can answer any more questions. I'd love to help."

"Who are you?" I said. "Where do you really come from?"

"I don't know what you're talking about."

"I think you do, and I'm going to find out."

"You're in for a lot of disappointment, then, I'm afraid. I'm nobody special, just a girl who happened to have a run of good luck. I had nothing to do with Cyrus's murder."

Two miles later, as rain fell out of the sky in large soaking drops, I was about to pull onto Flat Gulch Road. A large white Cadillac sedan came into view and put its blinker on for a right turn. I waited while it rocked carefully off the ledge of pavement onto Chugwater's rutted, hard-packed surface and rolled slowly past me, disappearing into the rainy morning in the direction of the Auberge de Joie. The driver looked to me like Cyrus's brother Samuel.

amuel Vaile on his way to visit his dead brother's paramour. He was clearly expected and, I could only imagine, excited at the prospect of a frolic in Gigi's gardens of delights.

What all did I have going on here exactly? I pulled my notebook out of my purse and flipped through it as the rain began to pound deafeningly on the Jeep's metal roof. There was certainly no shortage of suspects. I had put Bradford and Winston at the top of my list because I didn't want it to be George. I still knew he could easily be the killer, but what had been bothering me was the absence of solid female suspects, because, in spite of the fact that many of the master poisoners through-out history have been men, the landscape of poisoning is intrinsically feminine.

Women rarely kill the same way men do—instantly, spontaneously, passionately. They kill when pushed to the limit, when there is no other way to solve the problem or reach the goal. And then—whether the method is stabbing or shooting, or poison, which itself is extremely rare—they think about it for a long time, figure it out, plan it. And, ultimately, they seldom actually do it, because often just figuring it out, knowing it's an option, helps make whatever the situation is more toler-able.

Therefore, when women kill, ninety-nine percent of the time it's premeditated, even when it's in self-defense.

Nothing, I mused as I sat there in the rain at the stop sign, is more premeditated than a good poisoning.

I turned the corner and pulled over on the far side of the road. While I waited to see how long Samuel would be at the Auberge, I called my father in his office at the bank—I knew I'd catch him there working quietly on Saturday morning—and told him what I needed.

"Why don't you meet me for lunch Monday at the Cattlemen's Club, and I'll give it to you then," he said, once he'd noted my request and asked a couple of questions.

"Great. Thanks," I answered, relieved and wanting to push him to fax it over to me but aware not only that it was information of a highly confidential nature, but also that I was lucky to be getting it at all. I seldom asked my father for anything, because his answer was inevitably negative, still stuck as he was in the belief that women should not bother their pretty heads over anything but the household and their charities.

The second I hung up, the phone rang and it was Richard.

"How are you doing your first full day back at work?"

"Wonderfully," I answered. "Especially now that I'm hearing your voice."

"No, really."

"Really." It was true. Being in love with Richard was wonderful. Being loved back at the same time was terra incognito for me, and corny as it sounds, sometimes I thought I would simply explode with joy. Of course, there was always that little voice in the back of my heart that kept saying, You know he could be lying. This could be another one of those say-anything-to-get-the-money deals. But I knew it wasn't.

When you grow up as the target of fortune hunters, you learn to spot them—their gifts are a little too big, their gestures a little too lavish, they find you a little too funny.

Or else they're the absolute opposite—men with the attitude that they will teach you a lesson, who announce they will love you in spite of your money, as though it were a stumbling block or curse to be overcome, and who give you the impression they are doing you an enormous favor. Maybe even saving your life. They're the ones who give you sleeping bags for your birthday.

I've always preferred the ones with the too big gifts.

"I made a reservation at the Grand for lunch. Why don't you meet me at twelve, twelve-fifteen? Wait for me in the lobby because I might be running late. Actually, if you want to, why don't you go in and sit down, have a Bloody Mary or a glass of champagne and I'll be there as soon as I can."

"I can't," I groaned. Richard *never* invited me to lunch. And at the Grand of all places. My favorite restaurant in the world. "I have to meet my mother back at the ranch to go over some wedding stuff. But I could meet you there for dinner."

"Done. Six-thirty."

"I'll be there," I said. "I love you."

"I love you, too, Lilly."

So, if you love me so much, I thought after we hung up, where's the ring? I mean, let's get serious.

I took out my mirror and fixed my makeup and had just finished putting on a fresh coat of nail polish when, in the distance, through my rain-fogged windows, I saw the lights of Samuel Vaile's white Cadillac bouncing slowly down the muddy road through the downpour. I pulled off the shoulder onto the hardtop and was well down the road into town before he'd even gotten to the stop sign. He'd only been there forty-five minutes. Obviously he fucked faster than he drove.

SATURDAY NOON

My parents' house at the Circle B is in a rather secret, gentle valley—over a hill and around a bend and through a rocky draw. The valley is quite a lot smaller than the ranch's main one, more enclosed and private, and Mother has planted millions of wildflowers along the river in the graceful meadow below their house. They live at the ranch on and off from early May through the end of September.

Mother had been out here more than usual lately, because in just a week my twenty-year-old, orphaned goddaughter, Lulu French, would marry fifty-year-old German Baron Heinrich von Singen und Mengen, on the Circle B. Mother was in charge, and under her direction the event had taken on the international and diplomatic proportions generally associated with the opening of Parliament. She had never been happier.

I parked my car by the back door and Baby and I dashed through the rain, through the long pantry, past the old-fashioned cold cellar, and into the kitchen where their butler, Mañuel, was just finishing packing a large wicker basket.

"Buenos días," he said. "Your mother's out on the front porch."

"Thanks, Manny," I said, and grabbed a handful of powdered sugar-dusted macaroons on my way through.

Mother had never been exactly what anyone would call a "ranch" person, and whenever she was at the Circle B—when she wasn't picking wildflowers or taking long walks—she spent her time on the covered porch that extended the length of the house, talking on the phone, making arrangements for what she would do when she got back to town.

The porch was usually elegant and inviting and comfortable, with its heavy redwood furniture and sturdy, bright yellow canvas cushions, rough sisal rugs, and huge baskets of flowers, but as the wedding approached, it had taken on the attitude and appearance of a highly organized military Central Command and Control Headquarters. A large, heavy table, reminiscent of Mussolini's desk, served as Mother's command post and was stacked with long, speckled boxes stuffed with index cards of scrawled, illegible lists: of gifts, of seating assignments for the Tuesday Garden Dinner, the Thursday Square Dance, the Friday evening Rehearsal Dinner, the Saturday Wedding Ceremony, and the Wedding Dinner. Of RSVPs, of transportation and housing arrangements for the out-of-town guests. Of guest lists for parties friends were giving for Lulu and her bridegroom, of flower arrangements for the tables, houses, and guest rooms.

She constantly jotted notes on yellow legal pads for Mañuel and his kitchen and household staffs, dreaming up more and more assignments for him and all the temporary workers he was bringing in to pull off the whole four-day event. I wondered if he'd started taking Valium yet. He'd been hard into the sherry for two weeks now.

The storm was blowing itself out, but the branches from towering spruces still scraped across the roof, and Mother, who was slightly hard of hearing, was, predictably, yelling into the phone to her florist who, I'm sure, must have been holding his handset at least three feet from his ear. Two lights blinked on hold, and river rocks held down piles of papers that rattled in the wind.

I sat down, poured myself a cup of coffee in a tan ranch mug that had the Circle B brand fired in dark brown on its side, and arranged my cookies in a line on the table in front of me. I smiled at Mother. She frowned and shook her head. She'd always been thin as a rail, mostly because she didn't eat too much. I could be thin, too, if I wanted to be. If I wanted to eat as little and smoke as much as she did.

Finally she hung up. "Gracious," she sighed, smoothing back her gray hair with graceful hands. "This is more work than I've ever done. Nobody knows how to do anything properly anymore. I don't know what will happen when I'm gone. Everything will just go to hell, I guess." She smiled.

"Maybe if you gave them a chance," I suggested.

"Don't be ridiculous."

I read her the blurb about Gigi Dorrance-Downs out of the Social Register. "Do you know her?"

"Good heavens." She furrowed her high, pale brow and took the book from me to read it for herself. "You'd certainly think I would, wouldn't you? Never heard of her, except through the theater, of course. Wait a minute." She slapped the Register closed. "Of course. I'll call Mary Louise Wallace in St. Louis. She knows everyone."

Moments later her old finishing school roommate was on the phone, and after a conversation that went quickly to the point, they hung up. "Never heard of any of them," Mother announced. "No such family anywhere in Missouri, or Kansas either. Ever."

The phone rang and she grabbed it like an ill-tempered, this-better-be-important executive. "Yes? Yes. She's right here." She handed me the receiver. "It's for you, but don't talk too long, Lilly, we've got an awful lot of work to do."

It was Linda. Her voice was excited. "I couldn't find out anything about Gigi, but we got an *anonymous* call a few minutes ago." The words came out as though she were describing the most fabulous experience of her life. "And the caller—I couldn't tell if it was a man or a woman—said that Gigi Dorrance-Downs was really Molly Dolan from Waterbury, Connecticut, and that she was an escaped criminal and that she or he, the caller, had information that could prove Gigi was the one who murdered Cyrus Vaile. And that she would probably strike again."

"Strike again at who?" My heart began thudding.

"Didn't say. They hung up. I checked the caller ID number and it was a pay phone at the railroad station."

"Good going, Linda," I said. "Thanks."

The chief of detectives of the Waterbury Police Department was a good friend of mine from our days of whooping it up at the national police conventions when sexual harassment was mutual and we all thought it was fun. I called and left the name and info on his voice mail and asked him to get back to me as soon as he could.

"Well," Mother declared, taking to her feet, straightening her jeans and tucking her shirt in just so. "Just as I thought—a shopgirl with a big imagination." She arranged her sweater around her shoulders and hefted a canvas bag that bulged with wedding paperwork. "I've asked Mañuel to arrange lunch for us in the pavilion. I wanted you to help me with the seating."

We shrugged into our slickers and cowboy hats, and I followed her off the porch and down a steep, rocky, narrow trail through the aspen to the meadow.

"I can't wait for you to see," she said gaily as we splashed along the road. "It's finally finished."

And there, at the far end, alongside the river, sat the glorious structure my father had taken to calling Katharine's Folly.

Everyone in Wyoming knows that you never plan to do anything fancy in a big tent, because even if you do get the thing together, the wind just knocks it down instantly. Besides, I think this wedding pavilion—this folly of Mother's—had been a dream of hers, probably since she was a little girl and dreamed first of her own wedding and then, later, of her daughter's. And then, as the years passed and the light began to dawn that her daughter wasn't going to have a wedding, I think the dream of the light-filled pavilion next to the river faded, and she quietly dropped it off her list.

Last Christmas, however, when Lulu and Harry announced their engagement, they rekindled the ashes, and Mother blazed into action, mercilessly whipping her construction crew off their winter-plump behinds and their hockey- and basketball-watching beer bellies and into high gear, and into creating a composition of such special beauty, it seemed to have materialized from the waves of a sorcerer's wand.

The pavilion's gently sloping, green-shingled roof was supported by thick, peeled-pine logs. They, as well as the wide-board pine floor, had been varnished and shellacked so much they seemed to be encrusted in thick, clear glass, not yet cracked by thundering feet or shifting sands.

Pine railings, wide enough to sit on, surrounded the structure on three sides, while on the fourth side a large, fully rigged, stainless steel commercial kitchen and elaborately appointed ladies' and men's rooms twinkled in readiness.

In the center of the floor, Mañuel had placed a round table and set it for lunch with a yellow gingham cloth and a basket of red geraniums, adding two of Mother's specially constructed, brand-new, old-fashioned, straight-backed kitchen chairs, which gleamed with bright red enamel.

"There are three hundred of these in the basement," she said fondly, looking across the grand space out at the river, caressing the bright paint, taking in the sweet, sensuous feel of the flawless surface.

I didn't know whether to laugh or cry. The pavilion was beautiful and, to tell the truth, I'd never known her to put so much love and effort into anything.

"Do you like it?" Her eyes brimmed. "It's such a silly thing to do."

"I love it," I answered. "It's absolutely spectacular. Besides, you are seldom silly, so I think it's okay to go a little nuts every now and then. We all know—God knows—that you won't make a practice of it. This is going to be an incredible wedding. Lulu is very, very lucky."

Mañuel uncorked a bottle of cold white wine and filled our glasses. Chicken sandwiches with extra mayonnaise and the crusts cut off, sliced tomatoes, and clumps of fresh watercress sat on the plates.

"I don't want you to think for one second that I've given up on you." She smiled over at me as she shook her napkin into her lap. "But I've never had such a good time. What a stroke of luck for both of her parents to be dead, and her fiancé to be foreign—absolutely no interference. It's like a dream!" She sipped her wine and pulled two lists out of the canvas satchel.

"Tell me," I said, getting out my glasses, and asking the question girls never, ever tire of asking their mothers, "was this the dream for your own wedding? Is this how you had envisioned it as a little girl?"

"Good Lord, no." She laughed brightly. "Where did you ever get that idea? When I was little, I envisioned my own wedding as being in St. Paul's in London. I don't know exactly to whom I had thought it would be, someone very major, but then my father lost all his money in the crash, and even though he made most of it back, the war started, and your father and I were married at St. James Cathedral in Chicago when he was on a three-day pass. It was lovely, very simple, almost no one was there, except lots of women and all of our parents, of course. Everyone else was off working or fighting."

She looked beyond the river at the flowered hillside. "No," she said wistfully, "I don't think my wedding was what either my mother or I had pictured. It was slapped together and I wore a borrowed dress because mine didn't arrive from New York in time. The only perfect thing about it was the groom. I loved your father from the second I saw him, and he felt the same way. That was fifty-five years ago." Mother smiled at me and patted my hand and gazed around her creation. "No. I never, ever envisioned anything like this for myself. I'd never even been out West until I met your father, and now dynamite couldn't blast me loose."

She took a small bite of her sandwich and then signaled for Mañuel to take it away.

"Delicious," she said, and blotted her lips before continuing. "And I certainly never imagined a wedding like this for my own daughter. I was positive your wedding would be at St. Paul's, but I had to give that one up when that little Diana Spencer tricked Charles into marrying her. He was far too old for her in the first place, and now that dreadful Camilla is in the act. Never in my wildest dreams did I ever picture my daughter marrying a rancher or getting married here at the ranch."

The best thing about this part of the dissertation was that Mother was serious. She honestly thought I should have married Prince Charles. Does it matter that I've never even met him? Of course not.

"And now, at this point, I don't think we'd mind if you got married in a gas station in Chihuahua. To the owner, of course."

I laughed and finished my lunch, knowing she'd mind very much.

Mother rearranged her sweater and then lit a cigarette. "You don't think it's wrong to have both the square dance and the wedding down here, do you?" She smoothed the papers on the table. "I just hate to build this thing and have all these visitors here from all over the world and only use it for one party."

"No," I said. "I think it's perfect. The square dance is on Thursday and the wedding's Saturday, and they'll look completely different. I bet you'll find you use this place a lot."

"Oh, good. I'm so glad you like it. Your father, of course, thinks I've lost my mind. Now, let me see." She flipped through a stack of lists. "I know you're all ready for your bridal luncheon—Lulu is so excited about it. Tell me your plans—I'll bet they're lovely."

Oh, my God. Once I'd sent out the invitations, I'd completely forgotten about the whole thing. I was hosting the bridal luncheon the day before the wedding, and it was supposed to be as pretty and sweet and special as a bride's bouquet. Oh, dear.

21

The ringing phone startled me out of a deep sleep and I opened my eyes to see daylight still outside my bedroom windows. I wondered what day it was. The clock said it was three in the afternoon.

I'd come home from my lunch with Mother completely worn out. Not so much from her and the wine, but this smoke inhalation business was more serious than I'd given it credit for, in spite of the doctor's warnings. My strength was at maybe fifty percent of normal, and my lungs were as sensitive and tender as those of a tuberculosis patient.

"Hello?" I said, instantly fully awake. Years of practice teaches police officers not to have even a split second of residual sleep. It isn't that you're pretending to be awake. You *are* awake.

"Hello? Lilly?" I recognized the upturn at the end of his voice. It was George.

"George," I said, happy to hear from him. "How are you?"

"Wonderful. This Bertram is a dream. I don't know where you found him on such short notice, but I'll tell you something remarkable: he actually knows his Shakespeare."

I smiled, picturing Elias and his satchel full of Cliffs Notes. "Of course," I said. "We wouldn't send you a phony Shakespearean-scholar bodyguard. What can I do for you?"

"Nothing serious. I was just hoping you could come for dinner."

"Tonight?" I asked, thinking about my dinner date with Richard. "Yes."

"I would love to but I'm already busy."

"Doing what?" he asked gaily, the implication being that it couldn't possibly be more entertaining than coming to his house. "Meeting Richard Jerome?"

"Well, yes, actually."

"Wonderful. I'm just having a few friends over and maybe you both could come for cocktails. I'll have Shelley call Richard right now and see if he can join us. Where is he?"

"At the Opera House," I said. "He's in rehearsal for *Rigoletto.*"

"Come at six-thirty. Very casual. Sort of a fiesta."

After we hung up, there was a light tap on my bedroom door and Celestina waltzed in wearing a bright turquoise Mexican sundress and carrying a filter pot of French coffee and a plate of chewy macaroons. Her glossy hair was smoothed into a loopy, serpentine bun, and sunlight sparkled from her silver earrings and necklace and black eyes.

Celestina Vargas is not my leftover nanny and not my mammy—like we've all longed for since we were thirteen and saw *Gone With the Wind* a hundred times. She and I are about the same age and weight, and in spite of the fact that sometimes she likes to pretend she doesn't speak English, she is the fourth generation of Vargases to be born on the Circle B, and she attended Wind River Community College with an eye toward fashion design before deciding life on the ranch was pretty good. Celestina's been my cook and housekeeper for years and is married to our top wrangler boss.

She has two children, a son and a daughter, and now one grandchild—Elena—whose godmother I am. I don't understand why I'm always being asked to be a godmother. I'm not good at it at all—I'm not much interested in the children, don't give them fancy gifts or take them to church or Europe. But the fact is, if something happened to their parents, they know I'd be there in a heartbeat. I've also always made it a point to teach them all to appreciate good champagne, starting on their twelfth birthday, so what has happened over the years is that, as the children start to get older, they like me more and the parents like me less.

"Good sleep, chiquita?" she asked as she placed the tray on my bed table and opened the French doors, letting in the air, rich and invigorating after the thunderstorm.

"Perfect," I said. "Thanks."

She picked up Baby, who had been napping next to me. "You come with me to the mailbox, you little monkey."

I pushed the filter down, filled my cup with the strong black brew, and took a big sip before settling back on my pillows and starting to think about Cyrus and George and Kissy and if Gigi really was Molly Dolan from Waterbury, Connecticut, and if that would make any difference at all anyway. I thought about Samuel and all George's minions and tried to come up with how someone would get an overdose of digitalis into Cyrus without his knowing it. It couldn't have happened all at once; it had to have been administered gradually, and I reviewed our meeting that afternoon. Cyrus had wanted some whisky and Kissy had said no, only tea, and it occurred to me that might be it. The tea. The Chinese oolong that George had brought me yesterday as a gift and said he had imported directly to him.

I wondered if he gave it to everyone as a kind of board-of-directors, welcome-to-the-family gift. I imagined he did.

I slipped into my white terry cloth robe and slippers and sprinted down to the kitchen, where the only sound was that of a large pot of tomatillos Celestina had bubbling along for fresh salsa to go with her homemade hot tamales for our Sunday lunch. The beautifully wrapped, smoothly sanded wooden tea box, its top secured by a wide ribbon of dried seaweed and a strip of raffia, still sat on the counter. I picked it up and examined it closely. The seaweed appeared to be undisturbed. I took a sharp paring knife from the drawer and sliced the kelp on either side, carefully working off the well-fitted top to reveal a tin canister sealed with what looked like, and probably was, old Scotch Tape, sold as new in China. It, too, seemed not to have been tampered with. I ran the knife around the edge of the tin, pried off the cap, and scattered the fragrant black leaves on the kitchen counter.

It was brilliant. Keep adding digitalis—slowly, slowly—to a man on a daily dose of digoxin. Put it in his tea, because that's all the stimulus the doctor will allow, and sooner or later it will build up and, bingo, his heart will crawl to a stop. All it takes is patience.

I picked up the phone and called Kim Leavy, praying she'd still be in her lab this late on a Saturday, not off jogging a hundred miles to Lander. Thankfully, she was.

"Do you have that tin of Chinese tea from Cyrus Vaile's apartment?" I asked. "It might still be inside a smooth wooden box."

"Let me check. I'm sure we do, we moved practically everything from his kitchen and bathroom over here and we're working our way slowly through it. Hold on." She returned to the line shortly. "Got it. Is this where you think the foxglove is?"

"Yes," I said. "I'm positive. It would be a perfect mask."

"You're right. I'll call you back."

I felt terrific after my nap, completely refreshed, and I went into the bathroom and drew a deep, steaming eucalyptus tub and lay there inhaling the soothing, healing vapors as I concentrated on who all had access, not only to Cyrus, but also to the tea. I found it was pretty much the same bunch: Bradford, George, Gigi, Samuel, Shelley, and Winston, in alphabetical order. They were all there regularly and any one of them could deliver the spiked tea to the apartment. The beauty of it was that it wasn't poisoned. Foxglove digitalis wouldn't bother anyone who wasn't already on digoxin.

I ran some hot water, grabbed the remote, and flipped on the TV that sat across the room next to my old-fashioned, organdy-skirted dressing table. Joan Fontaine was answering the phone in a New York penthouse. It was dark and drizzly outside and she was sitting at her dressing table, a baby spot on her face, wearing a *gorgeous* one-shouldered chiffon gown (I'd like to think it was blue-gray), diamond clips as big as fifty-cent pieces on her ears, and diamond cuffs as wide as rulers on each wrist. A full martini glass sat among the crystal perfume atomizers.

"Oh, I'm not doing anything," she cooed into the clunky black receiver. "Just sort of a dreary Saturday night."

I love Joan Fontaine.

Just then, my phone rang and I answered it languidly from among my bubbles. "Hello?" I drew it out.

It was Richard.

"Hi, darling," I said dreamily. "Did George Wrightsman get hold of you?"

"Yes. I told him we would come just for cocktails," he said. "I get enough of these artists all week long. I just want to have a quiet dinner alone with you and get home early for a change."

"I agree. I feel like I haven't seen you for a hundred years. I'll meet you there," I said, admiring one of my long legs as we hung up. I've gotten so that it's not too jarring or depressing if I admire just my limbs, and only when they emerge—one at a time—above the edge of the tub in front of steamed-up mirrors.

I have mirrors all around my bathtub, and one time I was lying in the tub watching the movie about the *Sports Illustrated* swimsuit issue and one of the models was Cheryl Tiegs, close to my age, and she looked all right, not as great as the other models but all right for a middle-aged woman. And I was thinking I probably looked that good, too.

Then I stood up. And there in all those mirrors was the reality of my body, which looks absolutely *nothing* like Cheryl Tiegs's. We could be from different species. I screamed and fell down into the bath, way below the rim, I don't think the top of my head was even visible, and I haven't taken such a good look at myself since.

The phone rang again. Joan Fontaine had just tossed open her twenty-foot-tall front doors and thrown herself into Don Ameche's arms. He was dressed in a patched, limp jacket and a long, tattered and torn scarf, like a starving artist.

"Lilly, it's Kim Leavy." Her voice was excited. "You're right. It's so obvious, I can't believe it. The cut is about fifty-fifty. The foxglove leaves are just a fraction of a shade lighter, and you wouldn't notice unless you knew."

"Hidden in plain sight," I said.

"Exactly. Thanks. I owe you one."

"My pleasure."

I felt good. The discovery didn't get me anywhere big yet, but the simple act of reaffirming that all these years of ongoing study and hard work do pay off gave me pleasure. When you reach the point that your knowledge and experience finally begin to work together, you enter the full stride of your profession. Whatever that profession may be. I still worked on hunches and intuition, but now they were bolstered by more than twenty-five years of hands-on experience and hours of academic study. I actually *knew* what I was doing. Most of the time. Except when it came to men.

Foxglove in the tea. Talk about planning. Talk about patience. Talk about impressive. This was turning out to be one of those cases that required extreme diligence. Most of them were no-brainers.

George had said to be casual, but it doesn't make any difference to me between a full-blown evening State Department affair and casual when it comes to getting myself put together. It is always a major production, and to make matters worse, I've recently had all my makeup and skin care redesigned or whatever you want to call it, and now it takes me so long that, the other night, Richard said, "One day soon, you won't be able to leave the house. You'll get up in the morning and begin to put on your makeup and then it will be time to take it off and go to bed."

Very funny. But the thing is that I hadn't changed my look since I joined the force when I was in my early twenties, and as the makeup lady said, "That was about twenty-five years ago. You look different now. You need to change. Believe me."

So now here's what I do instead of forty splashes in boiling-hot water. I do steaming with lemon-lime essence, using a very special, very expensive, *pink* chamois: aromatherapy—good for my attitude, great for my skin.

Then I do a duet of glycolic acid, which is supposed to remove old skin, wrinkles, and spots. I have faith that it will. It's only been two weeks. Then I do a bunch of other stuff and finally put on the makeup, still referring to the chart she made for me because it's totally different from what I did for twenty-five years. And finally, half an hour later or so, I'm done. Is it worth it? Do I look better? I think so. But who knows. It's all just back and fill at this point.

I slipped into my new black silk crepe dinner suit and black patent high heels. I drove the short distance to the helipad and was airborne in the S-76, having a cocktail, by six-fifteen. Twenty minutes later I waved good-bye to the pilots, who had settled us like a feather in the parking lot of a tiny hilltop park just two blocks from George's.

George Wrightsman's apartment was the highest in a series of multilevel residences that descended down a steep hillside like some sort of modern white stucco Anasazi development, a Neo-Mesa Verde deal. You entered through an unobtrusive rough-hewn door in an out-of-the-way courtyard and then a small, steep, tight stairway led to the large marble-floored entrance hall. The space itself was huge and airy and the land simply fell away, leaving nothing but spectacular vistas.

"I can't get over your apartment," I said to him as we kissed hello. "I didn't think a place like this could exist in Roundup. It's out of the movies."

"Yes. Well, out of the theater, anyway." He smiled, his teeth as white as his dress sweats. "I'm so glad you're here, it makes me feel so safe. Did you bring your gun?"

"Yes," I said. "Always."

"Ooooh."

We looked into each other's eyes and I again felt that cosmic connection, a magnetic pull to him, and I sensed what people mean when they talk about the strong, charismatic, mesmerizing power that cult leaders exude and exert. He had it over me and I knew I could fight it if I wanted to. But this evening I didn't want to, I didn't feel like it, and that, at bottom, is the nature of that sort of power. It tosses out a warm bath of bright light like gold dust, with a taste as sweet and addicting as anything you've ever tasted; it makes you feel that things in your life have never been better and creates an irresistible longing to bask in it just a little longer.

He smiled at me again. Like the sun. I smiled back, aware that in many ways I brought with me my own sort of power.

"Amazing," I said.

"Yes. This place really is quite amazing, isn't it?" he agreed, breaking the spell. "But the truth is, most successful gay men have especially beautiful homes because they don't have wives to support, or children, or tuition. And then, since I'm in the theater business, I have access to unbelievably talented artists and artisans. They could convert my whole home to a Berkeley Square townhouse overnight if they had to. For instance," he said, "these columns."

I followed him across the black and white marble squares to the base of a wide staircase that led to a large landing. The bleached, pitted, marble pillars with their ornate, leafy, flowing cornices reached to the ceiling, about fourteen feet, and were either Corinthian or Ionic or Doric, I didn't want to embarrass myself by asking which because I should have known. Corinthian, I think.

He caressed the ancient stone as though it were a lover. "Doric. *Troilus and Cressida*," he said, knocking on it and making a dull, scratching thud. "Styrofoam. Nineteen eighty-three."

Even up close, without touching them, I couldn't tell the difference.

He took my hand and wrapped it around his arm and squeezed it close to him as he led me to a small sideboard above which hung a large, colorful, well-lit painting.

"But then, on the other hand, this Picasso is the real thing." George turned his rich melted-chocolate eyes on me, and although the nature of the gaze was open, it was neither happy nor friendly. He was tired and jaded. "In my world, you never know what you're going to find or get. But it keeps the burglars out because they think it's all fake. It's like living in Oz and being the Man Behind the Green Curtain. Remember him?" George swayed from foot to foot and circled his arms around, as though he were turning the big dials. "The most powerful man in the realm, and then the curtain fell away, revealing him, but he kept going nevertheless, turning his dials, making the show keep happening, and told them, 'Pay no attention to the man behind the green curtain.'"

"Of course, I remember," I said.

"That's me. The Man Behind the Green Curtain. Vanderbilt"—he turned to the dark-haired boy with the smoldering, James Dean looks who'd been staying close during our brief tour—"would you bring Miss Bennett a glass of Jameson's on the rocks?" He searched my face quickly. "I believe I've got it right."

"Perfect." I wanted to spend the whole evening talking only to George Wrightsman, learning more about him and his Byzantine world.

A small group of guests gathered in the corner living room, immune to the late spring thunderstorms that scudded across the city and plains and roiled along the mountaintops.

Elias, who'd left a message at the office that he'd checked into the Grand using his alias, Bertram Chiswick, had changed into a rumpled suit and was chatting at full speed with Shelley Pirelli, who, from the look on her face, seemed absolutely smitten. Unfortunately, Elias looked equally taken. I caught his eye briefly, trying to warn him off, but I could tell he pointedly ignored my message and returned to what I'm sure was a scintillating conversation.

I knew I should make an effort to visit with some of the other guests. I was, after all, a new member of the board, and then I decided they should probably be making an effort to talk to me; therefore, to kill a little more time while I waited for Richard, I crossed to the opposite side of the room and stopped to admire a small Degas bronze whose tattered tulle skirt desperately needed replacing, or at least mending. Heresy, I know, but the tulle didn't look that way to start with.

Out in the entry hall, Gigi Dorrance-Downs was making a grand entrance, kissing George, shrugging her lemon taffeta shawl into Cary Scott's waiting arms, to reveal a short, tight fuchsia cocktail dress. Then, with gleeful shrieks of recognition and outstretched arms, she disappeared into the dining room. She seemed to have arrived alone. Molly

Dolan from Waterbury, Connecticut. Queen of the Thespians in deep Wyoming.

Finally, Vanderbilt appeared on the far side of the living room with my drink, giving me an opportunity to study him for a moment.

Dark hair cut short, dark eyes with long lashes, thin angular face with straight white teeth. Gray flannel slacks, navy blazer, white shirt, striped tie. He was fairly short but had a lean, athletic body that made him seem tall, and he appeared to be only marginally stoned. He had a cunning about him, and I could tell he'd grown up on the streets, and that bringing cocktails to well-dressed, well-behaved people, and making conversation without trying to pick their pockets, was so newly and studiously acquired a veneer that it was still transparent and far from sticking.

"Where are you from, Vanderbilt?" I asked him.

"Modesto." He began to take a furtive bite of a fingernail and then yanked it quickly from his lips as though he'd just remembered George's admonitions. His nails were all gnawed to the quick. This boy had a hard past. "Have you been to see George's production of *Tiny Alice?*" he asked politely, as though he were reading from a script. "It's brilliant. Albee would be mad for it."

"Not yet. How did you end up here in Roundup?"

"Oh, I auditioned for George in Los Angeles. The company holds auditions there every spring, and I was acting with a small company at the Mark Taper Forum."

I could imagine the audition. It had no doubt taken place in a hotel room and the only thing it had to do with Shakespeare was a cat-o'-nine-tails. If Vanderbilt had ever been to the Mark Taper Forum, it was as a member of the audience. He was a street slut. A tramp. For money, he would be anything anybody needed him to be.

"How wonderful," I said, watching Andy and Sherri Beckett arrive.

It was true what I'd heard—she was a Barbie doll, with big, fluffy platinum hair, a perfect size 6 figure in a very curvy, tight, teeny-weeny, sparkly dress, extra high heels, and more jewelry than Queen Elizabeth. Compared to her, Shelley, in her long black T-shirt dress and long strand of cheap gray pearls, looked like a nun. She had turned her back to the room and faced Elias head on, standing close and speaking intimately. He was starting to sweat as those gigantic nipples poked into his chest like spikes on a mace.

George embraced the newest arrivals—Bradford Lake and Aldo

Franciscus—and laughed loudly at something Brad had said. A big stage laugh. A real HA! HA! HA!

"Excuse me a moment," Vanderbilt said. "I'd better get Mrs. Beckett's champagne cocktail or she'll go batshit."

Andy had dumped Sherri practically the second he was through the door, and she stood alone in the entrance to the living room like a glittering little time bomb that needed some damned attention pretty damn quick or it would damn well wreck everybody's damn fun.

I went over to introduce myself, and after a couple of false starts, conversation-wise, realized that while Sherri Beckett pretended she had no brain, no clue about anything, that she went where Andy told her to and did what he said, that she was an itsy, bitsy, ditsy party doll, she was nothing of the sort. This lady was totally in charge, and way, way too savvy to let anyone, especially her husband, know it.

"Andy said George has these dinners every Saturday night," she said in soft, high, Marilyn Monroe-ese. "And we never come, but when his secretary, Shirley—"

"You mean Shelley?"

Sherri looked at me blankly. "Maybe that's it. Shelley. Well, when she called me at home and said George really, really wanted us to come, I told Andy we should at least drop in for a drink."

"Have you ever met Shelley?" I asked.

Sherri shook her head. Her football-helmet hair did not move.

"I'd love to introduce you. Come on."

The looks on Shelley's face, in one corner of the room, and Andy's in the other, made one of those rare moments that cannot be choreographed. They simply occur and take on a life and momentum of their own. The gravity that descended on Andy's head, and the blood falling out of it way, way down, until he looked more basset hound than human, seemed to push Shelley's facial expression way, way up until you would have thought she was an olive-skinned leprechaun.

Andy set out, plugging toward us in slow motion like a man whose shoes had been glued to the floor. He was racing to stop a spill. To catch a vase of falling flowers. He would not make it.

"Shelley," I said with my biggest, friendliest grin, "do you know Sherri Beckett? Andy's wife."

Shelley put out a hand that looked like a bear claw in a beer commercial compared to Sherri's delicate paw. "No." Her smile was as huge as her capacity to deceive. "I'm so happy to make your acquaintance. Andy's said so many terrific things about you."

Sherri's vapid expression never wavered. "Oh? Like what?" She'd met a thousand Shelleys, and could have cared less if they thought she was a dummy. She'd signed on for the jewelry. The dummy was Andy.

He finally conquered the Sahara and burst onto the scene, gasping and out of breath from a twenty-foot dash that no doubt seemed like the longest of his life. "We're late, honey. Time to get going," he said, grabbing Sherri's arm and tugging her away, but not before giving me a death stare.

"Okay, honey." Sherri dug her lipstick out of her diamond- and onyx-studded purse, which looked like a little television set. "I'm ready." And as she took his arm, she turned and gave me a wink.

"Two-fifty, I think," I said to Andy under my breath as he led her past me, out of the room. Not bad. I'd just raised his annual gift from ten thousand, to one hundred thousand, to a quarter of a million, in about seventy-two hours.

Once they were gone, I chatted for a few minutes with Shelley and Bertram, a.k.a. Elias, whom Shelley introduced as the world's most famous and brilliant Shakespearean scholar, and thanked her again for saving my life on Tuesday.

"Wasn't that terrifying?" she said. "I sure hope they catch whoever did it."

"Me, too."

"We were just going to grab a bite," Bertram said. "Would you join us?"

"No, thank you. I'm fine for the moment."

The truth is, Richard had arrived, and I was so happy to see him, I wanted to race over and throw my arms around him. He and George laughed and smiled, and George gave him a large hug around the middle. Richard was so much taller, George just wrapped his arms around Richard's waist and hugged him like a child hugging his father. Richard laughed and hugged him back.

I started in their direction but had the indescribably poor fortune to be waylaid, ambushed really, by Maude Ballentine, whose personal hygiene was right out of a mud-floored Thomas Hardy novel when toothbrushes were still single pieces of straw used only when you got a wad of fur or a chicken feather caught between your front teeth.

"Do you know Theodore?" she asked, shoving, right under my nose, her scrawny, smelly husband, who stank of brandy and dirty laundry and immediately began to prattle on in his New Hampshire monotone about the Dartmouth-Yale lacrosse game, confusing me with someone who cared. And then Maude got started on wanting me to join some sort of damn guild or other.

"Over my dead body," I said, although I had stuffed two chili rellenos in my mouth and I don't think she could understand me.

I held my glass out for a refill, which arrived practically instantly, thank God, and watched George send his blond boy, Cary Scott, off to get a drink for Richard, then give very specific, meticulous instructions to Vanderbilt about going to the kitchen to get him something to eat. Vanderbilt nodded his head, his expression surly, as though he'd heard this particular instruction about a hundred times before.

Elias continued to refuse to catch my look begging him to come help me out, especially now that Shelley was practically doing it to him with her eyes right there in the middle of the living room. The collar of his shirt had grown as pink as his face from the rouge that had melted into it from his cheeks. Winston McMorris smiled and gave me a little wave hello, then joined Richard and George. They were all happy, happy, happy, talking shop, giving me the finger, so to speak, because they all knew I needed rescuing but the price wasn't worth it. The Ballentines were simply too much of an ordeal, and if you were stupid enough to get tricked, you were too stupid to save. Damn. I never get caught like this.

Vanderbilt had returned with a cocktail plate loaded with little tamales and was standing at George's shoulder, listening to the three men swap lies. Nothing to do with him, so he got bored and ate one of them, and then he ate another.

I had finally just walked away from Tad Ballentine in mid-sentence when Vanderbilt dropped his plate, scattering the little cocktail tamales like tubes of lipstick. His head wobbled on his long neck, and he staggered a step or two and then melted gently down onto the floor and went into convulsions. It looked to me almost like an epileptic seizure, except when I got there I could see that he was struggling for breath and his face was quickly turning blue. His hands tore at his throat.

George screamed and fell to his knees beside him as Vanderbilt's body began to toss and shake violently. His mouth was frozen open in a ghastly, silent scream and his terrified eyes bulged from their sockets, then his bladder and bowels evacuated volcanically as his system quickly began to slide into anaphylactic shock. It was clear to me that mouth-to-mouth would have no effect, even if I could catch him.

"Get the sharpest knife you have," I yelled. "And call 911."

Shelley appeared out of the chaos. "What's happened?" she cried. "What's going on?" It looked as if she were going to become truly hysterical until Bradford Lake grabbed her by the arm, yanked her away from the action, and spoke to her sharply.

"Oh, not the boy," I heard Gigi say to someone.

"Is it an overdose of some kind?" someone else asked, not unreasonably.

Elias shoved George out of the way and knelt down across from me. His steady hand passed me the hard nylon paring knife that the CIA counted on to be as sharp as a razor. "Have you ever done this before?" he whispered.

"Not exactly," I said.

He retrieved the knife. "I did it several times in 'Nam. Bring me two drinking straws," he ordered Cary Scott, whose blanched guppy face hovered nearby.

Elias made a single, definitive, deep, straight slash across the base of Vanderbilt's neck and inserted the straws into his air passage. Nothing happened. His lungs were somehow paralyzed and his body followed suit. The paramedics arrived and hooked him up to an IV and pounded on his chest, but it didn't appear that anything made any difference. They didn't say he was dead as they bundled him into the ambulance for the fast trip to the hospital. But he was. They knew it and I knew it.

That was pretty much the end of the party, and it occurred to me that, if George didn't look out, people were going to stop attending these lethal little theater functions, which had such dramatic, show-stopping finales they were clearly staged. They might have been okay to watch, but nobody wanted to end up as the body in the middle of the stage floor with the big pair of scissors sticking out of his back or the kitchen knife sticking out of his chest.

Bradford had been reduced to stone, unable to move in any direction, halfway up the staircase. His eyes looked dead and useless as a blind man's, and his chest did not move; he was as frozen in position as Noel Coward at a photo shoot, while below him Cary Scott and Shelley gathered up the spilled food and glasses through their tears.

Aldo hovered around them like a mother hen. "Don't worry, don't worry," he cooed. "He'll be fine. He'll be fine. You'll see." He shepherded them into the kitchen, where Cary Scott fell into the wide arms of a large black woman and cried like a baby.

"What happened?" he blubbered. "He was fine and then he was almost dead."

The woman soothed and rocked him in her arms and shot a dirty look at Shelley, who had dropped all her dishes in the sink, breaking most of them, and then ran crying into the big cushion of Elias's shoulder.

I spotted a tamale that had rolled under a potted palm, and picked it up and smelled it. It smelled like regular spices to me, cumin and chili powder. I peeled open the cornmeal skin.

Richard had been standing alongside me the whole time. We were alone in the foyer, except for Bradford, who still waited like an abandoned dog on the side of the road. I suspected that Quaaludes had nailed his shoes to the step.

"Odd," I said.

"What?"

"These are mushroom tamales." I folded the little tidbit into a cocktail napkin. "Would you put this in your pocket for me?" I said.

"What's wrong with your pocket?" Richard slid the small bundle into the pocket of his suit jacket.

"Newer."

In the living room, George huddled on the couch. He and Winston fired up joints with quaking fingers while Shelley, who had taken up her position in a chair, wailed into Elias's large handkerchief. She looked up as we came in, her face mottled and afraid. "Is he going to be all right?" she glugged out.

"I don't think so," I answered and turned my attention to George. "Do you know where the tamales came from?"

"Yes. My cook, Nora, makes them for me."

"What's in them?"

"Mostly eggplant, because I'm a vegetarian."

"Anything else?"

"Well, maybe a little Acapulco Gold. But they're just for me and the boys—I don't feed them to the guests or anything like that."

"Any mushroom?"

George wrinkled his nose. "No. Just eggplant, green chilis, and grass."

"These are mushroom tamales," I said. "Poisoned ones, I think."

George fainted dead away.

SUNDAY MORNING

The Circle B takes up two hundred thousand acres and employs so many hands—up to sixty full time from early spring through late fall, and more during the roundups—that one of the first things my great-great-grandfather built on the ranch in the 1860s was a small Anglican, now Episcopal, church. Since that time, people from ranches and country homes all around Bennett's Fort have attended Communion there on Sunday. It's a typically English country church, constructed of rough, hand-hewn stone with a slate roof and granite floor, beautiful stained glass windows, and dark wooden pews that glisten from hard-rubbed cedar oil.

I love it, especially on days like today when my cousin, the Very Reverend Henry "Hank" Caulfield Bennett, bishop of the Wind River diocese, performs the ceremony, because he stands up there in his crimson robes and bishop's miter—tall, white-haired, handsome—sunbeams flashing from his jewel-encrusted, antique cross, and thunders at all of us, scarcely pausing for breath.

And then my father, who in the summer months is always the lay reader, gets up and thunders along with him.

We still use the 1928 Book of Common Prayer, so everyone knows the service by heart—no surprises, no hugging, no guitars.

It's quite a sight, these two gentlemen—one a bishop, the other a business tycoon, both cowboys and Westerners. They are the culmination of several generations of Wyoming-born and -bred Englishmen. A lot of that old-time upper-class, public school noblesse oblige remains, the part that pertains to Duty above all else, but the doing of that Duty has been polished to solid, squinty-eyed rock by Wyoming's incessant grit-filled wind, where one is always, above all else, suspicious.

And now, when they visit England, they talk about retiring to live there, as though they'd just been gone for a few weeks. Done their time in the colonies and had now been captured by, or surrendered to, a primal pull that sleeps somewhere deep down in all of us. The instinctive longing for the gentler climate, gentler life, for Home. Like salmon.

Today I sat in the front pew with Richard and my parents, across the aisle from Christian and Mimi, who had on an electric blue Escada suit, had pulled her blond hair up beneath a pillbox hat, and looked better with no effort at eight o'clock on Sunday morning than I could after an entire day's dedicated grooming. I tried to pay attention, but all I could think about were Cyrus and Vanderbilt, and how I wished Hank would speed it up a little so I could get into town.

Although Jack Lewis said they'd already questioned Nurse Kissy— he kept forgetting to fax over her statement—and had come up with nothing, it would be unprofessional not to talk to her myself, ask my own questions, test her veracity. After all, she was the only one who had been a regular on the scene.

"I'm expecting all of you to breakfast," Mother announced once the family had gathered in the windblown churchyard where a few hardy roses clung for their lives to the rocky walls and where our ancestors who hadn't been cremated were buried.

"I can't," I said. "I have to go to work."

"I beg your pardon?" She glowered from beneath her wide-brimmed straw hat and took her best shot. "We won't have any of that. It's Sunday. And incidentally, has anyone seen Elias? We expected him for cocktails last night and never heard a word, and Marialita said she thought he'd gone out of town."

"He'll be back in a few days." I struggled not to bolt for my car. "He's doing a little work for me, and I need to get going."

"Honestly, Lilly." Mother took my arm and guided me away from the group. "You cannot expect to keep Richard if you continue behaving this way," she scolded under her breath. "A woman who works all the time simply cannot keep a man."

"That's a bunch of bull," I snapped. "Richard understands perfectly, and frankly, Mother, at the moment, I'm more interested in getting to work than in romance. I'm sorry, but I've got to go." I tore my arm free from her, stormed over to my car like a spoiled brat, and slammed the door, leaving her there to glare furiously at me.

Richard kissed me through the window. "Good luck," he said. "Don't worry, I'll get her calmed down."

"She makes me so goddamned mad sometimes, I just can't stand it."

"I know." He smiled and waved as I drove off. I felt like a complete shit all the way into town, filled with tears and fury and totally ripped up inside because I hate to fight with my mother; she's not only getting older and what if she died—that last fuss would haunt me forever—but also, *what if she were right?* Richard and I hadn't got home until one o'clock this morning and collapsed, exhausted, into bed. Richard's last words before I fell asleep had been, "I miss you. I don't think I'm ever going to get five normal minutes alone with you again."

What was I doing?

"I need some information, Curtis," I said to the doorman at the Grand. "And I know you can get it for me a lot quicker than I can get it for myself." I handed him a hundred-dollar bill.

"Shoot," he said.

"I want the name and address of Cyrus's nurse."

"Oh, you mean Franny," he said. "Coming right up."

Curtis picked up the house phone at his station and punched in a number, had a quick conversation, made a few notes, and was back at the car in record time.

"All the room service and bell staff guys know her," he explained.

"She's been around here for years. Her real name's Franny Sullivan and she lives right up the hill on Dakota. Seventeen-ten. Apartment D. One of the frontier's loveliest party girls."

Sunday morning traffic downtown is nonexistent and it took less than two minutes to reach the large, old-fashioned, red brick apartment house. White delphinium, red poppies, and blooming honeysuckle bushes filled the well-tended flower beds in the three-story U-shaped courtyard. It was very quiet.

In the small entryway, a bank of antiquated buzzers confirmed that Frances Sullivan lived in Apartment D. First floor. I took my Conoco card out of my pocket and let myself in through the security door, climbed a half flight of stairs through air thick with the Sunday smell of bacon frying, and knocked on her door. It opened almost immediately.

"Yes?" Kissy said. Her long hair was pulled into a pony tail and she was wearing running clothes and held a blue and white Roundup Police coffee mug in her hand. She was probably about twenty-five but looked fifteen. At first she didn't recognize me, and when she did, she wasn't too sure where it was from. "Yes?" she repeated.

"Kissy?" I said, holding up my badge. "I'm Lilly Bennett. We met at Cyrus Vaile's on Monday. When he died."

"Oh, right." She smiled, dazzlingly, and extended her hand. "Now I remember. I'm Franny. Come on in."

The apartment was tiny and neat. White and ruffly. Morning sun shone through a crystal vase of fragrant mock orange on a draped table.

"Have a seat." She indicated a love seat covered in a washed-out yellow and white slipcover. "Would you like a cup of coffee?"

"That would be wonderful, thank you," I said, making myself comfortable and taking my notebook and glasses out of my purse. "Has anyone from the theater company or the police department called or come by to talk to you since Cyrus died?"

Franny shook her head. "No. Why would they?"

"Well, I guess you haven't seen the papers."

"Sorry. Current events aren't my best subject."

I smiled. "I understand. Do you know that Cyrus Vaile was poisoned? Murdered?"

Franny opened her mouth, then closed it and frowned at me. "No kidding," she said. Then realization widened her brown eyes. "And you think I did it?"

"At the moment, I think everyone did."

"Do you work for Jack?"

"Jack?" I said, hoping I knew who she was talking about.

"Yes. Jack Lewis. The chief of detectives."

It took all I had not to burst out laughing. Oh, boy, Jack, old friend. Mr. Perfect. Now I know how you always get downtown so fast, even though you and your lovely wife live in the country.

"Sometimes we work together, yes," I told her. "On this case, for instance. As a matter of fact, if you'd like to call him right now and let him know I'm here, that would be fine."

"That's okay," she said brightly. She sat in a large armchair and tucked her long legs back under her. "I'll take your word for it. What do you want to know?"

"First of all, who visited Cyrus regularly, and where did the tea come from?"

"The Chinese oolong, you mean? That's the only time George Wrightsman came to visit was when Cyrus ran out of tea. That's what George brought. This special tea he had imported. Sometimes Winston came along and he'd sort of referee. Occasionally, they'd all laugh, have a good time, but usually it ended in a fight."

"Who else visited?"

Franny shrugged. "Lots of people. His brother. Gigi came by almost every evening there was a performance and had a cup of tea and short-bread cookies. Shelley would come by with papers and stuff—she came with George sometimes when they were getting organized for a board meeting or something. Bradford Lake and that Aldo guy came for dinner a couple of times a week, and they'd talk business. It was a great job." She smiled. "I'm sorry the old guy's gone because now I have to get back to actually working. With him, all I had to do was make sure he took his medicine and watch a porn movie or dance for him a little bit every now and then." She twirled her pony tail around her finger. "He paid me a lot."

"Was it always a new box of tea?"

"I guess. I never paid that much attention. Tea's tea, as far as I'm concerned."

"No," I said. "I mean was it always sealed with the seaweed and Scotch Tape?"

Franny thought for a second. "No. Never."

"And George always delivered it himself."

She nodded.

"What about Vanderbilt Belmont? Or Cary Scott Douglas. Did they ever come over?"

"Well, Vanderbilt, that's the darker guy, right? He did sometimes, but that's the only time Cyrus would ever tell me to go home, which was fine with me. That guy gave me the creeps. He always had one of those gym bags with him. I don't even want to think about what was in it.

"Look." She leaned forward, a serious expression on her face. "I know what you probably think of girls like me. And even though I'm making my living right now as an exotic dancer, I'm also getting my master's in microbiology at Bennett University."

I tucked my pad back into my purse and stood to go. "Miss Sullivan," I said, "you don't need to explain anything to me. I have a lot of sympathy and respect for you working girls. And I hope, for your sake, you can get out of this racket before you get killed."

"Me, too." She smiled her radiant smile. "Don't worry. I will."

"Thanks for your time. You've been very helpful."

Just as we reached the door, a key slid into the lock. The door opened and there stood Jack Lewis, holding a garment bag.

I gave him my biggest smile.

He was still standing in the hall, one hundred percent poleaxed, when I went down the steps and out the front door.

The first day of the Cody Gateway Rodeo was only a week off, and Richard and Christian and a handful of wranglers were in the main corral, practicing starts, when I drove past, so I stopped and joined my father at the rail. He was the official timer.

Richard sat comfortably astride Hotspur, twirling his lariat in lazy, low circles, his hat tilted against the afternoon sun, talking and laughing with Christian, whose lightning-quick small black quarterhorse gelding pawed the ground, anxious to get going.

Even from a distance I could see my brother's blue eyes flashing like thunderbolts above his black mustache as the cowboys rehooked the barrier rope across the front of his box. As the header, Christian was the only one with a barrier.

Richard, the heeler, whose box was on the opposite side of the cattle chute, could start out whenever he wanted, once things were in motion.

The black steer, whose horns curved up into graceful symmetrical points, gawked out suspiciously, knowing something was probably going to wreck his day. A thin rope lay loosely around his thick neck, because in rodeo team roping, as opposed to range roping, once the steer leaves the chute and crosses a certain distance, usually twenty to twenty-five feet, it is that line around his neck that pulls the pin on the header's barrier rope and starts the clock.

At a signal from the cowhand, the two men cut off their conversation, backed their horses into their corners, relooped their lariats, and leaned forward, standing slightly in their saddles. Their mounts' ears pricked, and they strained against the reins, squatting back on their haunches, tense and ready. And suddenly the chute flew open and the steer bolted into the ring. Seconds later, the barrier rope popped free and Christian's horse leaped after him, then Richard's, their hooves throwing huge clods of dirt into the air as thousands of pounds of horseflesh thundered and roared in a blinding, deafening blur of motion and sound, flying after the escaping steer.

Christian's lariat swung in a wide arc and settled smoothly over the sharp horns. He instantly changed direction, throwing the steer off course, making him pivot on his front feet and forcing his rear feet into the air so that Richard could lasso his heels. Then the steer was on the ground, fully spread, and the team of horses stood dead still, keeping perfect tension on the lariats.

"Time!" my father yelled, and it was over.

The horses stood down, and the confused calf, once freed from his lines, struggled to his feet and trotted around until Baby, along with Gal and Pal, Elias's two Australian shepherds, joined the cowboys and they all showed him the way out.

Here's the thing. A lot of animal rights people think that rodeoing is inhumane, and unfortunately a few rodeos are. Their livestock is not well treated. But the overwhelming majority of rodeo livestock is better treated than some range animals, and also, what many people don't understand is that these cowboying skills are essential to cattle ranching. Cows aren't roped to torture them or for the sake of the sport. The skill of team roping is the only way to doctor them in the field, to give them inoculations, or to brand them. They aren't pets. They won't come when you call them, and they're big—up to two thousand pounds. In fact, the only two rodeo rough stock events that are purely sport, showing off guts, muscle, athleticism, and lack of brains, are bull riding and bareback bronc riding. Those guys are get-down cowboys and they're nuts. Nuts but terrific. Everybody's darlings. And I can guarantee they aren't about to start wearing crash helmets to compete, no matter what those weak sisters at the National Institutes of Health say.

Richard and Christian rode over to the fence.

"That looked first rate," I said. "I bet you guys win."

"We'll see," Christian said.

Richard and I just stared at each other. He looked like heaven on earth and I wondered if he could read my thoughts.

And then he stood tall in his saddle, stretching his legs and back, turning to reloop his lariat, and I saw it. The tear in his pants, that small rip just below his rear, just off center, and I knew Richard and I had both been thinking the same thing.

I went into the barn and into the tack room, where I grabbed an armful of clean, wool, Hudson Bay travel blankets off the top of the stack, a bottle of champagne out of the cooler, and two yellow plastic mugs off the shelf, and climbed the rough wooden ladder to the hayloft, where the air was thick and musty with alfalfa and clover dust. I threw open the wide double doors to the meadow and let in the bright afternoon sun that carried with it the electric scent of a thunderstorm. The clouds were still way down the valley, but I could see the lightning forking down and hear the thunder's distant rumble.

I took off my stockings and stuck them behind a hay bale and put on a little lipstick.

When I got back to the corral, my father had gone home, and Richard and Christian had just bolted from the boxes for another round. I stood there in my sedate Sunday linen suit and Chanel pumps, trying to keep the horseflies off my bare legs, leaning on the railing, watching them, drinking in the noise and speed of the hoofbeats, the straining groans of the horses as they burst into action, the smell and sound of the saddles that shifted and creaked beneath the riders, and the whoops and hollers of the cowboys, growing as short of breath as if I were out there myself. They rode three more rounds, and I was starting to think that maybe the hayloft hadn't been such a great idea, when finally the wind started to kick up the dust and the lightning grew close, and they stopped.

Richard dismounted, and as he headed toward me, he pulled off his worn gloves and used them to slap the mud and dust off his legs, then shoved the gloves into his back pocket.

"I'm glad you're back," he said, placing one hand on the highest rail and leaning through the fence to kiss me. A deep, lingering, familiar kiss. "I was getting worried."

"Here I am." I smiled. "You guys look great out here."

"Getting better. But we're still a long way from where we need to be."

I walked beside him to the barn, tucking my hand into his back pocket with the gloves, feeling the hard muscles of his bottom flex as he walked. Christian was already working in the first stall; the coarse brushes in each hand flew like egg beaters across his horse's back and hindquarters.

"I am so late," he said, grooming his pony as fast as he could. "Mimi is going to kill me. She's got the governor coming for a steak fry."

"I'll do it," I said eagerly, anxious for him to be gone. "I'm going to wait for Richard."

"You sure?" He handed the brushes over, not waiting to find out if I was sure or not. "Thanks a lot. I appreciate it. See you tomorrow," he yelled as he grabbed his jacket from the seat of an old buckboard parked next to his horse's stall, dashed out the door, through the rain, and into his pickup. I watched him go but scarcely heard his words, because Richard had materialized behind me, reached his hands around, and put them on my breasts.

I thought I would melt from the currents that flowed through me. What are the words to describe them? Those feelings that are so close to pain, so deep inside, so strong and so centered? Feelings that weaken your legs and make you cry out with an agony that is too exquisite to bear? I lay my head back on his chest and placed my hands on top of his. I could feel him pressing against me through his jeans, and I reached back and slowly started to unbutton them as the rain began to fall in sheets. Richard kept one hand on my breast and moved the other down across my body until I was burning, every inch of me filled with heat and longing, my legs numb, my body arching forward. He pulled my skirt up around my waist and ran his fingers around the top of my leg, finding his way.

I turned to face him, ripping open the last button on his fly. We stood there, our hands caressing, stroking, faster and faster, without speaking, without even kissing, as the rain fell like a glass curtain, and his breath poured across me like a hot, tropical wind.

"I saw you come into the barn," he said later. I lay across him in the rough, plank bed of the buckboard, my skirt still around my waist, my head resting on his shoulder. "What were you doing?"

I laughed. "It doesn't matter. You didn't need any persuading."

He kissed me. "I never do."

"Want a drink?"

"Sure."

"Come on."

He followed me up the ladder to the hayloft, where the downpour on the corrugated steel roof obliterated almost all thought. Lightning cracked overhead as Richard expertly tore the foil off the bottle, untwisted the wire, and worked out the cork, which gave off a satisfying pop as I spread layers of blankets on the floor in front of the open doors.

"One of the things I like best about you, Bennett," he said, pouring the champagne into a mug, where it fizzed and threatened to overflow, "is that your solutions to any situation are always cocktails and sex."

"Yes."

We took off our clothes and snuggled side by side between the blankets, leaning our backs against a stack of hay bales, our bodies touching, watching the rain come down and sipping champagne.

"What's going to become of us?" I finally said.

"What do you mean?"

What do you mean? Isn't that like a man?

"Never mind." I drew closer to him, unwilling to press my case. Unwilling to face the consequences if he didn't see it the way I did.

Richard turned and kissed me and we fell back into the thick covers on the hay-softened floor and made love again, to the sounds of the horses stomping and shuffling below and the rain on the roof.

MONDAY MORNING

D estroying angel or death cap?" I said into the phone to Kim Leavy.

"Hard to tell, they're so similar," the pathologist answered. "I have more tests to do. His liver and kidneys are totally trashed."

Typically the super lethal varieties of mushrooms, the death cap and the destroying angel, are those used most often by organized poisoners, and whoever put the digitalis into the oolong tea was very organized and knowledgeable and skillful and probably just as surprised as Kim and I were that Vanderbilt's death had been so violent and fast. Usually the toxins don't kick in for at least six hours, not to mention the fact that I was certain he hadn't been the target in the first place.

"But it looks like they were already severely damaged." She continued on the subject of Vanderbilt's organs. "Pretty far gone. He had a chronic case of hepatitis and his blood looks like a hallucination, it's so loaded with drugs. I think these toxins were the proverbial straw—he wouldn't have lasted much longer the way he was going. What a waste."

I wondered if anyone would miss him.

"Between the foxglove and the destroying angels, someone in this crowd has a very interesting greenhouse," I said. "Thanks for the info."

What was it this person wanted? I wondered after I'd hung up. I leaned back in my chair and put my heels on the edge of my desk. The air rights? The allegedly missing endowment fund? Who would benefit most from George's death? All of them, it seemed.

I thrummed my nails on the side of my empty coffee cup and stared out the window, hoping to see a revelation on the wind. But before it blew by, Linda wandered in. She looked a little forlorn.

"What's the problem?" I said.

"Men," she said, sitting down with a whoomph, looking every one of her fifty years. Her hair was bedraggled and her Under-Eye Whisper Away Fatigue Concealer only made the bags under her eyes look like potatoes. "Your brother, specifically."

"Oh, no. What did he do?"

"More what he didn't do." Red patches spread on her cheeks and crawled up her neck.

"Like what?"

"Like he never called me once yesterday."

"Don't worry about it, Linda. You know he's on assignment. He'll call."

"I think he's met someone else. He always calls. Even when he's got a date with someone else, like Ellen, who I don't think he's seen now for a couple of months." Her eyes blurred with tears and little puffs of fog bloomed on her glasses. "I swore when I left the ranch that I was never going to let this happen to me again and now look at me." She pulled a wad of Kleenex out of her pocket and blew into it. "I'm a mess."

The phone rang and she started to get up to answer.

"Stay where you are," I told her. "I'll get it. Bennett Security," I said into the receiver.

"Hey, it's me." Elias's merry voice boomed through and I smiled at Linda who perked up instantly.

"What's up?" I said.

"Several items. First of all, as you requested, I moved into George's on Saturday night to keep a closer eye on him. This guy's guest room is awesome—it's done up like Africa or something. This big high bed with mosquito netting and stuff. Lots of animal skins and fertility statues. Cool. You know," Elias plunged ahead breathlessly, "how when you met Richard, you felt like it was love at first sight. Like you'd been waiting your whole life to meet him?"

"Yes," I said. All true. It hadn't exactly gotten me anywhere, but it was true nevertheless. *"Coup de foudre."*

"That's the one. I've got it, too."

"What?" I know my eyes widened because Linda looked at me with alarm. "You mean George?"

"Oh." He laughed uproariously. "Don't worry. I'm not turning gay or anything. It's not George. It's Shelley."

I closed my eyes and rubbed my forehead, picturing the girl whose wandering breasts and thick, common features men seemed to find so bewitching. "Actually, Elias," I said, "I'm not sure which one would be worse."

"You be nice," he said, hurt. "She's a terrific girl. I feel like I've known her all my life, everything clicks. And she says she feels the same way. It's as though everything is absolutely perfect. It all fits. Seriously, Lilly, I have fallen totally in love."

I held my coffee cup up to Linda and she grabbed it and went out to her office to get me a refill. "Does she know who you really are?" I asked while Linda was out of the room.

"No. Not yet. But I want to tell her. I don't think we should have any secrets."

"Do-not-say-one-word," I ordered him as succinctly as I could, wondering if my caution would have any effect. He was as blind and giddy as a schoolboy.

"You don't suspect Shelley, do you?" His voice was incredulous.

"Elias, at the moment there are so many loose pieces out there, I suspect everybody," I said sharply. "And don't forget it. Keep your pants zipped up and your eye on the damn ball."

Just as I hung up—thinking that if he brought someone like that home to Mother, it'd really hit the fan—my underbrained, oversexed deputy wandered in and half sat on the edge of my desk, dangling his booted foot.

"Sounds like trouble in River City," he said sagely.

"Nothing I can't handle, Dwight," I said.

He got up and walked around behind me and put his gifted, accomplished, ambidextrous hands on my shoulders and began to massage. "Sounds like Marshal Lilly needs to relax a little. Needs a little back rub."

I started to laugh, thinking about what had happened to me the last time a man walked up behind me. Dwight held no temptation for me today. "Deputy," I said, placing my hands on top of his and bringing them to a halt, "you're a day late and a dollar short. Go back to your side of the desk and sit down."

"If you say so." He leaned his bottom on the edge of the desk, on my side, instead. "But I know some pretty good stress relievers, and those blue pin stripes make you look a little tense."

"Chair, Deputy," I said.

"You're always pullin' rank on me, Miss Lilly." He ambled over and took a seat.

"Yes, and I expect I always will." I wondered, if I were ever to give in and do it, and, if he were disappointed—which, frankly, he could be if he ever got a good look at my body in daylight—if he would sue me for sexual harassment.

Linda came back in with a stack of faxes, one from the Waterbury Police Department saying that Molly Dolan was indeed a local girl, a cheerleader at Waterbury High School, president of both the French and the Fashion clubs, and that she'd moved to California to become an actress several years ago and changed her name to Gigi Dorrance-Downs. She still spent Christmas with her widowed mother, who now lived in a two-family house on Main Street in Naugatuck. She helped the nuns distribute Christmas baskets to the elderly, lost, infirm, and forgotten, handed out stuffed animals at the hospital, placed the crown on Miss Waterbury's head every spring, and was the biggest thing to happen to the Greater Waterbury area since the 1950s when the bantamweight boxer, Chico Vijar, and the Mad Bomber, George Metesky—who blew up a New York subway station—grabbed the local headlines. And would I please give Molly Dolan everybody's best from the Waterbury Police Department.

So much for Gigi Dorrance-Downs's dirty little secret.

"Did Elias hang up?"

"Yes. He said he'd call you later."

"I won't talk to him," she said petulantly and slammed the door.

MONDAY NOON

You know this is against the law," my father said as we sat down at a white linen-covered table at the Cattlemen's Club. He unobtrusively slid a sealed white envelope across to me. My fingertips met his midway and I slid the paper right off the edge of the table and into my purse, which sat open in my lap.

"Which?" I said, pulling off my white gloves and carefully straightening the fingers before laying them alongside the packet containing the Roundup Repertory Company's banking history, from which I expected little enlightenment but was, nevertheless, anxious to examine. I snapped the purse closed and placed it on the floor and then smoothed the skirt of my navy gabardine suit. "Handing me a business paper in a private club or passing on confidential banking information?"

"Both." His eyes twinkled. He and my mother secretly loved what I did for a living. "If I didn't know you had a court order in the works, I wouldn't do it, even if you are my favorite child."

When I was growing up, the Cattlemen's Club had really been a venerable old place, a wind-pitted red sandstone house with tall old doors and a snappy doorman. Then some brain decided to tear it down and build a high-rise and put the club on the top four floors and the poor doorman, now old and stooped, always looked so lost standing down there on the busy, windy downtown street in front of a modern office building, trying to pick members' faces out of the jostling crowd.

My father still likes it because it's called the Cattle*men*'s Club, "But," I've heard him lament, "you just wait, pretty soon it'll be the Cattleperson's Club or the Metropolitan Club or some other damn stupid thing. I just hope it's after I'm dead."

Today, the rain from a quick thunderstorm hurled itself against the windows, blocking the long view to the Wind River Range, and the cold Wyoming wind blew through the double-sealed cracks.

He ordered us both double Jameson's on the rocks and we spread soft butter on saltines and talked about Mother while we waited for our drinks.

"The wedding seems to have cast her into a permanent state of Full Bop," he said jovially. "And it's still six days off. I'm afraid her gaskets are going to start to blow if she doesn't calm down." He looked toward the bar. "Where're those drinks?"

I kept looking down at my purse there next to my foot, wondering if I should excuse myself and go into the ladies' room and open the envelope, because it was becoming quickly clear that my father was not going to be forthcoming with whatever he'd learned, and I knew if I asked him, he'd just dig in his heels and make me wait longer. "The pavilion looks like it's mostly done," I said.

"Yup. They're just putting the finishing touches on the kitchen. If there's a way to spend money your mother will find it. Thankfully there's enough to go around. Oh, good, here he is. Thought we'd lost you there for a minute, Emmett," he said.

"It's pretty," I said about the pavilion, smiling gratefully at the creaky old waiter who'd finally arrived and was transferring our drinks from his small tray onto the table in slow motion. We'd each taken healthy belts before he even turned to go.

"Yes," he said absently, looking longingly around the room at his friends. "Your mother has excellent taste."

My father and I love to be together, but we never say much, just take pleasure in each other's company. It had been that way since he taught me to ride and shoot and fish, starting when I was three or four. I remember perfectly standing in the river, casting out over the fast-moving water, when his only words would be, "That's right," when I'd land my fly in the shadows alongside a low-hanging willow branch. And then he'd say, "Now, reel it in slowly. There you go." And when I'd get a strike, all he'd do was stand next to me and say over and over again, "You're doing fine." On the days when there were no strikes, sometimes there wouldn't be any words, either.

He instructed me with the same low-key tips on the trap and skeet range. "Lead the bird, don't follow it. Shoot just below the arc." I spent hours there on the range by myself with one of the wranglers running the trap, and today it is still my favorite sport. My brothers and I love to spend an afternoon in friendly competition, but they've never been able to outshoot me. My father taught me well during those hours of silence. It was our way.

As Westerners, we don't talk much anyhow, since we're always busy looking into the distance for our cattle, even if we don't have any, and for some people, the silences can get pretty long. Not for us.

My father made a halfhearted effort at supporting women as equals, as partners in business. He did it to be gracious and a good sport. He really wanted it all to be the way it was before World War II, when the West was empty, the Cattlemen's Club was for men only, the Men's Bar at the Roundup Country Club was still the members' private domain, everyone dressed for dinner, and people kept their personal business private. Sometimes I wish it were that way, too.

So, in spite of the fact that my work might have entranced him, for us to have a business conversation was always a challenge, to put it mildly. After all, that's what my brothers were for.

"Look," I said. "I know it's not de rigueur, talking business in the club, but face it, everyone does it all the time. Don't they?" I looked him in the eye.

"Sure," he said.

"What's in the envelope?"

"The account is closed."

C losed?" I said. "All their accounts?"

"No." He shook his head, cheered to be off the subject of the wedding pavilion and back on familiar territory. "I requested their banking history for the past twelve months and found they keep a number of accounts at Roundup National—their endowment account has been managed by our trust department for years. But it was very small. Only about five million."

He paused to greet an old friend who'd stopped to say hello. I said hello to him, too, and was as nice as I could be without screaming for him to leave so we could get back to the point. He and Daddy exchanged pleasantries for a moment or two while I hatched my drink and signaled for another. Finally, the man left, and my father looked at me with a slightly blank expression.

"The endowment account," I reminded him.

"Of course," he said. "Then, three weeks ago, on a Friday morning, a large deposit was made—Cyrus's gift—twenty million. I remember when it happened, because obviously something that large would be brought to my attention."

"When was the account closed?" I asked.

"The following Monday," he answered. "I wasn't made aware of it at the time because your mother and I had left for France by then. But George Wrightsman had everything in the account pulled out in a single cashier's check. Twenty-five million dollars. I spoke to the trust officer—Grover Pendington—and he said that even though he'd tried to talk Mr. Wrightsman out of making such a significant withdrawal, there was nothing, legally, he could do to stop him. Wrightsman had full authority over the account."

The waiter brought our second round, and while my father exchanged pleasantries with him, I simply sat there, stunned, watching the thunderheads tumble around the sky. "Don't endowments usually have trustees?" I said. "At least double signatories?"

"Yes, normally. And this one did: Cyrus Vaile, as president of the board of directors, and George Wrightsman. Believe me, the signatures were all in order. I checked them and the endorsements this morning, myself."

He paused to greet another friend and then continued. "I remember when the actors first arrived in town and Cyrus brought Wrightsman to the bank to introduce him. I think there was something funny going on there between those two men. You know what I mean?" My father wiggled his eyebrows, sort of a schoolboy's oooh-la-la mug. His eyes twinkled.

"Yes." I smiled, not saying that Cyrus would do it with anything that still had the breath of life in it.

"Well." He gave a self-conscious shrug. "I told Grover Pendington you might be in touch with him. I asked him if Wrightsman had said anything about what he was going to do with the money. And he said no, he hadn't said a word. Just shoved the check into his shoulder bag and left. Said he had a sissy boy with him. Actor, I suppose." Daddy closed his eyes and shook his head. "I just don't get it. Never thought

I'd ever see things like this going on in Wyoming. You don't think Andy Beckett's one of them, too, do you? He's always around Wrightsman. On his board, I think."

"No." I laughed. "I don't think he's one of 'them.'"

"I'm in some business deals with him."

"I think you're safe."

"Oh, here comes your young man," Daddy said, sounding slightly as though he'd been rescued from the top of Everest or a desert island. Finally, someone to talk real business with, because in spite of the fact that Richard ran the Opera, which my father loathed but gave thousands to every year anyhow, Richard had a degree from the London School of Economics and had been a banker himself for years. They had a lot in common, and anyone who tells you that it doesn't matter whether or not your lover has anything in common with your family is full of it. If you want to be happy and have fun—it matters a lot.

It's like when I was dating this Jewish fellow—not David, whose grandmother died of a heart attack when she caught us in her powder room—and we liked each other so much. He lived in New York and his family's name is still on one of the country's oldest and most prestigious securities firms. He'd been to the ranch a couple of times and we went to spend a weekend with his parents at their winter home in Acapulco and then it all really began to get down to it: was this going to go anywhere? And for both of us, the fact remained that no matter how much we liked each other, and our families liked each other, over the long haul we were coming from two entirely separate foundations. The innate premises of our lives were different.

At least we had the guts to appreciate, and admit, that we didn't love each other enough to believe that when things got tough, as they inevitably do, we'd be able to withstand the big hits without a common faith to fall back on.

We're still good friends, and he married a beautiful girl, Jewish, and they have a wonderful, close family. I recently attended their daughter's wedding in Los Angeles, and while the ceremony was going on I watched him and asked myself if I'd made a mistake. No.

"I didn't realize you were joining us," I said to Richard, so happy to see him.

He leaned down and gave me a quick kiss. "I didn't either. I just came in to grab a quick sandwich."

"Please sit down," my father said. "We were just wrapping up a little business."

The two of them talked about a number of things. I didn't listen to any of it. All I could think about, as I ate my way through a Monte Cristo sandwich (I can't believe how self-destructive I am sometimes) was that three weeks ago George Wrightsman had withdrawn twenty-five million dollars from the bank. What did he think when he told me it was in the bank? That I wouldn't find out? What did he do with it? What do you do with a cashier's check for twenty-five million dollars? Who else knew? Obviously somebody who wanted him dead. I kept hearing what sounded like sirens screaming through the wind.

"I'm sorry to be rude," I said, suddenly gathering up my things, "but I've got to go." And I got up and rushed out in the middle of lunch, without any explanation. I was so edgy, I felt like a cat on the ceiling. Something was gnawing in my gut, telling me things were very wrong, and when I got outside, the sirens were clear, several of them, and to my ear, their sound was more than fire, more even than a conflagration. It had a catastrophic clamor, a keening wail that obliterated the senses.

I threw the doorman five dollars for keeping my car in front, and jumped in and tore off to the theater, bulling my way through intersections, running lights, leaning on my horn, and yelling at people to get out of my way, a familiar feeling spreading through me as though I'd accidentally drunk a glass of sour milk laced with adrenaline.

And when I rounded the corner to the theater, my breath caught in my throat.

"Oh, no," I said, out loud. Baby just watched quietly, her front paws up on the dashboard, her brown eyes alert.

A Rescue Unit fire truck with its lights spinning sat at the main entrance. An ambulance, siren blaring, was just pulling away, and I saw stretchers with bloody, wailing cargoes being carried to other ambulances. There were a half dozen squad cars parked at odd angles and a number of uniforms directing traffic.

27

I pulled my Jeep up onto the sidewalk directly behind the fire truck, leaped out, and started toward the doors.

"Sorry, ma'am." A uniformed officer held out his arm to stop me. "Off limits."

I held up my badge and hooked it onto my breast pocket. "U. S. Marshal Bennett." I kept going.

"Yes, ma'am," he said and stepped aside.

The lobby was a chaos of racing paramedics and white-faced staffers. "Who's in charge?" I asked another patrolman.

"Chief Lewis just got here," he said. "He's in there." He pointed into the auditorium.

All the house lights were on, turning the gold-leaf trim on the boxes and ceiling and around the proscenium arch into cheap, flat gilt. The raked, thrust stage looked like a war zone or demolition project. A long black metal catwalk and huge light batten lay menacingly across the center of the steep stage floor, having fallen, apparently, from just behind the proscenium arch. All around the periphery of the stage, actors in baggy warmups sobbed hysterically.

I looked for Elias and didn't see him. But I did pick out Winston McMorris talking to Jack Lewis down by the orchestra pit. I approached them as quickly and calmly as I could, swallowing a combination of fear for my undercover, older brother and intoxication at the calamity. George was nowhere in sight.

"What's happened?" I asked Jack. Winston's face was gray and he was chain-smoking and kept pushing his longish hair nervously back out of his eyes.

"Catwalk and lighting rig fell," Jack said. "Crushed George Wrightsman and Malcolm . . ." He looked to Winston. "What's his last name?"

"His name is Stephen Griffin," Winston said. "His character is Malcolm."

"Whatever," Jack said.

"Are they alive?" I asked.

"Barely," Jack said, grimly. I could tell from his expression that the injuries were graver than he was letting on. "A number of people were injured by flying lighting equipment and smashed wood."

"Was it an accident?"

"It wasn't an accident," Winston said in his vague, lost way, looking over at the scene with an expression of such total anguish, I reached over and laid my hand on his arm.

Jack didn't say anything, just rubbed his ear and looked more closely at Winston.

"It's obvious that someone's trying to destroy this company and kill George Wrightsman." He turned to me reproachfully, his big eyes full of anger and disappointment. "It was my understanding that you were supposed to help, but as far as I can tell, since George hired you, we've begun piling up more bodies around here than a Peter Shaffer play. Why don't you do something? Do what we're paying you for?"

Over the years, I've become accustomed to recriminations and accusations by survivors, and even grown my armor thick enough that the arrows don't pierce as deeply as they once did, but even so, I don't believe I'll ever be invulnerable to them. I wanted to say to Winston, "I'm doing everything I can. This isn't simple, or clear-cut, and this deal has obviously gotten way out of the box." But instead, all I said was, "How do I get backstage?"

My unresponsiveness didn't surprise or anger him further, because none of us expects anything from public servants any longer. He'd said his piece, knowing it wouldn't make any difference one way or the other. "Around through there." He indicated a curtained exit door at the end of the side aisle.

I pushed aside the curtain and walked down a short, dark, narrow passage and up a few stairs.

Because of hanging around the Opera House with Richard, I knew slightly more about the backstage of a theater than I did about being on a shuttle launch pad, which wasn't much, but at least I'd picked up enough to have a conversation on the subject without looking like a complete idiot.

Alongside the most technologically advanced lighting and cue boards was a mare's nest of ancient-looking contraptions—ropes, sandbags, weights and counterweights, grids and racks and towers of lights, scenery and curtains hanging way, way up near the ceiling, catwalks leading to more lights. And, in spite of the fact that all the stage and house lights were on, little illumination was shed. Every surface—walls, floors, and ceiling—was painted drab, flat black, so when I looked up into the fly loft, or back into the dark corners where two-story-high stacks of props and furniture for the three shows in repertory were piled, it was all an inky mystery. There were ladders everywhere.

After a moment my eyes adjusted and I could see where the fallen batten had come from. Far up in the murk, the steel rigging's moorings had ripped from the ceiling, bringing deadly clumps of plaster and roofing and lighting with them. Sodden daylight was visible through the jagged holes.

Accident? Normally you would think it was possible, or at least hard to say, but based on the events of the past few days, the chances of this being an accident were nonexistent. I sensed someone standing close by and turned to see Winston, looking up as I had been.

"How can I get onto the roof?" I said.

"Follow me."

We pushed through a black steel door, into a filthy, narrow, dead-end alley. A tall, locked, metal gate theoretically blocked the alley from the street, but even so, the ground was littered with broken bottles and dead pigeons, and in spite of the recent rainstorm, the air stank of the urine of drunken bums and their dissolving cardboard boxes.

I pulled the little Glock from my purse, and as I picked my way through the broken glass and detritus toward the fire escape steps that led to the roof, it crossed my mind that I was really getting soft. In my old life as chief, I never would have worn lovely, expensive, Italian high heels to work. Now I did it all the time.

"Wait here," I said to Winston.

"Don't be silly," he answered, and immediately began climbing the steep, old-fashioned, back-and-forth, rain-slickened, open-slat iron stairs. "There isn't anyone up here. Surely you've watched enough television to know that whoever's done this is long gone by now."

He was right, of course.

Following him required all my posture and balancing expertise—I felt like a stewardess in the 1950s wearing one of those extra-tight straight skirts with a sexy little kick pleat and a white piqué hat, walking sideways up the metal stairs into the DC-6B. I knew I'd have to take the shoes off to get back down, and prayed I wouldn't have to run anywhere, and that no other law enforcement professional would see me.

"Nice shoes," Jack Lewis's voice came from below.

Our weapons drawn, Jack and I climbed over the lip of the wall onto the tar and gravel roof. I went first, dashing quickly to my right in as low a crouch as a middle-aged woman in a St. Laurent pencil-slim skirt is able to muster, and found protection behind a large vent, while Jack did the same to the left, and after a couple of moments of confirming that we were alone, and securing the area, he and Winston and I gathered around the big, scary holes where the huge light batten had been anchored to the roof.

Several thick, foot-long, steel screw bolts had been tossed aside as though they were penny nails, and the holes were surrounded by wide scorch marks. Narrow black trails from burning det cord, like the lines left by a child's wood-burning tool, led to each bomb site from a point midway between them where a small servo with a Futoba transmitter and electric blasting cap sat undamaged, unruffled, undisturbed by the explosion. Tiny bits of what looked like confetti littered the roof.

I knelt down and put my glasses on and took out my magnifying glass to examine some of the debris more closely, being careful to disturb as little of it as possible. I put my nose at the edge of one of the sites and inhaled deeply.

"C-4," I said to Jack, who nodded. "Standard-issue receiver. Could be just about anything."

"Popped those gigantic washers through the roof right on cue," he answered as he squatted and peered down into a hole. He took a radio out of his pocket and called for the bomb squad.

"I didn't think detectives actually did that," Winston said.

"Did what?" I said as I regained my feet and brushed bits of gravel off my knees.

"Used magnifying glasses."

"You mean like Sherlock Holmes?"

"Yeah."

I was tired of Winston. And his tiredness. Just being around him made me want to go to sleep.

"What is really going on here, Winston?" I demanded angrily. "Tell me why this is happening. Two poisonings, a fire, and now a bombing. Who's doing this? Why aren't you telling me?"

"I swear to God I have no idea," he said, his eyes darting around furtively.

"Is it because of the money?"

"What money?" Winston looked at me blankly.

"Why is someone trying to murder Wrightsman?" I pressed aggressively. I wanted to punch him, to break through his fumbling demeanor and crack his egghead charm—see some damn passion, a little oomph. Something besides besieged weariness. "You're around this company twenty-four hours a day. You know everything that's going on. You must have some theory. For God's sake, stop keeping it to yourself."

"Lilly." Jack reached over and put his hand on my arm, but I shook it off brusquely. I was so frustrated.

"I don't know," Winston replied defensively. "Except Bradford. I've thought it was him all along."

"Who else?" I said. "This is no one-person job. Don't you agree, Jack?" He nodded. Both men appeared to be a little intimidated by my anger. Good. "Too many different things going on in too many different places, with too few of the same faces. Who else, Winston? What about Shelley?"

"Shelley?" He looked like he'd been slapped.

"How about Gigi?"

"Gigi?" he said in the same incredulous tone.

"What about Samuel Vaile?"

"Samuel Vaile?"

"What are you?" I snapped. "Some kind of talking doll?"

"Back off, Bennett," Jack warned.

"Look." I turned on him. "This man knows something he's not telling us." I spun back to Winston, my hands balled into fists. "Is it you, McMorris? Did you plan all this to get the air rights? Take over the company?"

161

"No. No." He shook his shaggy head. "I swear to God I don't know who it is."

"Take a guess," I said, wanting to add, "you son of a bitch."

"*Macbeth?*" he mewled.

"You're as useless as tits on a bull." I stomped back to the fire escape. "I'm going to the hospital." Just as I climbed over the edge of the roof, I spotted a tiny black hard rubber wheel that had survived the blast. I picked it up and stuck it in my pocket.

CHAPTER

28

Even though it was midafternoon, the outside entry ramp to the emergency room at Christ and St. Luke's still reeked of spilled blood and spewed vomit from the night before. Inside was the typical maelstrom of people in panic and fear and pain, jumbled in with indigent pensioners who had all the time in the world on their hands, happy to sit back and watch the show. They measured me with expert eyes, jaded and trained by "E.R." and "Chicago Hope" and "Ben Casey" and "Dr. Kildare." I raced in, desperately concerned about George and the actor, and full of questions and theories about this latest murder attempt, but more than anything wanting to track down my brother.

"Where is Elias Bennett?" I asked the Mexican girl at the desk.

She squinted at her screen and shook her head. "I don't have that name," she said. "When did he come in?"

"He was at the theater."

"No." She looked again. "I'm sorry. He's not here. We have all their names."

I struggled to remember the ridiculous Dickensian name I'd given him. Billy Fezziwig? Mr. Cruncher? Then it came to me. "What about Bertram Chiswick?"

"Bertroo Cheezewee?" she said. The name sounded funny coming out in her Mexican accent, and I'm sure I would have taken the time to laugh if I'd had it.

"Let me see that." I twirled the monitor around like an impatient schoolmarm snatching back a paper with a challenged grade. There he was. Cubicle 7. "Thanks." I raced down the hall, just in time to see Elias being wheeled on a gurney through the dun-colored curtain into the corridor. He had a large cast on his leg, a bandage on his cheek, and Shelley Pirelli holding his hand. She had on the tightest T-shirt and jeans I'd ever seen in my life not on a streetwalker.

I was so relieved to see Elias alive that it took all my energy not to grab him and say, "Thank God, thank God, you're all right." I rushed to catch up with them.

"Shelley," I said, "how's George?"

"Oh, hi, Lilly." She tried to smile, but her face was pale as gluten and she was clearly shaken and scared. Her brown eyes seemed especially large and had dark smudges under them. "It's just one awful thing after another, isn't it? First Cyrus, and then you and me almost getting burned to death, and then Vanderbilt getting accidentally murdered, and now this." Dime-sized tears spilled down her cheeks, and she wiped them away with the back of her hand. Elias gave her a Kleenex out of a box that sat on his lap. "George is in surgery. That's all I know. The thing hit him on the head."

Not good.

"It's like having our father being hurt," she continued, shredding the tissue between her fingers. She looked first into Elias's eyes and then mine. Her chin quivered. "That's what George is, you know. He's the father of our company, of our home. I never had one before I found him. Poor, poor George. If he dies, well"—she gasped for breath and blew her nose—"I think I'll die, too."

Elias squeezed her hand. "He'll be fine, Bunny."

"Bunny?" I wanted to say. "Give me a break. That is hardly the word you're looking for. We're dealing with something a little more feline here." But I bit my tongue.

"And my darling Bertie here has been like a rock. Even with this smashed leg." She turned to Elias. "You were so lucky. I'm never letting you out of my sight again."

Elias nodded and squeezed her hand again. His expression was that of a drooling goon.

"Do you know each other?" Shelley asked.

I nodded. "We met on Saturday night."

Shelley introduced us anyway—me as Lilly and him as Bertie. What is it with people that they don't use last names? They just say, "Hello, my name is whatever, what's yours?" I always say my whole name: "Hello, my name is Lilly Bennett."

"Are you badly hurt, Mr. Bertie?" I asked.

"Gads, no," Elias chirped back gamely. "And it's Chiswick. Bertram Chiswick. Just a multiple fracture. I should be back at it in no time."

"And poor Stephen." Shelley began to cry harder. "He looked like he was dead."

"Where is he?"

"Surgery, too," she sobbed. "He was just standing there, talking to George, and all of a sudden there was this terrible noise and the whole catwalk and all the lights came crashing. It was like an earthquake."

By then we were on the elevator, and as its wide doors slid silently shut and the orderly pushed the button for the third floor, Elias put his arms around Shelley and pulled her to him and stroked her dark, wavy hair.

"Everything will be fine," he said, evidently relishing being buried in cow udders.

"Where were you when it happened?" I asked Elias, itching to draw him aside and tell him please, please, please to keep himself under control, this girl was beyond bad news.

"I was on the stage, very close to George," he answered. "I can't believe how fortunate I was."

"And I was down in the front of the house," Shelley volunteered. "That's where I usually sit when George is in rehearsal in the theater. That way, he always knows exactly where I am, if he needs anything."

"Shelley," I said as I jotted down their remarks, "a few minutes ago you said Vanderbilt was murdered by accident. How do you know that?"

She stared at me for what seemed like a full minute without blinking. "I don't know. I just thought George was the target. Don't you?"

"Seems so."

"Well, you've got to catch him—whoever is doing this." Shelley started to cry again. "George barely escaped and they'll probably try it again."

Probably right about that, Bunny.

Aldo Franciscus and a small huddle of actors were in the surgery waiting room, which was filled with the fragrance of fresh coffee. Cary Scott Douglas sat off by himself, his hands balled between his knees. And I'm not meaning to belittle or make light of what I know was their legitimate concern, but face it, they were all actors, and as such, they looked more sorrowful and serious and frightened and suffering than any group of individuals I'd ever seen in a hospital waiting room in my life. I mean, these guys were DOWN. Low.

A few were crying and carrying on like Muslim women at a funeral. One kept saying, "George is such a fucking genius, he can't die." While another wailed that he was the greatest actor in the history of the American Theater, and another posed at the window in stoic, lonely resignation. I believe he was Laurence Olivier as Heathcliff in *Jane Eyre*. All the while, Aldo clucked and mothered and dispensed sheets of Kleenex as though they were life vests.

I poured myself a cardboard cup of coffee and went out onto the roof terrace where Bradford Lake had his foot up on the railing and an elbow on his raised knee and was smoking a cigarette held in shaking fingers. He was tightly, nervously composed. And dapper as an optimistic undertaker at the Harvard-Yale game. The sky had cleared, leaving everything bright and scrubbed of dust, letting the late afternoon sun shine cleanly on our faces.

"Hello, Mr. Lake," I said, taking a couple of big gulps of my coffee. It was just right. Strong and not too hot. I needed a big blast of caffeine.

He glanced at me with his smallish, navy-blue eyes and then turned back to the skyline. The mountains looked especially far away. I didn't like Bradford Lake. He seemed to me a phony, coldhearted bitch.

"Ms. Bennett," he said.

I also don't like it when people call me Ms. It's Miss. Or Marshal. Or Chief. Or Lilly. But Ms. looks bad and sounds stupid, and so when people like Bradford Lake call me Ms., it makes me like them even less.

"Do you know this wasn't an accident?" I asked.

Bradford froze his eyes on the horizon for a heartbeat and then turned his face to me. "What do you mean, not an accident?"

"I mean someone went up on the roof and pulled most of the bolts out of the suspensions for the catwalk and then planted plastique explosive on top of the anchor plates and then pushed a radio signal and poof." I held up the plastic bag that contained the little wheel. "This is all that's left. Looks like part of a toy."

"I don't believe it," he said, turning away and taking a drag from his cigarette. His hand had steadied, but his color was still lousy. He dropped the cigarette and ground it out with the toe of his shiny Bass Weejun loafer.

"Mr. Lake, it doesn't matter much whether you believe it or not. It is a fact. Where were you this afternoon when the accident occurred?"

A fleeting, arrogant look of contained contempt, the result of all those award-winning years as Caesar Augustus, whispered across his face. "In rehearsal. We were doing scenes in the Olivier across the street in the main building. *Uncle Vanya.*"

"The Olivier?" I said.

"Yes. You know. The black box." He frowned deeply. "I can't believe you claim this was on purpose. Who would do such a thing? It's fiendish."

I tried to recall the last time I'd heard that word. Fiendish. To me, it's the sort of word you need to think about, rummage around for. He just popped out with it. Cool, as Elias would say.

"That's a good question, Mr. Lake. Who do *you* think is doing this?" I finished the coffee and began to groove lines in the cardboard with my fingernail.

Bradford turned around, so he was facing the windows of the waiting room just as Winston McMorris walked in. "You might start there," he said and shoved his hands into the pockets of his gray flannels. "With that wheedling, ingratiating, brown-nosing, sycophantic little toady." He walked through the door to join the mourning wretches.

I stayed outside for a couple of seconds, wondering what a black box was, and how I would ever sift fantasy from reality when every move, every action, reaction, every cry, whisper, and word was choreographed, and the more I learned about the Roundup Repertory Company, the more I understood what Richard had meant when he said George had created a cult of insular, symbiotic, codependent, dysfunctional, wacked-out fanatics.

Just then a doctor in clean surgical scrubs entered the waiting room. Glasses hung around his neck and his mouth was set in a grim line. He looked around, unclear as to who, in this silent group, was in charge. Winston and Bradford, both jockeying to be boss, stepped over to him at the same time, and I watched him speak solemnly to them in phrases I hoped didn't sound as clipped and dry as they looked through the window. Winston closed his eyes and shook his head and buried his face in his hands.

Bradford reacted as though he'd been slapped. His mouth fell open and I heard him cry, "No!" He spun to Aldo. "He can't be dead." He fell into Aldo's arms. "This is a disaster. Malcolm doesn't die."

It was the young actor, Stephen Griffin. His head injuries had been massive. He never regained consciousness.

Stephen Griffin, assuredly an innocent bystander, had become the third murder victim in a week. Someone was out of control and making the situation at the theater very grave and very dangerous, and the small troupe of actors in the surgery waiting room wailed in direct proportion to the seriousness of the circumstances. Only Cary Scott remained alone, and composed, his hands still clasped and his lips moving in a silent prayer for George.

I took advantage of the hysteria to question them. Winston had been in his office. Phone logs could prove it. But the fact is that he had eagerly and easily led me to the roof and by that simple act had invalidated any evidence he could have left there earlier while planting the explosive. And he could have triggered the signal from the darkness in the back of the house. But then, so could anyone else.

Aldo? At home fixing dinner. Cary Scott? With his classmates, doing *Uncle Vanya* scenes, Bradford Lake, as I had already been informed, had been directing.

I went down the hall and pushed through the huge, swinging hermetic-seal doors marked AUTHORIZED PERSONNEL ONLY, into the hospital's surgical center.

"Has George Wrightsman come out of surgery yet?" I asked the nurse at the desk and showed her my badge.

"I don't think so. Let me call Recovery." She had a quick telephone exchange. "They're just bringing him in now. It's down there." She pointed the way.

George looked very banged up and tiny lying in a vortex of

monitors, rushing nurses, and noise. His doctor had accompanied him out of surgery and now picked up a chart tucked in the side of George's gurney, shuffled to a desk, and sat down heavily, splaying his legs. He tossed his glasses on the desk and rubbed his eyes before beginning to write.

"How is he?" I asked, once I'd identified myself.

"He'll be fine," he answered mildly, his expression as benign as his appearance. "His arm and shoulder were pretty seriously shattered, but we've got them pinned and I expect he'll recover full mobility. Got a nasty cut on his head, but no concussion. Mostly just heavy bruises. He's in terrible general physical condition—flabby, overweight—but he'll be back on his feet in good order."

"I need you to do us a favor," I said.

"Shoot."

"There have been two attempts on his life in the last forty-eight hours," I told him. "And I need you to put him in ICU where we can keep him safe."

The doctor gave me a give-me-a-break look. "No problem, but he doesn't belong in intensive care any more than you do."

"I understand." I liked this doctor; he had a sense of humor under all that responsibility. "And I appreciate your help. He's in jeopardy, and if we can keep him completely isolated and protected and out of the way until we get some answers, it'll make things a lot easier. We'll keep twenty-four-hour guards on him and they'll be instructed that if the chain of contact between them, the nurses, and doctors does not exist of their personal knowledge, then that person—doctor, nurse, orderly, whatever—will not enter."

"You've got it. How do you want us to report his condition?"

"Critical. And one more thing. I don't know George Wrightsman very well, but I do know he loves drugs, so he won't mind if you keep him sedated."

The doctor smiled. "We'll see what we can do."

Then I went back to Elias's room, thinking about the challenges presented by this gang of professional-liar suspects, and found him comfortably ensconced with Shelley, who was sitting on the side of his bed, still holding his hand. They had not yet heard the news that Stephen Griffin was dead.

"I knew it," Shelley said. Her face crumpled with despair and she started bawling her eyes out for the millionth time. I couldn't believe Elias was putting up with it. She twisted a corner of his sheet in her hands, around and around. "When they took him out I knew he wasn't going to make it. Poor Stevie. He was such a wonderful actor." She looked up at me. "Do you have any update on George? They won't tell us anything."

"He's out of surgery and in the recovery room. They'll take him into intensive care later tonight," I told them. "But he's not out of the woods by a long shot. He might not make it.

"Has either one of you ever seen anything like this?" I asked and held the little tire out for them to examine. I had so many technical questions I knew Elias could answer that it took all my restraint not to blurt them out.

"Some sort of a toy car, I would imagine," Elias preponderated in his half-baked Etonian accent. He held the wheel up to the light. "I believe my nephew received one of these for the holidays a while back. I believe my sister—what a jolly old girl she is—said she purchased it at some sort of radio shoppe. What ho?"

He was making me laugh and I wanted to punch him. Bunny and What ho? What next?

Shelley took the wheel from him and gave it a quick glance. She shrugged her shoulders and gave me a wide-eyed look. "I don't know," she said.

"Oh, look, Bunny." Elias had reclaimed it and examined it more closely through his glasses. "It's a miniature Pirelli. See here in the plastic? Pirelli Tires. It's a perfect replica."

She snatched it away and practically put the little black disk in her eye, trying to read the tiny words. "Yeah!" she said. "That's my dad's company. Back in Italy."

"How charming," Elias said, looking as though he believed her.

"That's where I grew up," she continued. "In Rome in a palace. That's where they make the tires."

"Is that right in downtown Rome?" I said.

"Un-huh."

This conversation was so outrageous, it was a full sixty seconds before I could trust myself to open my mouth. "I'd like to get it identified before the feds get in the picture." I pocketed the miniature Pirelli. No relation. No fucking way.

"The feds?" they exclaimed at the same time.

"Sure. The explosion was caused by C-4—plastique. You can only get it on a military installation."

"Wow," Shelley said. "The FBI."

Then I road-tested my theory about someone signaling the explosives from the back of the theater. They both listened to me with serious concentration.

"I think it could be two people," Shelley finally said.

"What do you mean?"

"Well, it's possible that one person could have planted the explosives and someone else could have pushed the button at the right time."

"Really?" I asked innocently, looking up from my notepad. "Which two people do you think it could have been?"

Shelley shrugged again, and I sensed some withdrawal on her part, as though she'd put herself too far into the game. "I don't know. It was just an idea."

"What's a black box?" I asked her.

"You mean like a black box theater? It's just a space, a totally empty room, that the director can block out in any configuration of stage and audience he wants," she explained. "It's called that because that's actually what it is—just a room with black floor, walls, and ceiling. Ours is named the Olivier; we use it for student and experimental productions—nothing public. Why?"

"Just curious." I made a couple of notes and thought about Bradford Lake's attitude. "Did you notice anything at all beforehand? In the main theater? Any unusual or unexpected sound, an expression on anyone's face? Any sort of warning?"

Shelley and Elias both shook their heads.

"No," Shelley said. "Nothing. It just happened."

"Did you happen to see Gigi Dorrance-Downs around the theater today?" I asked.

Shelley fiddled with a buckle on her high-heeled sandal while she considered the question. "Yes. Gigi came in and interrupted George during rehearsal and spoke to him about something. Whatever it was made him angry. But she's always doing that, always barging into his office, onto the stage, into a meeting. It makes George furious, but she could get away with it because of her relationship with Cyrus." Shelley paused, aware she did not have to elaborate on that particular situation. "Then she sat and watched the rehearsal for a few minutes."

"Do you remember where she sat?" I said.

Shelley thought for a second. "Maybe in the third row, on the aisle. Maybe the fourth. She was just in front of me." Shelley's face brightened. "She was there when it happened. Gigi could have pushed the button. It could be Gigi and Winston. I'm sure I saw Winston."

The door opened quietly, and Richard stepped in. For a second I prayed he would remember about Elias.

"Hello," he finally said, offering him his hand, a bemused expression on his face. "Richard Jerome."

"Bertram Chiswick," Elias answered. "We met the other night at George's party."

"Yes. You're the one who performed the tracheotomy. Interesting talent for a Shakespearean scholar."

Shelley looked deeply into Elias's eyes and ran her hand gently along the side of his face. "Isn't he wonderful?"

She picked up her worn-out tapestry sling purse and began rifling around in it, scattering its contents on the bed—makeup and keys, a garage door opener, a deck of playing cards, a church key, and an airplane-size bottle of Bailey's Irish Cream. "There's my wallet. Always at the bottom. I've got to go home in a while, Bertie, so I can get back here first thing in the morning and take you home, but what can I get for your dinner before I leave?" She removed three beaten-up dollar bills from the wallet, and I got the feeling they were all she was going to have till payday. I could not believe that Elias, with all his millions, even though he was undercover, did not offer to pay for his own dinner. "This hospital food's no good."

"Double cheeseburger, large fries, and a cherry Coke."

Shelley wagged her finger in front of his face. She had big hands and thick knuckles. "Oh, no, Sugar Bug. Remember, you and I promised to take care of each other. And I'm going to get you on a healthy diet—I want you to live for a very long time. What kind of a salad do you want?"

"You pick it out." Elias smiled at her like an idiot escaped from an asylum. "No one ever took care of me like this before," he said to Richard and me once she'd left the room. "No one's ever cared if I had a healthy diet or not."

"That is the biggest load of crap I've ever heard in my life, Elias Bennett IV," I said. "And you know it."

"Give her a chance, Lilly. She's had a lousy life. She's been married four times."

All I could do was stare and bite my tongue and think about what a complete boob my brother was around women.

"You know," Elias continued, "she really is a member of the Pirelli Tire family. What do you think Mother will think?"

"Has your brain turned into sawdust?" I said.

"No," Richard said, "his brain has relocated to his pants."

"Watch my lips, Elias," I said. "She is not a member of the Pirelli Tire family, and believe me, Mother will not be happy at all. I want you to keep a sharp eye on her. Something is not right with this girl."

I told him and Richard about the twenty-five-million-dollar withdrawal. "Shelley seems to know everything about George and there is no reason to believe she would not know about that."

"Let me look at that wheel again," Elias said. I handed it to him and he examined it closely. "Common device. Radio-controlled car. You can get it at Radio Shack. Not much to go on."

"I know," I conceded. "But it's just one more example of the kind of planning someone is doing. I know they—or she, or he—is a little like the gang that couldn't shoot straight because they keep getting the wrong person, but they're organized and determined and there's no reason to believe that George is out of danger, even if he survives this accident. You look out for yourself, Elias. Make sure all four of those husbands aren't dead."

"I guess you won't be riding in Cody on Sunday." Richard clapped him on the shoulder. "Christian and I will have to fight off all those hot-pantsed, adoring cowgirls by ourselves."

"Don't worry," Elias said. "I might not be riding, but I'll be there."

"Me, too," I warned Richard, teasing. "So don't go getting any crazy ideas. By the way, what did you do with all that weaponry?"

"Pockets of my sportcoat." Elias patted his pillow. A tiny edge of the checked coat was visible beneath it.

Shelley returned in record time with a tofu burger on nine-grain bread with sprouts, baked corn chips with no salt, and a carob chip cookie, or whatever it is those chocolate chip cookies made with margarine and fake chocolate are called, and some cherry-flavored soda water.

"We'll let you two lovebirds say good night," I said. "Enjoy your supper, Mr. Chiswick. It looks wonderful."

MONDAY EVENING

Can I buy you dinner?" Richard asked as we left the hospital.

Darkness had fallen and the sky was endless ultramarine with golden edges and a few bright early stars.

"That would be wonderful," I said and squeezed his arm. "Do you mind if we make one stop first? I'd like to go back to the theater."

Two squad cars, a forensics van, and the KRUN-TV Evening News van remained outside the Vaile Theater, but no broadcast personalities were visible, and when we entered the auditorium, only the work light on the stage remained lit.

"Will you look at that?" Richard said as he headed quickly down the aisle toward the stage. "I can't believe more people weren't killed."

Completely at home, he stood at the edge of the orchestra pit, his hands in his pockets, and looked all around, then passed through the small curtain that led to the backstage passageway and marched out onto the stage, not at all put off by its classical, steep rake.

"Watch where you step," I said. "It's hard to tell on that black floor if the blood has been washed off or not."

"Terrific," Richard said good-naturedly. "So if I start to slip, will you catch me?"

"Well," I said, "I'm trying."

We smiled at each other.

I joined him and made my way slowly around, examining the floor. There were chalk marks everywhere, but then I saw the one I was looking for. It was just a thin tick on the very edge.

Richard looked up at the ceiling, where stars were now visible, and then back at the ominous black steel apparatus. "These lighting battens weigh almost a thousand pounds."

"How long would it have taken to fall?" I asked.

"Not long, because it hangs low. See, just there." He indicated a spot slightly above the lip of the proscenium arch. "So even though it's suspended from the roof, it would only actually be dropping about twenty-five feet at the most."

I returned to the house and sat down in the third row on the aisle, where Shelley had thought Gigi had been. "Would you go stand over there where George was standing?" I pointed.

He walked carefully across to the lower right edge of the batten.

"Yes," I said, once he'd taken up his position. "The perspective on this slanted stage is very misleading. It looks like you're standing right under the edge of the arch, but actually, you're about a foot in front of it. Now step downstage about two or three feet to where Elias must have been."

In that position, Richard's body concealed the chalk mark, so it was conceivable that whoever ignited the blast had had to throw his best-laid plan out the window and eyeball the situation.

"Go back to where George was, please." I went up two rows to where I thought Shelley might have been, since she'd said Gigi was right in front of her. From the fifth row back on the aisle, it looked even more as though he were under the proscenium arch. But I didn't know whether or not she'd been on the aisle. I moved to the center of the row and the perspective corrected itself.

Richard climbed over the batten and crossed to the opposite side of the stage. "This spot here correlates exactly to where Stephen Griffin was standing," he said. "Go over to the other aisle."

I did as he said and saw. The spot where Stephen Griffin had stood and taken the direct hit appeared to be upstage enough to be out of danger.

"When your assistant sits in the Opera House while you're directing," I asked, "where does she sit?"

"Fifth row center," he answered. "I trust her eye. Her sense of balance is invaluable."

"Do you suppose George feels that way about Shelley?"

"Absolutely. She's a very sharp girl. I wouldn't mind having her work for me." Richard placed his hand above his eyebrows to block the overhead light and looked directly at me. "Listen to me, Lilly," he said. "It's obvious you don't like Shelley, but that doesn't mean she's guilty."

"Why?" I asked, slightly rankled that my professional judgment might be seen as being compromised by my personal feelings. Even if it were true.

"Well," he said, beginning to pick his way back across the stage, "she's smart, but she's not sophisticated. She seems to me more of a street girl."

Well, I thought, he's certainly on target there.

His voice stopped as he disappeared backstage. Moments later he reappeared through the maroon velvet curtain. "And these murders—poisoned tea, deadly mushrooms, plastique explosives—they're very dramatic. More grand opera than legitimate theater, actually.

"Another thing." He sat down next to me, picked up my hand, and plopped it on his thigh. "All performing arts companies are extremely incestuous and highly politicized, and the power struggles are legendary. Everybody wants to be The Star, closest to Daddy, closest to the top. But they're not necessarily obvious about it. This is an established company. The roots are deep and the history is extremely complex, and some of the players are veteran hardball politicians."

This talking-to was getting me mad and I was trying hard not to get defensive. "What exactly do you mean, Richard?" I drummed my fingers on his leg.

"I mean, I think you have to dig deeper than Shelley Pirelli—she's already as close to the top as one can get. Just because you don't want her as your sister-in-law doesn't mean you have to turn her into a mass murderer." He looked at me and smiled. "Know what I mean?"

Was he right? Possibly. "What about Bradford Lake?" I said.

"He certainly has strong motives, but I don't think he has the guts."

"Gigi?"

"She could be your Lady Macbeth. She's certainly played the part enough times."

Everybody's an expert.

"Private Investigator Lilly Bennett is just leaving the theater," said Evening News coanchor Tom O'Neil into the bright lights of the camera. He had on so much pancake, he looked like a Clearasil ad, and it stopped right at his jaw line, turning him, literally, into a talking head. "Let's see if we can grab her for a second." He thrust the microphone into my face. "This is the third murder in less than a week, Private Investigator Lilly Bennett. I understand you're helping the Roundup Police Department. Any new leads you're working on?"

"Yes, there are," I said. "I'm not at liberty to disclose them at this time, but we expect to issue arrest warrants shortly."

"Warrants," he repeated. "Is that plural?"

"Yes, it is. Good night, Tom."

"That was Private Investigator Lilly Bennett," Tom said as we walked to the car and got in.

Once Richard had given ten dollars to Curtis, the doorman, to walk Baby and give her some dinner, we went into the Grand's smoky tavern and sat on shiny red leather stools and ordered some whiskys and ribeyes and talked about nothing. Richard told some Henny Youngman jokes.

The television was on at the far end of the bar and Marsha Maloney, Tom O'Neil's KRUN Evening News coanchor, was saying, "A few minutes ago, Tom caught up with Private Investigator Lilly Bennett in front of the Vaile Theater, scene of today's bombing, which so far has claimed the life of one actor, Stephen Griffin, while the Roundup Repertory Theater Company founder and general director George Wrightsman remains in intensive care in critical condition."

I would kill myself if I had to be a television newscaster. They repeat everything fifty kajillion times, just on the off chance that one person out there arrived from Jupiter in the last fifteen seconds, and God forbid anyone should feel left out, that would be too politically incorrect—too irresponsible journalistically—to leave one single person out of anything. And we all know how responsible journalists are.

They rolled the tape of Tom and me and I studied it, deciding that I look better on television than I do in person. Especially with my new makeup.

"Yes, Marsha," Tom was saying. "Private Investigator Lilly Bennett said the police department expects to issue warrants for the arrest of at least two people later tonight."

"Did I say that?" I said to Richard. " 'Later tonight'?"

"No," he said. "But when did truth ever have anything to do with anything?"

We clinked our glasses.

"Jack Lewis is going to be mad," I said happily. "I'll bet my car phone's ringing off the hook."

31

L et's go past Shelley Pirelli's palazzo," I said when we left the hotel, much more relaxed than when we'd arrived, thanks to a bottle of Jordan Cabernet. "I want to see where she lives."

Shelley lived across the viaduct from downtown Roundup, a viaduct that crossed not only the Wind River and the railroad tracks, but also the world between blue- and white-collar, between day laborers and office workers, between G.E.D. high school certificates and college degrees.

"What do you know about Winston?" I asked as we drove.

"I've known him for years," Richard said. "He's from an old Boston family, about eight generations of Brahmin Yalies. Super brain. Super liberal."

"Is he married?"

"I don't think he's married at the moment. Has been, though, a couple of times. He's like a lot of those rich Northern liberal types," Richard said. "Likes his women beaten down and needy, unsophisticated."

"Nice." I laughed. "What about those rich Northern conservative types?"

"We like our women rich."

"Don't care if they're sophisticated?"

"Depends on how rich they are," Richard the Stud pronounced, and puffed a big cloud of cigar smoke in my face. "Winston's first wife—what a weather-beaten, old Cape Cod battle-ax she is—got full custody of his children when Winston ran off and married some black Jamaican actress who turned out to be a complete psycho who regularly set his house on fire in between episodes of slicing herself up with a kitchen knife."

"Nice," I said as I turned off the headlights and we coasted to a stop across the street from Shelley's white adobe bungalow.

"That was when he was at the Old Globe in San Diego, and she committed suicide by jumping off a bridge or drowning in their pool. I don't remember which. I think he was briefly suspected of murdering her, but it turned out he didn't."

"And you're just telling me this?" I said, perturbed. "When people are dropping like flies all around us?"

"I didn't remember until just now."

"Please tell me if anything else comes to mind."

"You'll be the first to know."

A table lamp glowed dimly through the open slats of mini-blinds that hung in front of Shelley's arched living-room window, and the top of her head kept flashing into view, as though she were riding one of those Hollywood movie giddy-up horse machines. A small tricycle was at the bottom of the porch, whose steps tilted precariously from the house, and a sleek, silver Mercedes 500SL sat by the curb at the end of the front walk.

"Wait here," I said to Richard.

"Oh, right," he said, and followed me out.

We closed the car doors silently, crossed the street, and concealed ourselves behind some large shrubs below the living-room window.

Shelley and Andy Beckett were in a large armchair with what looked to me like washable slipcovers—the kind you can buy through catalogues. He was fully clothed except for his Savile Row pinstripe suit pants, which were circling his ankles like a puddle of oil—the diamonds in his satellite-shaped cufflinks flashed off the windows like marquee lights at a strip joint. She was straddling him, and from the noise they were making—reminiscent of the monkey house at the zoo—it was pretty obvious they were close to concluding their business, at least he was. She kept looking at her fake gold Rolex, her only article of clothing.

"Holy shit," Richard said. "Will you look at that! It looks like she has boxing gloves attached to her front."

"Big deal," I said. "You've seen bosoms before."

"I thought I had, but I hadn't."

After one more look at the watch, she started moving faster and faster and his "Oh, babys" got louder and louder, and her hair danced like a dirt cloud in a tornado and finally, with one big convulsive shriek and a lot of surrounding commotion, it was over. Shelley collapsed across him and Richard tackled me around the waist and pulled me down on the ground behind the bushes. But it wasn't to be. All I could do was laugh. I don't think he'd even noticed the squirrels that lived under her arms.

"Now do you believe me?" Shelley sat up and slipped a transparent baby-beige negligee over her body. She smoothed his hair back gently, familiarly. "Bertram and I both *work* for George. I'm not doing anything with him. He's just one of those jugheads George is always hiring and making me look after."

Andy nodded his head and shook out a cigarette. I couldn't tell if he agreed, understood, or was simply too winded to speak. But then, suddenly, a door opened down the hallway and a bright shaft of light cut across their faces, silhouetting a small, maybe three-year-old, brown-haired girl. Andy and Shelley both jumped to their feet—he quickly zipped his trousers and she hugged the Saran Wrap closer around her.

"Hi, Uncle Andy," the little girl said, and went over and locked her arms around his legs.

"Hi, honey," he answered and patted her affectionately on the top of her head. "Do you want me to stay, Shelley?" he asked. "I wish I could invite you to come to my house."

The child released Andy's leg and began to pound a broken truck on the floor. Bam. Bam. Bam.

"Oh, yeah, that'd be just dandy," Shelley said sarcastically. "Tell me another." She wanted him to hit the road. She sounded aggravated and mean, and I got the impression it hadn't been as good for her as it had been for him.

I whispered this deduction to Richard, who poked me in the ribs. "Who cares?" he said.

I elbowed him back. Hard.

"Your wife would love it if you invited me over for the night. Rose Marie, stop that, please, honey."

Thankfully the child ceased with the truck and began to slap wooden blocks together and sing a little song. She was as grating and irritating and mindless as Mardi Gras.

"They said they're going to arrest two people tonight, so then this will all be over," Shelley said.

"You're really convinced it's Gigi?"

It was hard to hear them over the precious little concert.

"Shouldn't that child be in bed by now?" I whispered to Richard. "It's after eight-thirty."

"Sometimes children stay up as late as nine," he whispered back.

"Well, they shouldn't. They should be in bed by seven-thirty."

"Yes, Andy, I do," Shelley was saying adamantly. "She could easily have done all of it. She could have poisoned Cyrus's tea, because she was over there practically every day. She could have switched the mushroom tamales because I saw her fussing around out there in the dining room before Vanderbilt served them. And she was in the theater today when the lighting rig fell. I think she did all this stuff."

"I have trouble picturing Gigi Dorrance-Downs up there on the roof in one of her hostess outfits, planting explosives."

He and Shelley both laughed. He shrugged into his suit jacket and carefully folded his Hermès tie and tucked it into a jacket pocket.

Rose Marie had moved on to a little violin and in no time at all had it worked up to a mind-numbing screech. It had given me a splitting headache and I had no feeling in my legs from crouching for so long. I'd spent stakeouts in much more uncomfortable positions many times before for much longer, but I have to admit, it's getting harder to take.

Richard swiveled around on his haunches and sat back, leaning against the house. "I can't believe you make your living this way," he muttered. "I say we storm the battlements and shoot the child."

"Well, maybe she didn't do that part." Shelley gave it some thought. "Maybe she got Vanderbilt to do it and poisoning him wasn't really a mistake. Maybe she did it after he'd put the bombs on the roof. Rose Marie, stop that now, honey. Uncle Andy and I are trying to have a conversation and you know how much it upsets *you* when *you're* interrupted."

"For God's sake," Richard said. "She's talking to that child like she's a Harvard graduate. Just tell her to stop or you'll spank her. Can we go now?"

"Not yet." I laughed. "Now you know how I feel sitting through all those operas."

Rose Marie stopped her concertizing and once again attached herself to Andy Beckett's leg.

"Go on." Shelley pushed him toward the door. "I need to get some sleep so I can be back at the hospital first thing tomorrow morning. I don't want George to get too far out of my sight—I'm so afraid for him. This Lilly Bennett person, she's supposed to be such a hot shit, but as far as I can tell, she hasn't done anything at all. I think I've already figured this whole thing out and she's still got her finger in her nose talking to Bradford and me and Bertram, except the truth is that all this stuff started to stink big time when Bertram turned up on the scene."

No wonder I wanted her to be the perpetrator. I wouldn't have minded a bit if she got the chair.

Richard was very quiet, but I sensed his hackles rise, could tell that old testosterone Oh, yeah? had pumped up a notch, and it made me feel wonderful.

"I think she's okay," Andy said. "George trusts her. I think you ought to give her a chance. She has a brother who's a bachelor."

"Oh, yeah?" Shelley made no attempt to mask her interest. "Tell me about him. Is he as dimwitted as his sister? Marrying a Bennett could solve all my problems."

I jabbed Richard again in the ribs. "Hear that?" I said.

"I don't have any problems," he answered.

Oh, yeah? That's what you think.

Andy made his way to the front door with the little girl still attached to his leg. "I have to go to L.A. for a couple of days."

"Don't go. Don't go," Rose Marie screamed.

Shelley picked her up. "Tell Uncle Andy good-bye, Rose Marie," she said and lifted her little hand and made her wave.

"No," the child screamed, as Andy passed close to us in our hiding place and went down the walk.

"I'll call you as soon as I get back from the Coast," he called as he climbed into his car. He smelled mostly of Shalimar.

Shelley blew him a big Jayne Mansfield kiss before she closed the front door and turned the deadbolt.

Rose Marie just kept screaming and screaming.

"What a fucking jerk," she said over the caterwauling as she tucked a wad of cash into her purse, and as I watched her, all I could think was, in the words of the great Bill Murray, "This chick is toast."

"What a lowdown, sleazy, foulmouthed tramp," I said to Richard as he drove us home through the still night. "Poor Elias."

"Yup," he said. I could tell he was still thinking about Shelley's tits.

It made me sick for my brother, and the truth is, I was willing to sacrifice the whole case to keep him from further humiliation. That bitch.

Baby curled up in my lap and went to sleep, and once I'd called the hospital to reconfirm that the security on George was tight and absolutely no one—not his trusted personal secretary Shelley Pirelli, not his executive producer Winston McMorris, not his leading director Bradford Lake, not his personal assistant Cary Scott Douglas, and not his leading lady Gigi Dorrance-Downs—would be allowed anywhere near him, I looked out the window as the familiar starlit countryside sped past.

I decided not to call Elias until morning. Let him get a good night's sleep, dreaming about his fairytale future with the Pirelli Tire heiress before bursting his white-wall filled with happy gas.

"Do you suppose she knows who Elias really is?" I asked Richard.

"She's not stupid. Assume she knows everything."

32

TUESDAY MORNING

Do you want to go riding?" Richard asked as we lay in bed watching the edge of the sun begin to glow like fire through the trees of the distant hilltop. It was just five o'clock.

"Who?" I said sleepily, rolling over and reaching my arm across the covers and coming up empty-handed.

He was already out of bed and pulling on his jeans. "Your horse. Come on. You've slept plenty. Time to get up and get going." He tossed my bathrobe to me. "Up."

"I'm starving," I said.

"Un-huh," Richard snorted impatiently. "There'll still be plenty of food after you've had some exercise."

Before we left, I called Elias and told him everything we'd seen and heard the night before. "You can cancel out of this assignment any time," I told him. "Come on home."

He was silent for a few beats. I could hear the steam building in the boiler.

"Hell, no," he finally said. "I'm gonna see this through. It'll test my skills, pretending to be a fat old academic gull in love with a—well, I won't even say it. Besides, my assignment is to protect George Wrightsman, not ball his secretary."

"I'm sorry, Elias," I said before we hung up.

"Forget it. It's nothing."

He was mad as hell and I was glad not to be in Shelley Pirelli's shoes.

Then, once I'd left a message for Linda to dig up all the information she could about Ms. Pirelli and her four ex-husbands, I joined Richard, glad he'd made me go because the early morning silence always gave me an opportunity to sort things out. There were so many elements to this case, and until last night they had all sputtered and spun independent of each other, up there in the zone, like balloons with unlimited supplies of escaping air. Like little circling planes, each with its own landing pattern and airport. But something Shelley had said to Andy Beckett brought some definition as far as closing in on what was connected and what wasn't.

Power and money. Power and money. The only two things that matter to many people.

Shelley was right. It was hard to envision regal Gigi up there on the roof, but it wasn't hard to picture Molly Dolan, the do-gooder cheerleader from Waterbury, Connecticut, up there, or even Shelley herself. Or Winston, whose wife had died under mysterious circumstances. And it wasn't hard to imagine that Winston could be easily seduced by a beauty like Gigi Dorrance-Downs. She was apparently not the sort Winston was normally drawn to, but I couldn't help thinking that if she put her mind to it, got a little lost and needy—and larcenous—the sweetness of her perfume and the softness of her skin, the fineness of her bones, and ultimately her sculpture garden, would drag him like a magnet into her fine net. Gigi's attributes would have virtually no effect on Bradford or Cary Scott.

Possibly Gigi and Winston had hatched a scheme to take over the theater company because, as she aged, her status as leading lady became more and more threatened. And maybe Winston felt he had apprenticed long enough. Maybe they felt like New England Yankees—stranded, surrounded, about to be scalped in the hostile Indian territory of modern-day Wyoming—and had circled their wagons.

So far, I'd mentioned the missing endowment money to Bradford, Winston, and Shelley, and it was virtually impossible to tell who was legitimately surprised by its absence.

Everything was starting to narrow down. Not there yet, but getting so close I could taste it. What I needed badly was some hard evidence. So far there was none. Just the tiny plastic tire.

Furthermore, no one had made a mistake yet. But sooner or later someone would, and I would be there. Because I had the time—they had the pressure.

Richard and I followed a deer trail through a tight draw and pulled up on the rocky overlook of my parents' private valley, where their rough log summer house slept on the hillside, hidden by the woods. Bird song filled the air, and below, on the valley floor by the river, the wedding pavilion shimmered, beguiling us from across the meadow, sparkling in the morning sun like an enchanted palace floating on mist.

I turned Ariel back toward home.

"Don't you want to go see it?" Richard said. "I haven't seen it since it was finished."

"I've got to go to work," I called to him over my shoulder. I heard him calling behind me, but I didn't look back. I might have been crying a little bit.

s I'd explained to Shelley and Elias, there is typically only one place
that C-4 or Semtex, commonly known as plastique explosive, can
be obtained: a military installation. So, once I got put together, I
headed out to Fort Hickock Army Base, which lies outside of
Roundup, adjacent to the southwestern boundary of the Circle B.
Originally established to fight off the Indians, it was now a major artil-
lery training camp for the Army and housed a large unit of Rangers.

The commandant—John Taylor—was an old, very close friend of
mine, although we hadn't seen each other since those heady, wildly

oversexed, steamy Vietnam R&R days in Honolulu and Hong Kong and Sydney and every other place we could arrange to meet in the Pacific, when I was in much better shape. I was a little nervous and excited about seeing him again.

Although he'd been assigned to Fort Hickock before I moved back to Wyoming, we hadn't been in touch for years because he was married, and I am through with dating married men. Talk about a no-win situation. As one of my married lovers said to me, "If they'll do it for ya—they'll do it to ya." He was speaking of women in general and the word "screw" in particular. But you could replace the word "screw" with "lie," and the concept of women with married men, and the saying would still hold water. Who wants a guy with so little integrity and self-respect that he will live his entire life with a major lie and unhappiness at its core? Not me.

But even if I hadn't given up on married men, John Taylor had made it clear twenty-five years ago, when he got married, that from then on he'd be dedicated to his wife and uninterested in anyone but her. He had great integrity, which was why I'd liked him in the first place. Like Richard. How come all the good men are taken or don't want you back?

Now he was General Taylor, and when he walked around his desk to greet me, with those two gold stars gleaming like little head-lights on his collars, I saw that he was just as compact and handsome and squared away as ever. His closely trimmed hair was silvery on the sides, and his blue-gray eyes were as sharp as lasers behind wire-rimmed glasses.

I cannot tell you how relieved I was that I'd spent even longer than usual on my makeup and clothes to prepare for this particular meeting, because I returned instantly to the beach in Guam in 1967 where we'd lain breathless and salty in the sizzling tropical sand while fully loaded B-52s thundered just a few feet over our heads into the setting sun on their night missions to North Vietnam. The scream of those eight jet engines struggling to heave the mega-ton monsters from the earth churned up eroticism unique to war, to danger and death and youth. There on the abandoned beach we were the incarnate white-hot power of our country and its invincibility. The killing machines were our messengers.

Over the years, I've discovered that the only experience that begins to approach the power of war for its sheer animalism, for that erotic blood-lust thrill, is sitting ringside at a heavyweight boxing match, but that is a woefully decaffeinated punch if you've ever been young and made love to an American soldier on a foreign beach with American B-52s taking off over your head, delivering your message, bringing home your bacon.

John Taylor and I had a history and a connection we shared with no one else—irreplaceable, irrefutable, fired in that Pacific furnace—in spite of the fact that in that horrible war we did not, could not, and never would bring home the bacon.

He took my hands and kissed me on the cheek and then backed up and looked me up and down and in the eye. "Wow," he said, filled with the same memories and feelings. "The years have been good."

I smiled at him. "Yup," I said, admiring him back. "You're definitely right about that."

John looked past my shoulder to his adjutant. "Two coffees. Black." He looked at me. "I assume it's still black."

I nodded.

"Please have a seat." He indicated a chair and I sat down quickly, practically gasping from the charge of seeing him again. "I don't know what brings you here, Lilly, but I sure am glad to see you."

"Thanks, John. It's strange, isn't it?"

We looked into each other's eyes and I struggled to concentrate. Refocus myself.

"There was an explosion at the Vaile Theater in Roundup yesterday afternoon," I said. "An actor was killed and the theater's director is still in critical condition."

"I know. I read about it."

"The explosive was either C-4 or Semtex," I said. "And I'm assuming you have both on the base."

John nodded. "In great quantity. You think one of our personnel blew up the theater?"

I shook my head. "No. But I'm pretty sure some young E-5 supplied the means."

"Honey trap?"

"Un-huh."

"Let's find out." John jumped to his feet, grabbed his scrambled egg cover, and almost decked the aide who was just on his way in with the coffee.

I followed him out the door to where his driver waited on permanent call alongside a camouflaged, convertible Humvee sporting pennants with stars, and seconds later we roared off to the armory, flags flying. It was like riding in a royal carriage: Make way! Make way for the king! This was power at an excellent level.

As I described the theater roof and the heavy bolted anchors and the precision with which the blasts had been executed, the post flew past, and in five or six minutes we entered a section of woods and then came out into a gently sloping clearing that was surrounded by a high chain-link fence topped with concertina wire. Countless small steel doors were visible in the hillside, which was covered with the most perfectly green, manicured lawn I've ever seen. A guardhouse stood at the large gate, and when we came to a stop before it, a white-helmeted, heavily armed guard emerged and saluted the general. The gate slowly rolled open and then closed as soon as we were through.

"I'd like to see the log for the last four weeks," John said, once everyone was done saluting and sirring.

"Sir," a guard inside the shack answered as he handed him a black, plastic-covered notebook with a squadron insignia on the cover. "Here it is, sir."

These guys were extra strac, and if they were nervous at this unexpected visit, they didn't show it. John read slowly through the log, closed it, and handed it back, and we were almost immediately again in the vehicle heading for the Field Engineering Division.

"There haven't been any unusual dispersals in the last month," he explained. "The majority of the explosives are requisitioned by either the Warfare Training Units or Field Engineering Headquarters, so I thought we'd start at FEHQ because the supply sergeant is the only one who signs the order, as compared with different personnel in each WTU."

We had come to a stop in front of an old wooden barracks—white clapboard with green trim—and the second we stepped inside, the sergeant on duty called the anteroom to attention and everyone rocketed to their feet. It was fabulous.

Oh, my, I thought, watching John. There's something about a man in a uniform that gets me going. No wonder these guys hate to retire.

We were escorted immediately into the captain's office.

"Pleasure to see you, sir," the captain said once the general had told him to stand at ease. "Ma'am." He nodded in my direction. "What can I do for you, General?"

"I'd like to see the supply sergeant whose initials are B.B.," General Taylor said.

"That would be Buddy Butts, sir," the captain answered. "And I wish you and I both could talk to him, but he was reported AWOL yesterday morning."

"Was he in charge of all explosive requisitioning?" the general asked.

"Yes, sir, he was. Is there some problem?"

"The explosion at the Vaile Theater yesterday was done with either C-4 or Semtex," I said. "And as far as I know this is the only place in the region where those elements are available."

"Yes, ma'am. That's correct."

"What does he look like?"

"Sergeant Butts? Well, he is kind of short, and skinny."

"What about his coloring? His complexion? How old?"

"He just celebrated his twenty-fifth birthday—we had a cake and ice cream party for him—and I'd say he's sort of blond. Blue eyes. He has a pretty severe acne problem."

"Is he married? Have a girl friend?"

"No. Not that I know of, and I keep pretty close tabs on the men in my command. He is not what anyone would consider a good catch, in my opinion."

Such a boy would be putty in the hands of Gigi or Shelley. Or, who knew, maybe even Winston, or one of the other boys in the company.

"I'll call you as soon as I hear anything," John said once we were back in the Humvee. "I'll have the MPs fax Butts's vehicle information to your office. Registration, driver's license, so forth."

"Thanks," I said as we rolled along, now at a more dignified pace.

"Lilly," John said after a moment. The timbre of his voice had changed. "I've been meaning to call you."

I turned and looked at him. "Oh?" Feelings of confusion flooded me. What if he asked me out? What about his wife? How could he cheat on her after all these years? And what about Richard? I loved him with all my heart, and I knew he loved me back. But how could he be so dense as not to see that if he didn't take the next step he'd lose me? Tears stung my eyes.

"I don't know if you knew or not," John was saying. The wind blew our words into the air. "But Sheila died four years ago, just before I took command of Fort Hickock."

"I'm so sorry," I said. "I didn't know."

"I haven't seen anyone. Haven't wanted to. But every now and then, since you moved back to Roundup, I see your name or your picture in the paper, and I was wondering if you'd join me for dinner some evening."

All I could do was stare at him. "I'd love to," I finally said. "My goddaughter is getting married this weekend, but once I get that wrapped up, I'd love to have dinner."

"Great. I'll give you a call."

We'd reached my car and I climbed in and General Taylor closed the door for me and waved as I drove away, feeling sick. I didn't want to start this stuff all over again. All I wanted was Richard. He was where I wanted to stop.

Just before I went around a corner and out of sight, I saw Jack Lewis's car appear at the far end of the street. I felt better instantly.

I t took me two Radio Shacks before I found the one where a bulldog-looking woman remembered that last Friday she'd sold a Day-Glo-pink, radio-controlled toy car to a medium-height woman with lots of hair.

"It was bright red," she told me. "I thought it might have been a wig, there was so much of it."

"What color were her eyes?"

"No idea. She never took off her dark glasses. They were those big Jackie Kennedy jobs. She had on a ton of lipstick and jewelry." The woman squinted into the distance trying to remember. "She was real, real pretty. French or German or something."

"How did she pay?" I asked. "Cash? Credit card?"

"Cash, as I recall. Hey, would you like a cup of coffee? I just put on a new pot."

"No, thanks. I've got to keep moving." I put my notebook back into my purse. "Can you recall anything else?"

The woman considered for a moment. "Well, yeah, now that you ask. One thing sort of surprised me. I went and looked out the door when she left, 'cause she looked like the type that would have a chauffeur-driven limousine, and you know what? She left in one of those big-wheel pickups. You know, like the kids drive, with the Crocodile Dundee lights on the roof. Looked like a kind of scrawny-looking kid in a backward hat was driving."

Sergeant Buddy Butts.

I called Elias from the car on my way into town, but Shelley answered the phone and I hung up. That's good, I thought. Keep her occupied.

"He's been asking for you," the doctor told me when I met him at the circular central desk of the six-bed Intensive Care Unit.

It was midmorning juice and cookie time in the hospital, but that didn't make any difference in the ICU where every hour had the same importance as any other. Glass walls, with sliding glass doors, like porch doors, isolated the patients from the unit's constant noisy commotion, but gave the highly trained and skilled staff the ability to keep each of them in constant sight while their monitors and gadgets whirred and beeped and buzzed. The air didn't smell like anything—just hard and cold and slightly metallic.

"How is he?" I asked.

"It's just what I told you yesterday: except for a broken arm, he's fine."

"Has he had any visitors?"

The doctor shook his head. "A few people have stopped by but no one's been let in to see him. That boy hasn't left the waiting room." He indicated through a doorway, and I saw Cary Scott Douglas slouched back asleep on a comfortable-looking couch. He suddenly jerked awake and looked at me with frightened eyes.

"No change," I told him. "Go back to sleep." And he slumped

back as though he'd been socked in the solar plexus and rubbed his dry, gritty eyes with balled fists and then stared vacantly at the ceiling. I'm sure he'd counted the dots in the tiles a million times.

"We really appreciate your keeping Wrightsman here, Doctor," I said. "And for keeping the true extent of his injuries confidential."

"No problem. We understand the situation and the unit's pretty quiet right now anyway. Actually, he's a very funny guy. I never saw anyone who loves drugs as much as he does."

"It shouldn't be much longer. Just a day or two."

The two uniformed officers outside George's cubicle sharpened up a little when I passed, and we greeted each other amicably, which indicated an enormous improvement in my status, as far as the local beat cops were concerned, since just a few months ago. When I returned to Roundup—a chief disgraced, a sissy and a pantywaist, a girl who'd quit her job just because she'd been caught in bed with the chief justice of the California Supreme Court and his wife had threatened to turn the pictures of them in bed together, naked, over to the *National Enquirer*—their looks had held hidden sneers. Now they'd finally figured out I was saving their boss's butt every time he turned around, so they thought I was great.

I went in, and after drawing the curtain across the glass wall so we could have a private conversation, shielded from the rest of the ICU, stood by the side of George's bed. It looked like he was sleeping, or unconscious. Very quiet. Suddenly one of his brown eyes opened and looked at me and then closed. Then popped opened again. Like a five-year-old playing peekaboo.

"Oh, I'm so glad it's you," he said. "I'm scared to death." The bruises on his face were starting to darken visibly around the edges of the bandages.

"I don't blame you." I took his hand.

"What am I going to do?"

"We're going to try to flush these folks out," I said. "And it'll probably take a couple of days. I've asked the doctor to keep you isolated, with round-the-clock guards, so you'll be safe."

"Oh, thank God." He smiled tentatively, painfully. "I feel much better now that you're here. Who's doing this?"

"I think I know, but I'm not going to tell you. It would be completely counterproductive. Have you ever met a fellow named Buddy Butts?"

"Buddy Butts?" George perked up. "Is that an actual name?"

"Twenty-five, scrawny. Bad skin."

He shook his head. "Not my type."

"I didn't think so," I said. "Are you in much pain?"

"Excruciating. But the drugs are fabulous. The nurse just gave me some more Demerol."

I sat down on the padded metal chair near his head, took my gloves off, and laid them across my knee. "Now," I said, "what did you do with the money, George?"

"What money?"

"The twenty-five million."

He was caught and he knew it. "How did you find out?"

"My family owns the bank," I said. "Surely you knew that."

He frowned and shook his head. "I've never been much of a businessman."

"Where is it now?"

"Under my bed."

"What's under your bed?"

"The money." He looked slightly embarrassed. "I bought gold with the money and it's under my bed."

I couldn't believe my ears. "You bought gold?" I said. "Twenty-five million dollars' worth of gold?"

"Yes."

"And you put it under your bed?"

"Yes. Well, the bed in the guest room, actually."

He and I both started to laugh. What he was telling me was preposterous. Incredible. I put my head in my hands and stared at the floor. I was completely speechless. "Are you serious?" I finally said.

"Yes."

"Where did you get it?"

"A dealer, of course," George answered, like I was a jerk for not knowing.

"Why?"

"We need the money for our pensions. Actors never have anyone to look after them when they're old or sick."

I loved listening to George when he got riled up like this and started putting on the show. It reminded me of my mother. Ferocious as a bear.

"This was the first time anything like this had happened, to get a gift like this," he railed. "Our ensemble would have an actual retirement fund. But, with Cyrus, there were always strings attached. It was common for him to come back and find a way to rewrite the terms of his gifts because they were always given with strings. I couldn't let him do that with this endowment. We finally had a secure future, and he had threatened to take it back if I didn't concede about the air rights."

"Who else knows it's there, George? Who helped you carry it in?"

"The dealer delivered it, but Vanderbilt was there," he said, and if there were any sorrow in his voice over young Vanderbilt Belmont's demise, I could not detect it.

"Not Cary Scott?"

The bandaged head shook. "I would never endanger him that way. He's too special to me."

I could tell he was getting drowsy from the shot, his heartbeat on the EKG monitor was getting slower and slower.

"Not Shelley? Or Winston?"

No again.

"Cyrus knew the money was gone," I said, knowing he wanted to believe, and also convince me, that his injuries were severe and he needed to slide into a sweet opiate euphoria. But I wasn't going to let him off that easily for bruises and a broken arm. "That's why he called me in the first place. Is there any chance Vanderbilt might have told him and he might have passed the information along to Gigi?"

The heart monitor noise picked up and George looked at me with incredulity. "Ooooh, that Vanderbilt," he said with disgust. "He was such a slut."

"Are you positive Shelley doesn't know? She seems to know everything else about you."

"Yes." He nodded. "Everything. But Shelley would never do any of this, because I rescued her. I found her in the street, and if she lost her job she'd end up there again. She takes care of everything for me. My whole life. But she doesn't know about the money."

"How do you know?"

"Because I don't operate that way, especially when it comes to money. That's one thing I don't joke around about."

George was showing me a new side. The survival side of maybe not a hard-boiled, worldly-wise, big-time, wheeler-dealer executive, but a shrewd, canny, and cunning one, certainly.

"I do most things on a need-to-know basis, although most people aren't aware of it, because they think I'm too much of an artiste, too fey, too precious. I trust Shelley implicitly within the boundaries I've mentally set for her. If she betrayed me, well, so be it. I've been hurt by bigger talents."

"What about Cary Scott?" I asked, thinking about the exhausted boy who had become George's sentinel.

"He is my stuffed animal, my baby, my angel. I adore him but I have no expectation of his loyalty. He's too young to choose for life. But again, the money wouldn't register with him. I swear to you, Lilly, these murders and attempts on my life have nothing to do with the gold. If that's what all this is about, then why don't they just steal it?"

George was right and I told him so. "Cary Scott has not left the waiting room since they brought you in," I added.

"And you know"—George's expression was contented and peaceful—"he won't leave until I do."

We talked for a few more minutes, and then I could tell he wasn't paying attention anymore, so I crept out of the cubicle, quietly sliding the door closed behind me, and was instantly almost flattened by Gigi, who was rushing headlong across the ICU with a huge bouquet of white lilies.

O h," Gigi said, startled. *"Excusez-moi."*

She wore the modern version of one of Christian Dior's beautiful, famous day dresses—the ones that personified life in the fifties—full-skirted, crisp navy-blue organdy with a low neckline surrounded by a wide white piqué collar. She looked prim and elegant and
very glamorous and the bouquet's flowing yellow ribbons set everything
off like an Arthur Penn photograph on the cover of *Vogue.*

She tried to blow around me, but I blocked her way.

"Excuse me, *chérie,*" she said with a wonderfully patronizing gran-
deur. I swear to God, she must have memorized every word Maureen

O'Hara ever said and every move she ever made. "I'm trying to get past. I've come to see George."

"I'm sorry, Gigi," I told her. "But George can't have any visitors."

"Oh, he'll want to see me." Her green eyes flared with disdain. "I'll just give him the flowers—they're his favorites and they'll perk him up *tout de tout*—and then I'll be on my way."

Tout de tout? I thought. I held my hands up, palms toward her. *"Non."*

"Goddamn it." Gigi raised her voice. "Let me by. This isn't your hospital."

One of the uniformed officers came up behind me. "Is there some problem, Marshal?" he said.

"I don't think so." I looked Gigi dead in the eye. "Is there, Miss Downs?"

She glared back and forth between us, blazing, absolutely brilliantly. Vivien Leigh as Scarlett O'Hara—foiled—but, as always, only temporarily. "Certainly not."

"Will you join me for a cup of coffee?" I said to her. "There are a few questions I'd like to ask." I indicated with my hand. "We can go right down here to the doctors' lounge."

"Of course. Anything I can do to help. Here." She thrust the flowers into the guard's hands. "Get these in water immediately," she ordered him, and led me down the hall, a ship of indignity at full sail, into the doctors' lounge, which was reminiscent of every staff waiting room in every nonprofit institution.

No matter how beautiful or outstanding or well endowed the college or hospital or school or opera company, or whatever, is, the staff always gets the shaft, accommodation-wise. The Christ and St. Luke's doctors' lounge was no exception.

Two brown, Formica-topped metal tables, surrounded by a jumble of padded metal folding chairs, ran end to end down the center of the long narrow room. They were heaped with several disassembled copies of the morning paper and littered with half-empty Styrofoam cups of cold coffee. On one wall was a chrome-framed couch with brown plastic cushions and at the far end was another, dreary and bereft, beneath the row of windows where the recent rains had carved splotchy streams through a thick, ancient coating of dirt and dust.

A young doctor, who had been dead asleep on the grungy sofa, leaped to her feet when we came in, quickly reshuffled her clothes, and left without even acknowledging our presence.

Gigi and I helped ourselves to strong, stale coffee from a stained pot on a wobbly stand next to the door. Then she went over to the far side of the table and did something I've always wanted to do: she took her arm and simply swept the newspapers, coffee cups, doughnuts, everything, off the table onto the floor. She removed a handkerchief from her purse and dusted off one of the chairs and sat down and looked me in the eye, her back as straight as a string, and said, "I can't stay for long. I have to get to rehearsal, *toute suite*. And I have a performance tonight of *Cat*."

I took this to be lingo for Feydeau's *Cat Among the Pigeons,* and then I remembered about actors. That all they really care about is the show. They are people of such deep emotion and vulnerability and sensitivity that the only way they can handle the mess of their own lives is to hide inside someone else's.

They all probably cared about George, and whether he made it or not, but they cared more about the show, and worried, if George didn't make it, where their next show was going to be. To miss a show standing by his bedside would be unthinkable. "Oh, George wouldn't want that," they'd say. Not giving a rip whether George would want it or not.

Her answers were smooth, well rehearsed. She'd left the theater before the accident, and when I told her that Shelley had said she was there, sitting in the third row, she called Shelley a bald-faced liar. Said she was nowhere near the theater when the lighting batten fell, and when I asked her about Radio Shack, I thought she was going to punch me.

She squeezed out a few tears for Stephen Griffin and called him the most brilliant actor of his generation, a phrase that gets used at least four times on every "CBS Sunday Morning" about whoever the interview subject is: actor, musician, mechanic, author, doctor, cook, makes no difference. The mention of Buddy Butts drew only a distasteful reaction to the vulgarity of his name.

As to the missing twenty-five-million-dollar endowment fund, she stared at me blankly. "I have absolutely no idea what you're talking about," she said.

"Tell me about Molly Dolan from Waterbury, Connecticut," I said, expecting some reaction to my knowledge of her true identity and getting none.

"If you're expecting me to be surprised, or impressed, that you know my real name, don't waste your breath. My identity is no secret, and I'll tell you about Molly—me.

"My father worked for American Brass and when they went out of business he went to work for Uniroyal and when they went out of business he went to work for Scoville and by the time they went out of business, the town had died and he did, too. My mother is a simple, lovely, Irish lady who goes to mass every day and would not leave her home or friends for anything in spite of my begging her to move out here with me or at least to let me buy her a place in a nicer part of town. As for me, I was discovered in a beauty pageant when I was fifteen and I grabbed that brass ring for dear life. It happened to be a ring a rich, older man was wearing and you can criticize advancement through the casting couch all you want but it started working for me that afternoon on his settee that had such a thick coating of old semen on it, it was like lying on a sofa covered with cellophane, and it's worked for me ever since. I am completely the product of my own imagination. Now, does that answer your question?"

I grinned over at her. "That was great," I said.

"Thank you. Now, if you don't have any more questions, I really must be on my way."

"Just a couple more things. Tell me about Samuel Vaile."

"That is none of your business," she informed me.

"As a matter of fact, Gigi, it is my business," I told her. "If you'd rather wait to be subpoenaed, that's fine."

At least that threw her off balance a little. Not much, though. She was such a pro. Face it, anyone who could sleep with Cyrus Vaile on a regular basis would have to be the Sarah Bernhardt of her generation. Talk about acting with a strong stomach.

"Samuel has always been one of my greatest patrons. We fell in love the moment we met."

"Did Cyrus know?"

"*Absolutment pas.* That wouldn't have been good for anyone."

"Does Samuel's wife know?"

"*Je ne sais pas de deux,*" Gigi said. "She's not on our schedule when we're together." She said it like "shed–jewel."

The doctor's decided to keep me under observation for a few more days," Elias said, looking disgruntled and discouraged. "But"—he pretended to perk up—"Shelley has brought this little angel to keep me company."

Rose Marie, Shelley's daughter, sat on the edge of the bed next to her mother and had a doll cradled in her arms. She was rocking it and singing a little song.

"Isn't that crummy that he has to stay?" Shelley said. "I was looking forward to getting him back to George's and taking care of him."

Right, I thought. Right on top of the twenty-five million in gold bullion. I was sure she knew it was there.

She had hitched up her skirt and crossed her legs as though she were a secretary on the stand in a Perry Mason movie. Whenever I looked at her, all I saw was brown—skirt, blouse, stockings, shoes, Neapolitan olive skin. Even her lipstick was the color of dirt. Her brown hair waved along her shoulders and her brown eyes were as sly and quick as a ferret's. But, hey, I told myself, remember what Richard said: "Just because you don't like her doesn't mean she's guilty." She was guilty and I knew it, and it didn't matter if I liked her or not.

"Shelley," I said, "do you know a young man, an Army supply sergeant, named Buddy Butts?"

She wrinkled her nose. "Buddy Butts. Ick."

"Butthead, butthead, butthead," chanted the child. "What a icky name."

"Do you know him?" I repeated, ignoring Rose Marie.

"May I have some aspirin, please?" Elias asked plaintively.

Suddenly the door burst open and my mother blasted into the room like some kind of wild-eyed Storm Trooper empress. She had on a gray chiffon day dress, pearls, and white gloves.

"What in the—" she began to proclaim, her voice loud and commandeering, and we all could finish the sentence if we wanted to, but the only thing I could think of to do was slap my hand over her mouth and spin her around and power her right back out into the hall.

I don't know where I got the nerve to do it, but I did.

And she was just as floored as I was. Once I'd removed my hand, we simply stared at each other, aghast, for a moment or two.

"I'm so sorry," I finally said. "But don't say a word. Please."

Mother brushed her hand down her front, straightening her bibs and tucks and gathering her dignity. She never took her eyes off mine, and after a moment or two they stopped shooting death rays. But I could tell her feathers were ruffled in a major way. "May I ask a question or two?" she said.

"Yes. Let's get a cup of coffee."

I set off back down the corridor to the doctors' lounge.

"Oh, heavens, let's not go in there," Mother said. "It's so dreary. We'll just go to the directors' private dining room."

Mother was on the board of Christ and St. Luke's, so she didn't have to use the doctors' lounge, and we certainly didn't have to descend to that horror of horrors, the subterranean cave they called a cafeteria, which had bug zapper lights on the walls. I swear to God, it did. I never asked why.

Once we'd filled our green- and gold-trimmed white bone china cups and sat down in brown leather club chairs by sparkling Palladian windows, I apologized. "I hope I didn't hurt you."

"No, you did not. But you certainly could have, grabbing me like that." The feathers were all still pretty much at right angles. "I'm an old woman."

"I'm really sorry," I said. "Are you all right?"

"Of course I am, I'm perfectly fine. But please tell me what's going on."

"How did you know Elias was here?"

"Well, I didn't exactly, until I put two and two together. Did a little detective work of my own." Her cornflower-blue eyes started to twinkle. Oh, dear. Snoop Sisters on the loose. "I got this sorrowful call from him at about five-thirty this morning. He didn't tell me that he was in the hospital but he sounded so sad and just wanted to talk and talk, and that's so unlike him, and then about nine o'clock the head of the hospital called and said someone who looked just like Elias, but with some sort of insane name, was here with a broken leg. And you had said he was doing some sort of undercover work for you."

"Ah," I said, and nodded my head; so much for confidentiality.

"Well, I was on my way to Aunt Nancy's linen shower for Lulu anyway, and just thought I'd stick my head in. Incidentally, what are you wearing this evening?"

"This evening?" I stared at her blankly.

"Lilly," Mother said incredulously, "where are you these days? You are off in some other world. Don't tell me you've forgotten about our dinner tonight for the Westminsters? They arrive this afternoon."

"Of course I haven't forgotten," I said defensively. "I just can't remember what I'm wearing."

The truth is, I'd forgotten completely. It was wedding week. Every noon and night was some affair more dazzling than the one before. And even though I'd probably never admit it, if she hadn't said something, I wouldn't have forgotten the party but I probably would have completely forgotten to pick up my dress.

Mother was off and running. "I just don't understand why you can't participate in some of these wedding activities, Lilly. Like this lovely luncheon today. Lulu is your goddaughter, not mine, and it's so transparent that you're being a bad sport because she's getting married and you're not. Aunt Nancy's shower is going to be perfectly lovely and I think you should stop in for at least a couple of minutes."

"I'll try," I lied, biting my tongue not to say something I'd be sorry for. "Let me be perfectly clear about something, Mother." I took a deep breath. "I am not jealous that Lulu is getting married. I've had lots of opportunities, just never to the right person."

"And now you have the right person, and he's not asking?" Her voice was suddenly filled with gentleness and understanding.

"Something like that," I said. I could feel my eyes burning and I willed the tears not to come.

I hated and loved it equally when Mother was tender, because her strength was mine, and mine hers. The same with weakness. So how could I be strong if she wouldn't be? Sometimes I felt we could not be linked more closely if we were twins.

"Don't be nice to me about this, Mother," I finally warned her. "I don't want to think about it."

"May I make one small suggestion?" she asked, not bothering to wait for an answer. "I think if you tried being a little nicer to him. You're always running off—look at the way you left practically in the middle of communion on Sunday. And you're too bossy. You'll never be able to keep a man if you're always telling him what to do. Let some of these things be his ideas. I truly think, my darling, if you seriously want to get a husband, especially a big catch like Richard, you need to change your career, do something a little more feminine."

I looked at her and shook my head. Answering simply wasn't worth it, especially the part about "you'll never be able to keep a man if you're always telling him what to do." It was not worth it to point out to her that she controlled and manipulated and choreographed every breath my father took outside his office, but it was all sub rosa, behind the scenes, backstage marionette stuff. I didn't point it out, because it wasn't her fault. Women of her generation were too vulnerable to deal with their men head on. They had no fallback position because, if the men left, they could find themselves high-ended and abandoned like old wagons out there on the Oregon Trail.

On the other hand, with women like my mother, who are as tough as old boiled owls, I think it probably crossed all our minds a hundred times that even if we were to take her out there on the range and tie her to a stake and cover her with honey, the ants would die and she'd beat us back to the ranch house and fill all our butts with buckshot.

"Don't worry, my precious. It'll all work out. It's all up to you."

She patted my hand and gathered her gear together. "And who's that floozy sitting on your brother's bed? She looks as cheap as they come."

"She is," I said. "Smart and cheap. You'll grow to love her one day, Mother. I think Elias is going to ask her to marry him."

"Don't be ridiculous."

There. Now we both had something to chew on.

'm on my way to the bank," I said to Linda from my car phone. "Anything big going on?"

"Remember that Countess Louisa de Rochefoucauld?"

"Yes," I said, recalling the three dead Burgundian vintners.

"She just called again and wants to know when you'll be available. What should I tell her?"

I thought about it carefully. "Tell her next week," I finally said, feeling a small burn on my heart, as though someone had touched it with the tip of a cigarette.

"The Cody Gateway starts on Sunday."

"Tell her next week, Linda," I ordered.

"Yes, ma'am," I heard her answer as I slammed the phone nose first into its cradle.

Mother's words had stung deeply—hit an old nerve I supposed would smart for my whole life like an undone root canal: I was never going to get a husband because I would never be willing to pay the price. I loved my life, my career, too much to give it up, and no man in his right mind wanted his wife making her living the way I did. An adrenaline addict who preferred crime scenes and stakeouts and morgues to country club dinner dances and gardening and Gucci. Straight whisky and expensive champagne to spritzers and Chardonnay. Red meat to sushi, and shotguns to golf clubs. Who the hell would want a woman like that? I thought, as tears streamed down my face. Who the hell was I kidding that Richard Jerome would propose to me? Better to spend my life in occasional affairs with men like him and John Taylor than to claw up those stupid little-girl white-dress dreams.

Elias and I would die of old age on the Circle B—never married, no heirs. Just each other and our dogs and our money and our liquor-soaked lies. Christian's children would cash in, big time.

No matter that at the start Richard and I had both claimed we had no interest in long-term, serious relationships. I could no longer hold up my end of that bargain and I had to end it. It wasn't fun anymore. The futility was killing me—I had to get back to my own reality.

What better way, I told myself, to change my perspective than to spend a couple of weeks sleuthing around three or four lovely châteaux in Burgundy in June?

"We'll go to France and find a count," I said to Baby, who barked. She had such a great attitude. I decided not to think about General John Taylor and the heyday of our youth. I think I read somewhere the other day that all the B-52s had been grounded, their years of proud service complete. Their day was done, and now John himself was no doubt getting ready to retire. The thought of golf on a regular basis made my skin crawl.

I blotted my cheeks and put on some lipstick at a stop light, and moments later pulled up in front of the old granite and marble Roundup National Bank, where my father's secretary met me at the front door with a packet containing copies of the checks and the signature cards on the accounts of George Wrightsman, Winston McMorris, Shelley Pirelli, and the Roundup Repertory Company. Then I swung by the First National Bank, which, as a courtesy to my father, had agreed to provide copies of the signature cards for the accounts of Cyrus Vaile, Gigi Dorrance-Downs, and Samuel Vaile.

With this crucial information tucked safely into my purse, I went to one of the locations where I always get some of my best thinking done: the ladies' bar at the Roundup Country Club, because there's nothing like a country club bar, or the lobby of a great hotel, for privacy. I took a window table and ordered a Bloody Mary and a club sandwich, and waved hello to a few of the ladies playing their regular Tuesday morning bridge.

As I waited for what seemed forever for the waiter to return with my drink, my heart pounded so hard, I was sure they all heard it, and once he'd departed back to the morning paper behind the bar, I pulled out all the cards and studied the signatures carefully through my magnifying glass.

My first piece of solid evidence stared back up at me. All of Cyrus Vaile's signatures at the Roundup National Bank, for the theater's accounts, were forgeries. And unless I was losing my powers of observation, I was pretty sure that my guess as to whose hand it was would be confirmed by expert examination.

At least we had bank fraud. It was a start.

I sat back and looked out at the busy golf course and laid all the pieces out. All the ones that had been played already, and all the ones I would play now.

Then I went into the powder room and called Elias. Shelley had gone to her office, so he was alone for a few minutes and we could talk. And then I called Jack Lewis and briefed him. He, of course, wanted to execute the warrant right away.

"Let's let things develop just a little more, all right?" I said. "We'll end up with hard, convictable evidence if we just stay cool. Besides, just because we have a forger doesn't mean we have a killer."

"If we end up with any more murders, Bennett," he said, "I'll hold you personally responsible."

"We won't. But you've got to make sure those tails stay in place," I said. "Do not let her out of your sight. And do not leave George Wrightsman alone for one second. And find Buddy Butts."

"Done," Jack said, and hung up.

After lunch, I drove to Belle, our loveliest shop, for the final fittings on all my wedding party clothes. One thing I've learned after giving away thousands of dollars' worth of one-size-too-small designer clothes is: Never buy clothes or go for a fitting on an empty stomach or when you're feeling especially thin.

When I moved back from Santa Bianca, I put my nose up in the air about the level of fashion available in Roundup. But that was before I'd been back into Belle, where my mother had always done all her shopping. Or maybe my change in attitude had more to do with my maturing change in taste. When I left Roundup, it was as a girl who thought her mother's old Chanel luncheon suits were stupid, and now that I'd returned twenty years later as a woman, I thought they were terrific, except that by the time I started liking them Chanel had stopped making them.

Belle was located downtown in a four-story brownstone, and inside it was all gray velvet walls and drapes and gold rope trim and crystal chandeliers and curving staircases that swept from one floor to another, and enormous dressing rooms and, unfortunately, mirrors angled so you could see your entire body.

There hadn't been many events in Wyoming like this upcoming wedding celebration, at which a lovely young woman, girl really—Lulu is just twenty—will marry an older, and important, German baron who is related to lots of important European royals who all want to come to the American West and see what we Westerners are really like. See if we're going to spit on the floor and whoop and holler and draw down on a rustler here and there. And when the elegant French saleswoman, Miss Phillips, and her two assistants came into the dressing room with the rack of my clothes and the list of what went with what on which day, I was impressed.

I'd never done anything before when everything I was going to wear every second for five days—starting today with my parents' small dinner for the Duke and Duchess of Westminster, through the wedding Saturday afternoon—was completely planned and perfected in advance.

"Now," Miss Phillips said. She had pale skin and dark red lipstick and wore a plain black Chanel suit. "For your parents' garden dinner for the duke and duchess this evening, here is the copper organza." She held it out. "You'll wear your large pearl earrings and pearl necklace with it. The shoes are here." She pointed with a short red nail. "Box A—Tuesday. Your gown for the Thatchers' dinner dance tomorrow night is here."

We oohed and aahed as she let the slinky black jersey flow across her arm like black water. I'd never owned a more beautiful dress.

"Don't forget," she reminded me in an exquisite Parisian accent that Gigi Dorrance-Downs would kill for, "your grandmother's diamond earrings and brooch with this. Very simple and elegant. For Thursday's square dance, you'll wear your buckskin skirt and starched white bib blouse. Is that correct?"

"Right," I said, trying to remember whether or not I'd given the blouse to Celestina to wash and iron. All these parties and murders had jumbled together in my mind, and I could keep the murders straight, but not the parties.

"Taupe suit for Friday's bridal luncheon. Shoes are here, standard Chanel pumps. Black silk column for the rehearsal dinner Friday night at the baron's. Put on every pearl you own. You'll wear your hot pink linen for the luncheon Saturday at the club. Have you had it cleaned?"

"I think so." I was dazzled by the display.

"And finally the navy chiffon for the wedding with your grandmother's emeralds. We'll have everything delivered in the next hour." She smiled at me. "This will be the most beautiful wedding in the history of Roundup," she said. "Until you decide to marry, of course."

"Don't hold your breath," I told her.

I had been so carried away with how exciting it all was and how pretty I was going to look in all my new things that I had forgotten for a moment I was going to leave Richard on Sunday morning. That Baby and I were going to climb into Christian's fancy new Gulfstream 5 and fly nonstop to Nice.

I went to the beauty salon for a manicure.

I love to get my nails done, probably because it's time spent brainlessly and I can't talk on the phone. I love the looks on people's faces when I say, "Oh, I can't do that because I have to get my nails done." And they're thinking: She is a complete idiot. She's going to miss this or that because she has a *manicure?* I don't care. My best friends and I are all there at the same time and that's the way it goes.

Mary Paul "Polly" MacArthur and Pitty-Pat Palmer (Texas) and Sparky Kendall, all of whom I turn to for guidance on domestic issues, were already there. Polly and Pitty-Pat were finished, just hanging around talking while their nails dried, and Sparky had one hand soaking in deep cream and the other extended across one of the manicure tables. They were my wedding experts, since they'd all been married before, several times.

"How is it going?" they all asked at the same time.

"Well, aside from the fact that my mother calls me every fifteen seconds to consult me about the seating for tonight and at the square dance, and believe me," I laughed, "when we get to the actual occasion, the seating will have nothing to do with my suggestions—"

"Well, that's a given with mothers," Pitty-Pat drawled. From all she'd told us, her mother made mine look like Little Bo-Peep.

"—and to make sure that all the out-of-town guests and dignitaries have got the right rooms at the Grand or are staying with the right people, it's all great." I sat down, gratefully disengaging my brain. "Most of the guests arrive tomorrow in time for the Thatchers' party."

"I think it's so exciting that all these royals are coming to Wyoming," Pitty-Pat said. "I hope that bachelor, Marquis whatever his name is"—she said it like "Marcus"—"is good-looking. I'm needing a new husband about now. I have all my clothes lined up."

"What did you decide to serve on Friday for the luncheon?" Sparky asked. Her blond hair was parted in the middle and held back with tortoiseshell combs. She was the perfect Peck & Peck woman.

"Well," I said, "I'm doing all the tables in pink and white, with lots of roses and satin ribbons and ivy curled all over the place."

They all smiled and nodded.

"Pretty," said Pitty-Pat.

"For cocktails, we'll have margaritas and little sliced quesadillas, and then for lunch I'm serving a Mexican grilled chicken salad, with black beans, jalapeños, cheese, chopped lettuce, and cilantro and Celestina's salsa. And banana coconut cream pie for dessert. What do you think?" I grinned around at them; my mouth was watering. "Doesn't it sound fabulous?"

"Good God," said Sparky. "You can't serve that."

"Why not?"

"All these little teeny, size-two bridesmaids? And the bride? You'll have them blown up like balloons from all the salt." She frowned at me like I should be shot. "No one will be able to fit into their clothes." She practically was yelling. "Have you gone crazy?"

I started to laugh. Polly and Pitty-Pat rolled their eyes.

"Well," I said, "what would you serve?"

"There's only one thing to serve at a summertime bridal luncheon," Sparky decreed. "Chicken à la king in patty shells, fresh asparagus, angel food cake, and iced tea. Although, knowing you, you'll probably want to offer wine, too."

"Probably," I said.

"For-*get* the margaritas," Sparky ordered.

The WGB Electronics shop was just a little, shabby hole in the wall on a busy downtown street, not the sort of place anyone would go to buy a new computer or upgrade anything fancy. It was little known, patronized primarily by surveillance hackers, legitimate private investigators, and occasional city or state detectives when they could pry the money out of their departments for the most advanced gear.

The man who ran it was in his late twenties or early thirties and was fat and dirty and smoked cigarillos. Long, thin, oily hair lay plastered across his scalp and reached almost to his shoulders. He also had a beard, which I'm sure still carried the remains of his first college drinking binge. He wore a long-sleeved, collarless shirt, buttoned to the neck, and a dark velour vest that had Velcro closings. He was a total nerd. Just a giant brain sitting surrounded by heaps of gadgets.

We had a long conversation about bombs, and Semtex, and tiny radio-controlled cars and a variety of detonating devices from electronic joysticks to walkie-talkies to timers to garage door openers, and then I headed back to the Fort, turning the Beach Boys up so loud, thought was not possible.

Buck was in his booth at the saloon talking on the phone. He already had a shot waiting for me. I tossed it off while he talked.

"All right, Bob," he was saying. "It's a deal. We'll look forward to seeing you after Labor Day. Righto." He hung up and sipped his whisky. "Redford." Buck's white teeth twinkled through his beard. "Shooting a big new Western here this fall. My business has doubled since Old Tucson burned down." He took another sip and drew his breath in through his teeth as the liquor made its familiar way down his tubes. "You're lookin' good, girl. You going to that deal for the duke and duchess?"

"Yup," I said. "Sure am. You?"

"Hell, no."

About five-thirty, as the sun laid long carpets of warmth across the white-painted wood of my bathroom floor, I had just climbed into the tub and sunk beneath a cloud of rosemary-balsam bubbles, when I heard the helicopter settle in the meadow. Five minutes later, Richard strode into the bathroom with glasses of champagne.

"How was your day?" He handed me a flute and gave me a sweet, quick kiss before sitting down at the end of the tub and crossing his long legs. I didn't care a bit that he was getting mud and manure all over my bathroom floor. Baby jumped into his lap.

What in the hell do you think you're doing? I said to myself. You really think you're going to run off and leave this guy? It sure was a lot easier to do in theory than fact. All I had to do was look at him and I melted. I ran the hot water to plump the bubbles back up, and a few minutes later, when he'd gotten out of the shower and I was sitting at my dressing table, swathed in a pink silk robe, we looked at each other in the mirror and knew we'd be late for the ride into town with Christian and Mimi. I followed him into the bedroom, and lay on the sun-drenched white damask coverlet, welcoming him back into me as though he'd been gone for a hundred years. Resolve can be such a tricky, elusive thing.

Christian and Mimi called three times to ask what in the world we were doing, but we finally floated our way on board the chopper and sailed through the late evening light toward the mountains, settling as though on a feather in the park in front of my parents' big house in Roundup.

The circular driveway was filled with limousines, and the rosebushes that climbed up the brick columns and branched out along the top of the estate's surrounding wall had burst into thousands of bright red blooms. At the main gate the Union Jack, which had replaced the Wyoming colors for the evening, snapped in the wind alongside Old Glory.

Flowers of every shape and color filled the beds on either side of the open front door, and all the living-room doors to the rear terrace stood wide open. The military standards and flags emblazoned with the family's various brands, which encircled the grand room from the upper-level gallery, fluttered in the breeze.

"Thank God you're here," my father said, kissing my cheek and shaking Richard's hand. "We have all these goddamn horsy types to-night. There's no one to talk to." He was decked out in his white ducks, white bucks, and navy blazer. "Come on." He took Richard's arm. "I'll get you a drink."

I went over and greeted Lulu and Harry, who also had on white ducks. Except his navy blazer had his own royal family crest embroidered on the breast pocket—most of us have to settle for Ralph Lauren's. He looked trim and handsome and relaxed.

"Aunt Lilly," Lulu said. I loved that she called me Aunt, even though I was her godmother. Her brown hair was full and swept back, caught by diamond combs. "I cannot thank you enough for all you're doing, everything is like a fairy tale."

"I'm so glad, but the truth is, my mother is doing virtually every-thing. I'm just along for the ride. Speaking of which," I said to Harry, "why did my father say it's all the horse crowd here tonight? I didn't know you were interested in horses."

"Me? Heavens, no. But you know the Westminsters—they would have ridden horses into the party if your mother had let them."

I looked over to where the duke and duchess stood, surrounded by friends and admirers, and they looked the way they always did, a little rumpled. She had on a saggy old bright blue bouclé knit suit, a little sprung out in the seat, with a white silk blouse tied in a long bow at her throat and low-heeled, bone-colored shoes. Her shoulder-length gray-blond hair was dry and disheveled and she wore no makeup on her ruddy skin. A platinum brooch with pavé diamonds and sapphires that would probably cost a million dollars to replace was pinned haphazardly to her jacket.

The balding duke, whose pate was sunburned and peeling, had on white ducks, an old navy blazer, a club tie, white eyelashes, and a bright red nose.

They were both drinking martinis from stemmed glasses.

"Philadelphia," I said, once we'd kissed hello (that was her name: Philadelphia), "welcome back to Roundup."

"Oh, my dear, I'm so glad to see you," she trilled in her perfect English. "Mr. St. John here was just telling us about your hunt. We're going to ride with him tomorrow."

"Our hunt?" I said, giving old Malcolm St. John the once-over.

He is an aging Main Line transplant, the president of the country club, and always, excuse-my-French, shit-faced.

Furthermore, what is loosely referred to as The Hunt out here in Wyoming means a bunch of homesick Easterners and northern Virginians getting all done up in their Pinks, which smell to high heaven of mothballs, climbing onto their oversized hunters, and chasing coyotes across the prairies. It's never a question of the fox outwitting the hounds or dodging around corners, or hiding on the mossy far side of a charming rock wall. No, because there aren't any trees or walls. It's just flat nothing. So The Hunt is actually an endurance race: whoever can run farthest, fastest, straightest, wins. And it's always the coyote.

I began to say more but then realized that Franny Sullivan, Cyrus's erstwhile Nurse Kissy, was standing at Malcolm St. John's arm, and before I could open my mouth, she extended her hand and said, "Good evening, I'm Francesca Frescobaldi."

"Francesca Frescobaldi?" I repeated, wanting to tell Richard to kindly close his mouth and take his eyes off her dewy lips.

"Yes," Malcolm said. "She's an old classmate of my daughter's from

Bryn Mawr, just visiting for a day or two, and your mother kindly consented to my bringing her along."

First of all, Malcolm St. John has no daughter and nobody—and I mean, nobody—who looks as glamorous as Franny Sullivan has ever attended Bryn Mawr.

"Really?" I said. "I'm pleased to meet you, Miss Frescobaldi."

It wasn't all horse people, fortunately. Richard and I wandered around and spoke to a number of good friends, including Andy Beckett and his Barbie doll, whom I liked more every time I met her.

Just before dinner I went to the powder room, and on my way back I found Franny waiting for me in the hall. The volume of her Opium perfume almost knocked me out.

"Thanks for not giving me away. I really appreciate it."

"No problem," I said. "We all need to make a living, but I really don't envy you yours, Franny. I mean, Malcolm St. John?"

"It's not so bad." She shrugged. "Pays my tuition, and I only have a year to go. But listen, I remembered something and wanted to tell you. One time, George Wrightsman and Cyrus were having a terrible fight and I heard George say he would see Cyrus dead before he'd let him sell the air rights."

"Anything else you can recall?" I asked.

"No. Just that."

Mother appeared.

"This is the most beautiful party, Mrs. Bennett," Franny said smoothly. "Thank you so much for including me at the last minute." And then she stepped back out onto the terrace and rejoined her blithering escort.

"Do you really think she went to school with his daughter?" Mother asked.

"She didn't," I said. "She's a call girl."

"I beg your pardon?"

"You know, a prostitute. A hooker."

Mother's eyes twinkled. "Really? I've never met one before." And for the rest of the evening I could see her chatting up Franny Sullivan every chance she got.

The party was lovely, not only because the duke and duchess were always such delightful guests and added such a special shine, but also because Lulu and Harry were so totally happy. So beautiful. So handsome. So enthralled with each other. Sort of like Richard and me. Except that we weren't getting married on Saturday, and they were, and the whole thing just made me mad all over again.

WEDNESDAY MORNING

T he next morning, when I got to the office, Dwight was in my chair. Leaning back with his feet on my desk talking on my phone.

"Okay, boss is here," he said into the receiver as he jumped to his feet. "Gotta go."

"Well," I said, "isn't this a treat?"

"Sorry, Marshal. Linda said I could use your phone." He ran his hand across the top of his head, ruffling his short hair. I swear to God, he looked so good in his deputy's uniform, he could be the poster boy for the U. S. Marshal Service.

I started to say something, but Linda whistled in and saved me from indiscretion.

"Look at these," she was saying. "I've never seen anything so beautiful. I tell you, that Richard Jerome is the most wonderful man I've ever known. You are some kind of lucky girl."

"You need a younger man, in my opinion," Dwight said.

Two dozen long-stemmed red roses in a crystal vase, and Linda was right, they were absolutely splendid.

"What does the card say?" She handed me the small envelope.

All I could think as I tore the envelope open was: My life is so fucked up. I can't stick to a single hard-line decision when it comes to that man. Richard Jerome has got me hog-tied. I am doomed.

Darling Lilly [the note read], *I'll not make the same mistake by letting you go twice. See you next week.*
John

Oh, sweet Jesus.

"So?" Linda said. "Did he propose?"

"Not exactly," I said. "Right flowers. Wrong guy. Anything new going on around here?" I pointedly changed the subject.

"Well, I've just had a call from your brother." Linda would no longer say his name, she was so mad and hurt. "He said Gigi Dorrance-Downs was storming around the hospital, completely hysterical, something about commandos breaking in and searching her house. She is such a prima donna."

"What do you mean, 'searching her house'?" I could feel my blood pressure rising. That goddamn Lewis, he could not control himself for one second. He had the imagination of a slug.

"I don't know," Linda answered. "That's all she said. All they probably found were truffles, Petit Beurres, and flimsy underwire bras."

"Get Chief Lewis," I said, and moments later Linda had tracked him down at the hospital and had us connected.

"How's George?"

"Uh," he said. "The doctor's not saying much. At least if the guy kicks, we still have the bank fraud."

"Gee, Jack," I said, not bothering to point out that what we had was *possible* bank fraud. "Some guys are all heart. I understand you decided to search Gigi's house. I thought we agreed you'd hold off."

"Yeah, well, *you* agreed we'd hold off," he griped defensively. "My job is to arrest criminals. Not sit around at some rich–girl tea party with my finger in my ear waiting for them to spill."

"So tell me what you found," I said sarcastically. "Any plastique? Or timing devices? Poison mushrooms? Books on bomb making? Maybe you can arrest her as a long-sought Weatherman fugitive."

"I don't think you're funny, Bennett."

"So tell me what you found."

"Nothing much."

"Really. Now isn't that a surprise." I hate short-term thinkers.

"Except"—Jack drew it out—"some funny-looking six-foot-tall weeds and scary-looking mushrooms and a Radio Shack receipt for a radio-controlled car."

"No shit."

"We caught up with her here at the hospital a few minutes ago and are just about to take her into custody. Three charges of murder one, and three of attempted homicide."

"Want me to help out?" Dwight asked after I'd hung up. "I don't have any shootouts till noon."

I shook my head. The scent of the roses filled the room. "No, thanks. There's nothing you can do."

"Knock, knock," a little-girl voice called tentatively from the doorway. It was Shelley Pirelli.

She ambled across the room like Mae West, never taking her eyes off Dwight's for one second. "I just thought I'd drop in and say congratulations."

"Congratulations?" I asked, thinking I'd like to boot her ass back to North Denver, or wherever it was she came from. "For what?"

"For catching the murderer. Aren't you the one who told the police to arrest Gigi? Who gave them all the evidence?"

I had to think about all this for a second, which fortunately didn't seem to bother Shelley a bit, occupied as she was with Dwight's belt buckle and holstered side arm. "Shelley," I said, "who told you that Gigi'd been arrested?"

"No one. But I know it's just a matter of time."

"How do you know?"

"Because she has a greenhouse and that's where they're going to find all the foxglove and the mushrooms. She knew about George's special tamale stash, and I'll bet if they hurry they'll find all the bomb stuff at Winston's. They've been in cahoots for ages." She sat down and ran her finger across the top of a sugar doughnut and then licked it slowly off her finger, looking very pleased with herself.

And here's what interested me: Dwight just studied her as though she were a laboratory specimen. I would have thought he'd be on his knees by now. Maybe he did learn something after all back there at the academy.

"In any event"—she opened her purse and removed an envelope— "we had an emergency Executive Committee meeting last night, and the committee's unanimous vote of thanks for your services has been entered into the minutes, and they asked me to deliver this check and to say the services have been successfully completed and they hope you'll stay on the board."

"Let me get this straight. There was an Executive Committee meeting last night?"

"Un-huh," she answered, her finger back in her mouth and her eyes on Dwight's.

"As I recall, the Executive Committee is made up of George, Bradford Lake, Gigi, Andy Beckett, and the late Mr. Vaile. Is that correct?"

Shelley nodded, looking a little taken aback at my abruptness.

"Now, unless things have changed in the last thirty seconds, George is still in the hospital, Cyrus is still dead, and last night Gigi was onstage in a show Bradford was directing. Did you and Andy by any chance have this meeting at your house in your bed?"

"So what if we did?" She was smart. She moved quickly into an offensive position, showing no surprise at my knowing about her and Andy. "He's the president pro tem."

"Let me tell you something, Shelley," I said quietly. "Women like you are a dime a dozen. You are cheap through and through. I see your hand in every aspect of this ridiculous, deadly game and I'm watching every move you make and pretty soon I'll have all the goods I need." I pushed the envelope back across the desk to her. "So why don't you just keep the check—I'm doing the work pro bono anyway—and start making plans about who's going to look after your little spoiled brat for the rest of *her* life, because you'll be spending the rest of *yours* behind bars.

"Oh," I said. "One more thing. FYI: I spent the evening with Andy Beckett, you didn't. You'd better look out, you're starting to make mistakes."

Old, tried-and-true tactic: people, whether they're guilty or not, cannot withstand having their children brought into a situation. It's an easy, and foolproof way to gain the offensive.

"I had nothing to do with any of this." Shelley had jumped to her feet. "I almost burned to death trying to save your life." Tears flooded her eyes and began to film across her cheeks.

"In a nickel-and-dime fire I suspect you started."

"Cary Scott and Vanderbilt started it. I saw them."

"I don't know exactly how you've done all this, Shelley, but I know it hasn't been alone. Someone besides Buddy Butts is your accomplice. Why don't you just tell me now, and save everyone a lot of time and money and maybe another life or two? Who is it? Winston? Bradford? Cary Scott?"

"It's not me," she cried, clutching her purse. "It's not me. I'd never even heard of Buddy Butts until yesterday." Mascara ran down her face in long black lines.

"Who is it, then?" I said.

"It's Gigi and Winston. I can prove it. They've been plotting together all along, because the Japanese air rights offer expires on Friday at noon and so they know they have to hurry because George isn't going to invite either one of them back for next season. They're the ones who have the money."

"What money?" I said.

"You know, the missing twenty-five million."

"You know about that?" I said. "You told me the other day you didn't."

"Well, I was lying, because I didn't want to let on in front of Bertram. But everyone knows it's missing. George and Winston and Cyrus can sign on all the accounts, and everyone knows that Cyrus's signature is actually Gigi's. She has his power of attorney for everything."

"Who else is involved?"

"Bertram Chiswick. That's why I've been staying so close to him, to keep him away from George. I heard him and Winston talking about the real estate deal. And he's always hanging up the phone just when I walk into his room."

Oh, brother.

CHAPTER

40

D wight," I said, once Shelley had sobbed her way into her car and headed it in the direction of Roundup, "I would have thought you'd be doing anything you could to help Miss Pirelli. She certainly would have done anything she could to help you."

"She looks kind of dirty to me," he said. "I like my women clean, Marshal. Like you."

"Well, I've got my hands full at the moment, honey, so all I can tell you is, take a number and get in line."

I called Paul Decker, Roundup's wildly flamboyant, ridiculously expensive, very successful criminal defense attorney, but his secretary told me he was already down at the courthouse trying to arrange bail for Miss Dorrance-Downs, so I went across the street and had a quick cup of coffee and a doughnut with Buck to clear my mind. Of course, he had coffee, a doughnut, and a shot.

"I don't like it when my mind's clear," he told me. "Too many bad things going on in there. Where's Elias, anyhow? He hasn't been by for days."

"He's doing a job for me, but I think he'll be back soon."

Shelley had tipped her hand one time too many. A time line. A deadline. Friday noon. She'd been trying to show off for Dwight and had inadvertently dropped a plum. We now had a schedule.

This whole deal of arresting Gigi stank to high heaven. Someone had obviously planted evidence in her greenhouse, because it hadn't been there when I searched it on Saturday, but I didn't think Shelley had been gone from the hospital or her office long enough to get out to Gigi's and back.

I rolled the strong black coffee around in my mug, and while Buck hammered out another movie deal, I recalled something Bradford Lake had said: that he'd been in rehearsal for *Uncle Vanya* in the black box, the small empty-space theater in the administration building across the street from the Vaile main stage. Before I drew my circle any tighter, I wanted to see exactly what that meant.

I waved good-bye to my cousin, but he was deep in the slash-and-burn aspect of his negotiation and didn't even notice I was gone.

Morning rush hour was long over, but even so, downtown traffic was still heavy, so I pulled two wheels up on the sidewalk in front of the theater, flipped down my U. S. Marshal Service visor, and pushed through the front doors of the Rep's office building.

Even with the company's *patrón*, George Wrightsman, theoretically on his deathbed, the air was as charged as ever. Students—changing classes, rushing to rehearsals—shoved past me in the narrow corridor at the main entrance, but I was finally able to corral one and ask where the Olivier was.

"Right there." He pointed down the murky hall to a scarcely visible doorway. A sign, printed in white on a black card, stood on a stanchion before it: REHEARSAL IN PROGRESS—DO NOT DISTURB. "They won't be done until noon, though."

"Thanks," I said as he rushed off. I went to the door and shoved gently. It whispered open soundlessly and I slipped into the dark, pushed the padded door to behind me, and held my breath. A screen of black drapes blocked my view of the performance area, although I could hear a girl speaking. My eyes grew accustomed to the blackness after a moment or two and I stepped into the space.

On the far side of the room, the young woman stood alone in a single spotlight. A wide white ribbon held her sandy hair in a low pony tail that fell straight down her back. She wore a long khaki skirt and a white blouse with a lacy jabot, and her face looked freshly scrubbed. The stage was bare except for a ladder, an unvarnished kitchen table and chair, and an empty window frame suspended in space. She was doing the scene from *Our Town,* where Emily talks about having fallen in love with George, and having to let him go—because she has died—and she was incredible. The actress wasn't really a bit pretty, but she possessed that special dramatic gift—the transcendent power to immobilize—and I was so completely drawn in by her monologue, by her love and her pain, I forgot what I was doing there.

"Excuse me, Jane," Bradford Lake's lordly voice suddenly commanded from the darkness nearby on my right, interrupting and wrecking everything. "It seems we have a visitor." All the stage lights came to life, flattening and flooding and ripping away the magic. "What can we do for you, Miss Bennett?"

"I'm so sorry, Miss, uh, Jane," I said, humiliated and furious at Bradford Lake. What a cruel bastard he was. "I didn't mean to intrude. Several people have told me how superb your delivery of Emily's monologue is, and I thought I'd be able to sneak in here in time to see the whole thing and not disturb you. Please forgive me."

She rewarded me with a smile, and I hoped my sincere praise and quick cover-up would disarm Bradford.

"I think you've probably come in here to see just how dark it is during a rehearsal." He emerged from his inky corner dressed in a black turtleneck and black jeans, rendering only his face visible, like Banquo's ghost. "To see if I could sneak out undetected, run across the street and wait for the moment when George Wrightsman would be beneath the lighting batten, push the button, and dash back over with no one the wiser."

"You're a smart fellow, Mr. Lake," I said. "You're right. That's exactly why I'm here, and for the looks of it, it would be very simple for you to leave and return with no one the wiser."

"Simple? Yes. But did I? No." He clapped his hands at the small company of students. "That's all for today, kids," he said. "See you tomorrow."

Winston materialized next to me, and I had no idea if he'd just entered the room or had been there all along. He hovered alongside me, nervous, agitated, aggravating.

"I'm sorry," I said again to the actors as they began to shuffle around and pick up their backpacks. A couple of students were congratulating Jane on her performance. "I really didn't mean to wreck your rehearsal."

"You didn't." Bradford seemed cooled off. He pulled on a tweed sport coat, picked up a stack of loose-leaf books, and shoved them into a canvas bag. "I have to go and meet with the stage manager across the street. *Macbeth* opens tomorrow night, and with George temporarily out of commission, I've taken over. Is there anything I can do for you before I go?"

"George has taken a turn for the worse," I said. "He's developed a fever."

Winston studied me carefully, expressionless, but Bradford's prissy little eyebrows raised and his tight little mouth curved sinisterly. "Oh?"

"You don't seem surprised."

He looked at me directly. Shadows cut deeply across his face, making him look old and haggard, and his teeth caught the light like a row of chrome-plated spades in a hardware store. He emanated the faint, acrid odor of nervous sweat. "With the way George lives, I'm surprised he didn't develop a fever years ago. This is a man with what could be called a high-risk life."

I sensed this was my first glimpse of the real Bradford Lake. Not Julius Caesar, not Henry V, not Henry Higgins, and not Professor Harold Hill, but possibly someone who could be as vicious and ruthless and malevolent as Titus Andronicus. A man who took no prisoners, who fed the queen her slain sons baked in a pie. A man who would never realize his full potential as long as George Wrightsman was alive.

"How much do you know about the financial operations of the company?" I asked.

"Virtually nothing. I do not even carry my own checkbook. Aldo takes care of all that. So if your question is, can I read a balance sheet? The answer is no. Winston is the money man."

Someone had switched on all the work lights, and now I could see Bradford's eyes, and they were distant and distracted. Dark circles smudged beneath them and his color was terrible, as though he hadn't slept for weeks.

Winston was frowning at me and I suspected he somehow knew George's true condition and had decided to keep it to himself.

"Gigi Dorrance-Downs has been arrested," I informed both of them. "But she told me a few days ago, Bradford, that you have the most to gain by George's death. That you were Cyrus's and the board's heir apparent, and if that's the case, I'm just curious how much Cyrus discussed finances with you. He must have said something. I understand the air rights offer expires in less than forty-eight hours."

"Why can't you just leave it with Gigi?"

"Because there was more than one person involved."

"Let me be perfectly clear, Miss Bennett," Bradford snapped perniciously. "I have been with George Wrightsman for most of my life, ever since we were undergraduates at Yale. We have a very deep and true friendship, and we have always had disagreements, some personal, some business, some artistic. And there have been many times I've wanted to kill him. As a matter of fact, if you would let me in to see him right now, I would tell him that if he dies I'll kill him." Bradford's eyes and face reddened as though he were about to cry. "I love him. But if he dies, especially from this 'fever,' well, so be it. He'll have taken some better men down with him and he deserves it."

Bradford Lake picked up his satchel and left the room quickly. His performance was great, but he never answered my question about the money.

"Do you think Bradford is responsible?" Winston asked hopefully, the faithful old retainer wanting everybody to be happy.

"I'm not sure. The only thing I do feel certain about is that Gigi was not involved. I think Shelley Pirelli is, and you are as well, in some way."

"Me?" Winston looked stunned.

"You keep the books. You know the endowment account has been emptied. I haven't uncovered the whole trail yet. But I will."

"You're wrong," Winston said quietly. "I would never do such a thing."

"Are you and Shelley lovers?" I asked, and I could see it stopped him.

"Why do you ask?"

"Are you the father of her little girl?"

Winston shook his head, sadly, I thought. "No."

"Who is?"

"I'm not too sure. She just sort of appeared." He shouldered his backpack. "Do you need me for anything else? I'd better get back to work."

I shook my head and remained in the brightly lit black box, staring into a black corner at a pile of forgotten litter, shoving the pieces around with my mind.

Why did I believe Winston? Because I'd watched him with George and I could tell he really loved him—wanted to protect him. As opposed to Shelley, who observed those around her the way a cat does—distantly, analytically, arrogantly. I knew that Shelley was the ringleader, but unfortunately, she was also like a big raw egg yolk: very, very slippery. And slimy.

A minute or two later I followed Bradford and Winston, crossing the street and entering the Vaile, and I was surprised to see that the stage was not a Scottish moor and crumbling castle, but in the process of becoming an opulent, belle époque Parisian boudoir. As I stood in the dark in the back of the theater, two stagehands unrolled a Persian rug while two others stood by with a carved dolphin-based round table, which they placed and adjusted precisely in the middle of the rug. Another positioned a large vase of red roses in the middle of the table and a tall stand with a champagne bucket alongside. This looked like my kind of play.

There was virtually no sign of Monday's accident, and I realized that it had been no coincidence that it had happened on a Monday when the theater was dark. The show is everything.

41

We built a new main, downtown police station a few years ago, and a few days before it opened the city held a big benefit fund raiser for the Police Widows and Orphans Fund and had a dinner dance in the new jail facility on the roof. It cost one hundred dollars per person to attend the party, but for five hundred dollars patrons could spend the night in the spiffy, streamlined, gleaming stainless steel cells where the air still smelled like fresh mortar and paint. They dressed in the facility's brand-new, bright orange prison garb with the word PRISONER stenciled across the back, and received new fiber-fill pillows with clean fiber-paper pillowcases and pure polyester blankets from the requisitioning room, and they slept on the new rubber-coated, three-inch-thick mattresses, and had freshly brewed Colombian coffee and crisp, buttery croissants before they went home in the morning.

Once the new central station opened for business the next day, it probably took about fifteen minutes for the jazzy new jail to look and smell the way it did today, like every other big-city detention facility, with feces-smeared walls and urine- and vomit-puddled floors.

This was not a good spot for Gigi Dorrance-Downs, and I did not expect to find her in especially good shape, but human nature being what it is, I was happy to find I was wrong.

She and Paul Decker were ensconced in a small conference room, smoking cigarettes and sipping coffee. He had on ostrich-skin boots and so many turquoise and silver Indian rings, I was surprised he could pick up his hands. They had already finished processing her and the jumpsuit looked fabulous. A steady stream of uniforms, male and female, passed needlessly by the door and peered through the small, square, wire mesh window, trying to get a look at one of Roundup's most glamorous citizens. I asked her how she was doing.

"*Merveilleux, chérie.*" She smiled, tucking back an escaped tendril of red hair. "I've visited the jail before on a VIP tour, but this is a totally, what should I say, *je ne sais quoi,* a whole different research aspect. But Paul, here, is my knight in shining armor and he's promised to stay with me." With that she reached over and patted his hand and looked into his eyes, and I could see him melt like a snowball on a hot stove.

"If you can just keep that positive attitude for a couple of days," I told her, "you'll be able to star in a Brian de Palma film."

"*Pas de problème. Tout de tout.* Marie Antoinette experienced much greater hardships than this, and goodness, I don't think they're planning to guillotine me."

"I think you're right." I laughed, admiring her sangfroid. I knew that deep down she was undoubtedly scared to death, finding little solace in Susan Hayward's courageous Oscar-winning, you-can-kick-me, spit-on-me, have-your-way-with-me-but-you'll-never-make-me-cry performance in *I Want to Live* as she sucked it up and awaited her appointment in San Quentin's death house. "What's the situation?" I asked Wyoming's most illustrious attorney, who had been reduced to a drooling fool.

"At the moment"—he smiled and sat up a little straighter—"the charges being what they are, bail will be very tough, although I've gotten the arraignment scheduled for three o'clock today, so we'll see. Do you have anything useful to contribute?"

"Yes. The evidence was planted," I said, "and I can prove it. I was out there on Saturday and there was absolutely no foxglove in the greenhouse. It's big and impossible to miss. Also, I located the Radio Shack where someone in a big red wig, impersonating Gigi, bought the radio-controlled car used to rig the bomb."

"Unfortunately," Paul said, "Gigi says she has no alibi for Saturday afternoon. She was home alone."

"Is that really true?" I asked her.

She looked away.

"Let me put it this way, Gigi. Would you rather reveal the identity of your lover or have people believe you're spending time with an eighteen-year-old Army private named Buddy Butts, who has a serious complexion problem, drives around in a big-wheeled truck, and wears his Chicago Bulls baseball cap backward?"

"Mon Dieu," she giggled.

"Exactement." And once we'd settled the subject of Samuel Vaile, who, as it turns out, had returned shortly after I left—he'd gone to town on a champagne run—I asked her if there was an easy way to break into her house.

"No. Not at all."

"What if someone got into the garage?"

A startled look crossed her face.

"And your garage door opener was missing for a couple of days?" I said.

She nodded, her mouth hanging open. "How did you know?"

"That's what I do," I said. "Figure this stuff out. I'll see you guys later."

"Au revoir," Gigi called.

If I hear anyone, ever again, call Gigi Dorrance-Downs a third-rate actress, I'll deck them. She was better, and braver, than Meryl Streep. Well, just as good as, anyway.

My car phone rang just as I turned off the two-lane into Bennett's Fort.

"Two things." It was Linda. "Your mother called and said absolutely do not be late to the Thatchers' party tonight, and there's a young man here to see you. Won't tell me his name."

It was a terrified Buddy Butts, and once we were done talking, I convinced him to go ahead and surrender. Dwight placed him under arrest and led him across the street to our little jailhouse.

"Linda," I said, once they'd left, "would you call General John Taylor's office and tell him we've taken Private Butts into custody, and they can come get him whenever they want but I'd appreciate it if they'd keep it under their hats. I've got to get home. If we're late two nights in a row, my mother truly will kill me."

The fact was that I didn't want to talk to John Taylor. Not yet, anyway.

42

THURSDAY MORNING

Jack and I talked at about seven o'clock and decided to make the
morning line on George cautiously optimistic. Try to get some action out of Shelley and whoever was helping her, now that they had
the hollow comfort of knowing Gigi had been apprehended for their
crimes. The Roundup police still had no lead on Buddy Butts; I guess
word of his surrender hadn't filtered back to them through the U. S.
Army bureaucracy.

I called Elias.

"If you don't let me out of this place pretty soon, I'm going to go crazy," he yelled into the phone from his hospital room. "I want to come out to the ranch, I've got a lot to do. I'm homesick." His voice echoed out of my speakerphone and off the walls of my office.

All the windows were open and the air was as sweet as it can get, just rich with manure and dirt and General Taylor's two dozen red roses. I looked at the clock on my desk, almost eight. The tourists and their trailers and the big tour buses would start to roll in in the next half hour, and Bennett's Fort would look and sound and smell like Manhattan until Cousin Buck closed it up at nine o'clock at night.

"Elias," I said, and began to explain for the millionth time, "you've got to stay close to George. I know you want to come home, and I swear to God it won't be much longer. Oh, thanks," I said as Linda placed a fresh cup of coffee on my desk.

"Tell him I don't want him anymore," Linda said to me in a very loud voice that Elias didn't need the speakerphone to hear, even all the way from Bennett's Fort, "now that he's been hanging around with that slut. Tell him also I hope he's using triple condoms, because from what I hear, you could count the people she *hasn't* slept with on one hand."

"You tell her," Elias yelled, "I'm not using a goddamn thing because I'm stuck in this stupid hospital when there's nothing wrong with me except a broken leg. And I may be dumb but I'm not so crazy that I'd ball anybody in a hospital where my mother's on the Board of Directors. And tell her also that Shelley Pirelli is *not a slut*. She's a very nice girl who's had a tough time and made some bad decisions."

"BULLSHIT!" Linda roared as she left my office, slamming the door behind her.

I waited a moment or two before continuing. "Flushing this lady out is getting very complicated," I said. "Did she come back last night?"

"Yes, until late. I still don't think she suspects anything," Elias said, happy to be talking business with his sister rather than romance with Linda. "I don't know where she gets her stamina, but she's here all the time when she doesn't absolutely have to be at the theater."

"I have a feeling we're looking at some major cocaine energy."

"Unfortunately, I think you're probably right."

"How're you doing, Elias?" I asked. "Are you in much pain?"

"None," he answered impatiently. "I just want to go home. Have some fun."

"I thought you and Shelley were having fun," I teased him. "She sure seems to be."

"Yeah, well. It's not too much fun anymore. And I'll tell you another thing—I'll beat the hell out of anybody who ever mentions tofu to me again." He paused. "I am sort of missing Linda. Would you tell her for me?"

Poor Elias. He was always in a big mess with women. You could write a book about it, but who'd want to, until you could see a happy ending somewhere in the picture?

"This can't go on much longer," I told him. "She's going to make a move pretty soon. The Japanese clock only has about twenty-eight hours left on it."

"Yeah. But in the meantime I'm missing all the parties," Elias grumped. "And I'll tell you, I'm not missing that square dance tonight. One last thing—I went in to see George a while ago and asked him if he had a greenhouse, and he said he only has a roof garden that Cary Scott and Shelley look after, so I don't know if that'll make any difference or not. What're you doing today?"

"I'm about to leave for George's apartment, check in with the guard there, and then I'll come to the hospital."

"Bring me something to eat. Bring me a goddamn cheeseburger. . . . Oh, hi, Shelley," I heard him saying as we hung up.

Sunlight poured into George's living room through the picture windows that wrapped around the corner, giving a peak-to-peak view of the mountain range and all of downtown Roundup. Off to the right was the dining room, and directly ahead was the wide staircase to the second floor.

A police guard sat at a small desk at the bottom of that staircase, next to one of the phony Doric columns. He had placed a television set on a chair next to him and had strung a long line of TV cable from the kitchen. A Winchell's Donut box sat on the desk next to his phone. Empty. Just my luck.

He stood up and brushed sugar glaze off his chin and shirt and trousers as I rounded the corner coming up from the front door.

"Good morning, patrolman," I said and picked up his coffee-stained call log. "Much going on?"

"No, ma'am. Quiet as a morgue. Well, the secretary, what's her name?"

"Shelley?"

"Yeah, Shelley—she is one available babe—she comes in to pick up the mail, but, like you said, we don't let her go beyond the landing."

"Great. Thanks. I'm going upstairs to look around."

Framed, autographed pictures of the world's greatest actors and a number of their unknown—at least to me—colleagues hung on the walls of the second-floor landing. Light glittered off the glass that covered them.

I turned left into the guest room, where the air smelled strongly of old, burned incense, and it was just as Elias had described it, a sort of safari arrangement, zebra rugs and fur throws and a high, mahogany double bed with a canopy, draped with mosquito netting. Or gauze anyway. We don't have many mosquitoes in downtown Roundup. A brown and black batik dust ruffle hung from the bed frame to the floor, and I got down on my hands and knees and looked underneath it.

The whole area was solid with sanded wooden crates, the kind that fine wines are packed in, except that these were all about a foot long and four inches tall. I tugged a box off the top and after some hard effort with my Swiss Army knife, the nails screeched loose and then gave way. Inside, wrapped in thin sheets of snow-white tissue paper, were nestled three layers of one-kilo gold bars, a dozen in each layer.

I pried one of the ingots out and held it for a moment. It was heavy and had a deep, smoldering glow and a good, solid heft in my hand, well balanced, like a good shotgun. It was amazing. Twenty-five million dollars' worth of gold bullion. It would be so easy for someone to walk out with a couple of boxes, but it appeared to me that the stockpile was intact, because I carefully placed my fingers on each crate all the way around the edge of the stash and the dust level was consistent. I sat back on my heels, the ingot warm in my hand. A clock ticked on the night table.

Whoever else knew the fortune was there—if, in fact, anyone did—had a lot of patience. Of course, it was possible no one else knew. The secret might have died with Vanderbilt. But what George had said was true: Vanderbilt had been a slut, he would have done anything for self-advancement, money, or drugs. However, Cyrus had wanted me to find the money; he hadn't mentioned gold, only that the fund was missing. Maybe he hadn't known either.

I replaced the box of bullion and dropped the batik ruffle back into place, carefully straightening it. Then I got back on my feet and went into an upstairs sitting room off which was the roof garden. A thick white stucco wall surrounded the terrace, and brightly planted pots of red and pink geraniums and fuchsia bougainvillea dotted the red flagstone floor—the products of a loving gardener. I wondered if it was George or Cary Scott. I probed each pot carefully with my fingers and found nothing.

It had to be somewhere.

I went back inside. George's bedroom held no surprises, at least none that were germane to the search, but there were some interesting props of a sexual nature to be found, if that's what one was in the market for—feather boas and spangled, sequined underpants and gallon-sized jars of Vaseline and several miles of satin ribbons, mostly red, a number of boxes of new Ping-Pong balls, and condoms of every size, shape, scent, and color imaginable—but nothing resembling what I needed to find.

Defeated, I returned to the terrace and looked around some more at the terra-cotta pots of plants. I was about to give up—it was getting hot as Hades—when I noticed a long ladder leaning against the wall behind a rattan screen. I had assumed it was to escape to the roof below in case of fire.

"Of course, you idiot," I said out loud. "The ladder's to get to the roof."

I leaned it against the stucco overhang and began to climb, and when I reached the top, there it was: another roof, concealed from sight below by the high adobe walls, with a good-sized greenhouse. I climbed over, tearing my skirt, and looked inside.

Only one crop: marijuana.

At least it looked, at first, like solid marijuana, but when I stepped inside, I realized the light was slanting through tall, graceful stalks of foxglove, and their pinky-purple, bell-shaped flowers bowed me in, like geishas who'd been expecting me. And, on the floor, in the moist, shady accumulation of years of spilled dirt and manure beneath the counter, grew the destroying angels, looking as innocent as little mushrooms for soup. Their sinister presence made my skin prickle, and I pictured Vanderbilt's blue face as he struggled for his life while his liver was in the process of melting.

This was where the poisoning agents came from—the agents that Shelley had so adamantly insisted would be, and had been, uncovered at Gigi's. As I stood there, twirling a small sprig of foxglove between my fingers and inhaling its undistinguished, mild scent, the glass to my right suddenly shattered and a bullet whizzed right under my nose and smashed into the wall next to my ear.

Jesus Christ! I dropped to my knees and reached for my weapon, freeing it instantly from its holster. The reverberation from the shot had caused a number of the greenhouse's small panes to disintegrate, and they fell around me like dangerous slivers of rain. I crouched on the ground and tried to shield myself from them by throwing my left arm over my head, but I could feel them pricking my skin and one or two sticking in my back like tiny needles. And although it seemed forever, it was probably just seconds before the glass stopped falling. I stayed in my crouch and pivoted slowly, searching each direction. No one was there returning my gaze from across the wall, but I realized the ladder was gone. I raced to the ledge. The ladder now extended down to the roof two floors below me and there was no one in sight.

My first call was to Elias. "Where's Shelley?" I practically yelled into the cell phone, picking splinters of glass out of my arm.

"She just went downstairs to get us some coffee," he said. "Why?"

"She's been over here shooting up the place. How long has she been gone?"

"About ten minutes."

"When she gets back," I said breathlessly, "do not let her out of your sight."

"Roger," Elias said and then added in an ebullient voice, "Oh, I've got to hang up. Shelley Pirelli just walked in with some coffee. Hi, darling," I could hear him say as he hung up. "I've been missing you."

"Don't drink it," I yelled as the line clicked off.

My next call was to Jack Lewis. "Where in the hell have your guys been?" I shouted at him, and I'm sure he was holding the receiver away from his delicate little ear.

"What's the problem?" he asked calmly.

"Who in the hell is supposed to be watching Pirelli?" I screamed. "I'm on the roof of Wrightsman's apartment building and she's been taking potshots at me."

"I'm on it," Jack said, and hung up.

Police quickly blanketed the neighborhood. A very good-looking young fireman brought another ladder and came up it. "We have to stop meeting like this, Marshal Bennett," he said.

"I beg your pardon?"

"I'm the one who rescued you from the fire at the theater office."

Now I could see his face as he stood beside my bed in the hospital while I thanked him profusely for saving my life. "I'm sorry I didn't recognize you."

"You were pretty doped up," he said. "Do you want me to carry you down?"

Wasn't that sweet? And to his credit, he didn't show his relief when I said no, knowing he'd just saved himself years of lying on a chiropractor's table and forced retirement at a young age with a back disability. Nobody should have to lift me up twice.

Shelley Pirelli, I thought as I drove to the hospital, was as quick and as smart as a snake. But why would she miss at such short range? That miss was on purpose.

S he was here the whole time." Jack and Elias met me at the entrance to the ICU. "But now she's gone."

"What do you mean, she's gone?" I looked at both of them. "Poof," Jack said.

Elias swung slowly from side to side, balancing on his crutches, looking chagrined.

Things were bad, serious, but not so bad that I didn't take enormous pleasure in seeing Jack Lewis sweat. For the last few days he'd had squads of men whose only assignment was to watch Shelley Pirelli and wait for her to make a move.

"All you had to do was watch her." I couldn't help rubbing it in a little.

"She was here," Jack said. "We've been on her the whole time. But when you called and said someone had taken a shot, we turned our backs for one second to beef up the watch on Wrightsman, and she went right into thin air. But I can guarantee you, she has not left this building, and it's starting to look like you've been up the wrong tree the whole time."

"No, goddamn it!" I felt absolutely frantic. I could feel my face flush with anger and frustration. "I know she's behind it. But who else? Who's helping her?"

Both men watched me quietly.

I looked through the door into the waiting room where Cary Scott's eyes, gray with dread and exhaustion, had never left us. Poor kid. He'd chewed off all his fingernails and now had started on sunflower seeds; their cracked shells dusted his shoes like globs of paint.

"Time for Plan B," I said.

"George," I said, once I'd explained the situation to him, "as you can see, the stage is set. You've got to do it."

"I won't. I won't. I won't." He pulled the covers over his head and sank down under them.

"Can't you just pretend to be brave? I mean, you are an actor."

"No. Not that brave. Not that good an actor."

"Are you sure you want to do this?" Elias asked me. "It could be dangerous."

"Well, here's the choice: We can either do this and catch them in the act, or we can keep jerking around letting them kill people off one at a time for the rest of our lives. Just do me a favor," I said to Jack. "Keep a better eye on me than you have on Ms. Pirelli."

"I can't wait for this to be over," Elias complained. "This whole week has been lousy. And another thing, I can't stand being around all these cultured assholes all the time. If I ever have to watch 'Masterpiece Theater' again, I'll throw up."

That is a perfect example of why Elias should never stray too far from the Circle B.

44

For a long time nothing happened. The business of the ICU hummed along as usual, lots of quiet rushing and bright lights. I almost went to sleep, and then I heard the guard talking to a man, a doctor, whose soft footsteps entered the cubicle. Seconds later the glass door whisked soundlessly closed, and the privacy curtain clicked along its track, blocking me from view. The sounds were magnified, the way they are when you're half asleep in a car and small bumps become dull thuds and the turn indicator is as loud as a metronome.

I could hear my heartbeats on the monitor—bleep, bleep—as I lay there in the bed—a big, swathed-up blob with an IV tube passing to nowhere through the bandages.

His tenuous footsteps made tiny squeaks and I could make out the approaching white shoes. They were old Tretorn tennis shoes, for heaven's sake. I couldn't quite make out who was wearing them, my vision was so restricted by the bandages, but his aftershave smelled of lavender.

"George," the small voice said, "I'm so sorry. None of this was my idea."

I closed my eyes and struggled to keep my breathing regular, but in spite of my efforts, my heartbeat on the EKG picked up. It was Bradford Lake. He had on a doctor's starched white jacket and baggy green surgery pants. The earpieces of a stethoscope dangled from his pocket and a drab green surgical cap covered his dark, curly hair. He perched his reading glasses on the end of his nose and then tugged a little on the IV, looking for the insertion link.

"It was Shelley," he said conversationally, his head tilted back as he examined the unfamiliar tubing. "I want you to understand and I want you to forgive me. She is blackmailing me. Ah, there it is." Bradford let go of the plastic tube and began fumbling around with something. It sounded as though he were trying to tear open the paper wrapper on a syringe.

"You know how much I love Aldo, of course you do, we've all been together for years. Oh, George . . ." He suddenly began to weep.

"It's all so cheap. So unbelievably common. Three years ago, when we were all on tour in Hawaii with *Hotel Paradiso,* and Aldo couldn't go because of *Henry V,* I got very drunk. I went home with Shelley. Back to her hotel room." The words came out in a sob. "And I went to bed with her. Oh, God. I can't even believe I did it. That disgusting little brat of hers, Rose Marie, she's my daughter. And Shelley has held her over my head like the sword of Damocles ever since."

Bradford slumped down on the edge of the bed. "If Aldo finds out, he'll leave me. And you know I can't live without him."

He pulled a starched white handkerchief from his pocket and patted his eyes and blew his nose, and after a couple of moments he had calmed himself down.

By sheer will and determination, I had forced my heartbeat to return to normal, to that of a sleeping person, and so Bradford Lake and I stayed there for a moment or two, me wrapped in claustrophobic, sterile gauze, he wrapped in guilt.

"Shelley laid out this whole plan," he continued presently. "We get rid of you and Cyrus, then the three of us—she, Aldo, and I—take over.

We'll have the air rights, we'll have the money, and we'll have the company. She's as sharp as a tack in the business end, I will give her that. Besides, the company really needs a new artistic mission, George," Bradford lectured. "It's gotten tired and hackneyed. You've completely ignored the way subscriptions have dropped off and how ravaging the reviews have been."

He rambled on and on, and I wanted to ask him, "Could we please get on with it?" I could feel streams of sweat running past my ears and through my hair into the bandages. Finally, he got back on track.

"It was going to be so *simple*." Bradford began to laugh, and I could hear the giddy clatter of building hysteria. "Then everything started to go wrong, and suddenly I found myself caught in this nightmare. Killing innocent people, planting bombs, breaking into Gigi's house. Even to-day, Shelley told me to kill Lilly Bennett, and I did. I climbed up and shot her right there in your rooftop greenhouse. Why did you hire her, George? Why couldn't you just sell the air rights, the way Cyrus wanted, and take your pension package—Cyrus was planning to be so generous—and pack Cary Scott off to Tahiti like Marlon Brando and smoke dope all the rest of your life? It's all your fault.

"Well," he said philosophically, and stood back up and picked a piece of fuzz off his cotton pants and tucked the handkerchief neatly back into his pocket. "I guess I might as well get it over with. I did feel a little badly about losing Vanderbilt that way, probably about as badly as you felt about giving Patrick AIDS." He laughed bitterly. "Patrick was like my son, you miserable bastard. And poor Stephen Griffin. Oh, God, George, why couldn't you just have died in the accident? Why'd you have to get better? Make me do this?"

The door slid open and closed again.

"What are you waiting for?" Shelley's voice said menacingly. "Stop screwing around and do it. You owe this guy nothing."

"I can't," Bradford wailed. "He's my oldest friend."

I heard a gun cock. "Don't make me kill both of you," she warned.

This made me nervous, and I wondered where in the hell my backup was. I peered closely at her from behind the gauze. She was dressed in a nurse's uniform and staring intently at Bradford, and I could tell she planned to kill him as soon as he'd gotten rid of George.

Come on, Bradford, I kept thinking. You can do it. Make your move.

With shaking fingers and shoulders shuddering with sobs, Bradford pulled the plunger out from the syringe as far as it would go and inserted the needle through the membrane into the sealed injection point on the IV tube. "Good-bye, my friend," he said. "This isn't my fault. She didn't give me any choice."

He pushed the plunger. And he and Shelley stared at the swaddled body, waiting for the coup de grâce—that big air bubble—to get to George's heart and kill him instantly. Nobody breathed.

And then the lights came on.

"That's all," I said, sitting up, placing the business end of my pistol on the bridge of Shelley's nose, cold and hard, right between her eyes. "Don't move a muscle, either one of you. You're under arrest."

"Drop the gun, Miss Pirelli," Jack said from behind her.

"It's not me," Shelley said. "It's Bradford. I saw him sneak in and I followed him. I caught him for you, for heaven's sake."

The door leading to the adjoining cubicle opened, and, although there was nothing wrong with his legs, George limped into view. He was dressed in his sweats and except for a cane, a row of stitches in his head, his arm in a sling, and a few colorful bruises, he looked pretty good.

"George," Bradford gasped. "What the . . . ?"

All Shelley could do was stare.

"I've always told you," George said to them angrily, "pay no attention to the man behind the green curtain."

"Oh, Christ," Bradford said.

"But what I really want to know"—George's voice began to rise—"you sorry, driveling, little snake, is: this is the opening night of *Macbeth* and what are you doing up here trying—totally ineffectually, I might point out—to murder me, when you should be at the theater? I thought you were directing for me. WHO'S LOOKING AFTER MY PLAY? CAN'T YOU DO ANYTHING RIGHT?"

Bradford Lake burst into tears and collapsed across the bed.

I looked at Shelley and shook my head. "What was the point of all this?"

"None of these people know what they're doing," she said scornfully, indicating George and Bradford with a toss of her head, as Jack's young lieutenant pulled her hands behind her back and clicked the cuffs around her wrists. "I'm ten times smarter than they are. I didn't kill anybody—Bradford did it all."

"Why?" George regarded her with a look of sheer, incomprehensible horror, as though she were the devil and he had just escaped from the jaws of hell.

"I have a genius IQ," Shelley bragged. "And I got sick and tired of nobody getting beyond my body. It's my turn now. They can't make any charges stick to me."

I stepped forward. "Number one," I said, "whoever told you you were a genius was pulling your leg, probably to get into your pants, and number two, your turn is now up."

"You can't prove I did anything. You've been out to get me from the start."

"Not entirely from the start," I acknowledged. "But certainly from when you started screwing with my brother."

"What brother?"

"Bertram Chiswick." I smiled at Elias. "He's really my brother."

"You're a Bennett?" Shelley's eyes widened.

"Sure am," Elias said.

"You mean I could have had a Bennett?" she cried over her shoulder as Jack's boys led her away. "I did all this when I could have just been a Bennett instead?"

Elias and I looked at each other and laughed. "No way," we both said at the same time.

CHAPTER

45

THURSDAY NIGHT

an't I have just one little joint?" George whined when we arrived back at his apartment. It was close to midnight, and I wondered vaguely how the square dance had gone.

"Not while I'm here," I said. "But I can leave."

"No. No. No. I don't ever want you to leave."

"We'll stay for a while," I said, and collapsed into a small settee next to Richard.

George had ensconced himself in the goosedown cushions of his sofa like a pasha in his palace, his damaged arm cradled in a tower of satin pillows. Cary Scott sat on the floor beside him, his cheek resting on George's thigh and his arms wrapped around one of George's legs as though it were a life preserver. He reminded me of a puppy who'd been temporarily lost, and now, found, would sleep forever.

George possessed the largest selection of whiskies I'd ever seen outside of an Edinburgh tavern, and in no time at all the six of us—he, Cary Scott, Winston, Elias, Richard, and I—were well on our way to getting totally smashed on straight-up single malts.

"I'm usually a better judge of character than this," George said. "I had no idea Shelley hated me so much. I thought she loved me. I did everything for her."

"She hates everyone," Winston pitched in. He couldn't help feeling a little smug. There had been a major power struggle in the palace—an attempted, and foiled, coup d'état—and he'd survived. The loyal lieutenant who would be well rewarded. "She thinks she's owed by the world."

"Owed what?"

"Everything," Winston said calmly. He lit a cigarette and pushed his hair back, relishing his new stature. "I've never known anyone who used people so skillfully. She was just working her way up the ladder. She started with me, a long time ago, and got her foot in the door, and then after that everyone else was just cannon fodder."

"Why didn't you tell me?"

"Would you have believed me?"

George shook his head. "I don't know," he admitted sadly.

"It was a pretty smooth plan," Elias said from his comfortable roost with his leg in its big cast stretched across an ottoman. "She sure tricked me at first."

"Face it, Elias," Richard said, "a ewe with red lipstick and false eyelashes could trick you."

Elias roared. "Many have."

"How come you were so sure all along it was Shelley?" Richard asked me. "She really had me fooled."

"Two things." I leaned back against him and pulled his arm around me. "And they both happened the night of the accident. The first one I didn't pay much attention to—it seemed so unremarkable. But remember when she was sitting on Elias's bed, searching through her purse for her wallet, up at the hospital?"

"Sure," Elias said. "She dumped everything out all over me and it hurt like crazy."

"One of the things she spilled out was a garage door opener and then later that evening Richard and I went to her house, and she clearly had no garage. It didn't take long to make the connection. A garage door opener was definitely on the list of possible signaling devices to detonate the bomb. And yesterday, when Gigi told me her opener had been missing for a couple of days, that clinched it. And then, of course, when we were hiding in the bushes outside her living room, she told Andy Beckett that Gigi had poisoned Cyrus's tea."

"So?"

"At that point no one except a small handful of us knew it was the tea that had been used to poison Cyrus."

"You've known all along," George said. His voice and his chocolate-brown eyes brimmed with admiration and awe, and he made me feel as though I were sitting alone in a strong spotlight—the most wonderful person in the world.

"Yes," I said. "But proving it was a challenge. She's a fairly cunning girl. She kept Bradford out there in front the whole time, like a goat."

He nodded his head. "Bradford and Shelley. I've never been so betrayed."

"At least it's over," I said.

But, evidently, it wasn't.

Suddenly it seemed as though a bomb were going off. A huge crashing, tearing, thundering explosion filled the living room with plaster dust and debris, and the chandelier in the entry hall crashed to the floor, shattering its crystals into millions of bits.

George and Cary Scott screamed and ducked under the cushions, and while Richard jumped to his feet and Elias struggled to his, I drew my weapon and dashed to the wall next to the door and signaled for everyone to remain quiet and stay where they were. For a change, they obeyed.

Nothing but dead silence.

I edged slowly along the wall to the archway and peeked around the corner, through the dust-filled air, past the destroyed chandelier, across the entry hall into the dining room.

"Oh, my God." I started laughing. "I don't even believe it. Wait till you see this."

Everyone raced to look.

The ton and a half of bullion had strained the guest-room floor beyond its limits, and now the big wooden bed sat on top of what was left of the flattened dining-room table. The wooden crates had smashed open, scattering gold bars around the floor like glittering dominoes.

We all gaped as a few final shards of glass from a watercolor of a castle in Scotland fell onto a sideboard. I looked at the writing at the bottom of the painting: "Dunsinane Castle overlooking Birnam Wood." It was the opening night of *Macbeth,* and once more Malcolm had prevailed.

George bowed and kissed my hand. "You are my Athena," he said. "My dea ex machina."

CHAPTER

46

FRIDAY MORNING

The rising sun drilled straight into our eyes as we drove home. Richard dropped Elias off at his house where his cook, Marialita, welcomed him into her arms and helped him up the steps to the front door. Gal and Pal leaped and twisted and twirled around him, jumping as high as his shoulders, like windup dervishes.

Then, instead of taking us home, Richard turned down the road toward my parents'.

"Where are we going?" I asked sleepily, holding his hand against my cheek. Even at five in the morning it smelled of good soap and Old Spice.

"Field trip," Richard said. "It'll just take a minute."

The heavy roadster bumped slowly along the dirt road and then angled down toward the river and pulled to a stop at the end of the small valley.

Richard turned off the car and got out. "Come on," he said. "I want to show you something."

"Can't you show me later?" I asked "I want to go to bed."

"No."

We crossed the meadow through the deep morning shadows, holding hands, toward the wedding pavilion. Tiny bluebirds, red-breasted robins, and barn swallows sailed around us, singing their hearts out, and I didn't even want to think about what we were doing there, because the setting was so perfect.

A deep sense of dread hardened my heart. I began to think about how the maharajah who built the Taj Mahal must have felt when his girl unloaded him before he could even show it to her, and I commiserated with him strongly. How humiliating. Obviously, the roles were reversed but, like the Taj Mahal, the Circle B's wedding pavilion beckoned to us like Brigadoon.

Morning's clean, pure light turned the varnished pine floor to gold as we went up the stairs, our footsteps sure and solid.

"Here," Richard said, guiding me to one of the side railings. "Have a seat. There's something I want to tell you."

"It's okay," I said. "I understand. You don't have to explain and you don't have to apologize. It's the story of my life."

"Will you be quiet for a change and let me talk?" He stood in front of me, his hands deep in his suit pants pockets. "I don't think you've noticed that I've been trying to get you alone for about ten days."

"We've been alone plenty," I said.

"I mean alone when you were in a halfway decent mood and not consumed with murder. And now at least the murdering is behind us and you seem fairly happy."

"Well, yeah," I said, wanting to get the conversation over with. Wondering if it was too late to call John Taylor back. "I'm mostly exhausted."

"Happy. Exhausted. Whatever." Richard was getting exasperated. "Look, Lilly. I love you more than anyone I've ever known in my life. You make me a complete person—it's as though I've found my other half."

"I know. I feel the same way." I started to cry. "I just don't see why you don't want me," I blubbered along. "I love you so much, and I can be a really nice person. I would probably be a lousy wife, but we'd always have fun."

Richard started to laugh, dug deep in his pocket, and held something out, but I of course was too carried away to notice what it was. "Will you marry me?" he asked.

But by then I was on a roll, reciting all my positive attributes, minimizing the negative ones.

"Hey," Richard yelled, "do you want to get married or not?"

It was then that I noticed the ring. Big. It was an emerald-cut diamond as big as a rectangular Scrabble tile.

"Oh, my God," I said. Right ring. Right guy. It was a miracle. "Yes."